OVER THE HILLS AND FAR AWAY

OVER THE HILLS AND FAR AWAY

MY LIFE AS A TELETUBBY

Nikky Smedley

SANDSTONE PRESS

First published in Great Britain in 2022 by
Sandstone Press Ltd
PO Box 41
Muir of Ord
IV6 7YX
Scotland

www.sandstonepress.com

Editor: Nicola Torch

ISBN: 978-1-914518-05-8
ISBNe: 978-1-914518-06-5

Sandstone Press is committed to a sustainable future.
This book is made from Forest Stewardship Council ® certified paper.

FSC www.fsc.org MIX Paper from responsible sources FSC® C171272

Cover design by kidethic
Typeset by Iolaire, Newtonmore
Printed and bound by CPI Group (UK) Ltd, Croydon, CR0 4YY

Dedicated to the memory of Simon Shelton
Keepin' it up! Keepin' it up!

CONTENTS

INTRODUCTION

EH-OH!

If you were – or had – a young child in the second half of the 1990s, you probably don't need any help translating what that means. For those that have no idea – where have you been for the last twenty-five years? It is a phrase that springs to many people's minds when they think of *Teletubbies*, and was at the heart of the initial controversy our programme stirred up when it premiered on BBC Two on March 31st 1997, before eventually becoming a well-loved feature of the cultural landscape. At its peak, *Teletubbies* had total global viewing figures of around three billion per annum, showing in one hundred and twenty countries and being translated into forty-five different languages, making it the second most internationally successful television programme on the planet. The only show at the time with more viewers was *Baywatch*, but we achieved our popularity while remaining more than modestly covered up.

Welcome to the story of how a scraggy dancer from South East London found herself part of that global television phenomenon, while at the same time remaining almost completely anonymous. This is an intimate look at the secret world behind the scenes of Teletubbyland through the eyes of Laa-Laa, the real human story from inside one of the world's most recognisable puppets. It's a strange claim to fame, and mine is a unique perspective on a surreal world. It's the story of how putting on a giant furry suit can propel a person to Number One in all sorts of charts and at the same time bring them insight, courage and love.

I wouldn't have got the job if I wasn't a funny person, so this is quite a funny book. I was also deeply emotionally invested in the show, as were many of my colleagues, so there are touching moments too. I was part of a bizarre family working in a field in the middle of the English countryside for six years of my life, but the impact of that time stretches beyond that place and those years. Somewhere in the world, right now, a child is looking at Laa-Laa and laughing. I count myself as pretty damn lucky to be able to comfort myself with that thought.

Everything in this book happened quite a long time ago. I've endeavoured to recount events as accurately as possible, but inevitably it is written through the filter of my own memory and my own point of view – which is as good a truth as any, I guess. I gave a copy of the manuscript to John Simmit, who played Dipsy, to make sure it chimed with his recollection and indeed it did, both factually and emotionally. He told me he found it strange reading a collective story, but that's the thing: although there were only ever five people who knew what it was like to be the original Teletubbies, we were such a close-knit filming unit that those six years were very much a shared experience for all involved. That sense of community shone out of the television and we formed a deep personal connection with our audience, the earliest cohorts of whom will now be all grown-up. I'm eagerly waiting to see how the world shifts when Our People come to power – remember all those predictions of doom for the children who were exposed to the perils of *Teletubbies*? Personally, I'm expecting the best generation yet!

Beyond the impact on the individual, what *Teletubbies* did more widely was open up the debate about the place of television in people's lives, in their homes, in their worlds. It generated a conversation about how often we expose our children to screens and what we allow them to watch. This broader discussion came out of the criticism we endured. I believe the original series stands up to scrutiny as much as ever, if not more, in these strange days.

At the very core of the programme is love, and I find the warmth people across the world have in their hearts for the Teletubbies a constant source of gleeful surprise. I realise that *Teletubbies* is just a TV show, but it has brought a lot of joy to a lot of children – and to me. I do hope you enjoy reading this book, and that it reminds you of happy times. Most importantly, I hope it puts a smile on your face.

CHAPTER 1

FIRST, FIND YOUR TELETUBBY

Four green vinyl body bags are lying on a concrete floor, arranged in order of size. My body is second from the left and I haven't seen it in seven years. Behind each bag is a large square wooden box, colour coded: red, yellow, green, purple. The boxes contain our heads.

I shouldn't really be feeling as emotional as I am – I am here to do a job after all, and frankly I am a little surprised at myself. Okay girl, take a deep breath, get a grip, be a grown-up, swallow down whatever that's all about and get on with the task in hand.

It's the summer of 2014, almost twenty years since I first became a giant yellow puppet, and I have recently been employed as a consultant on the new, rebooted version of *Teletubbies*. The show is being produced by Darrall Macqueen, not Ragdoll Productions, the original creators. The rights are now owned by Canadian company DHX, who had tried to make a new version, in-house, the previous year. When they failed in their attempts, they decided it was because there was something inherently English about the show: it needed to be made in the UK. My role is to ensure authenticity, to inject some of the spirit of the original, so I was asked to come to Twickenham Studios and assist with auditions for the new cast. I've rarely felt as well qualified to do a job, so my usual nerves are somewhat alleviated by an unfamiliar level of confidence in my own abilities. I am also very excited. Do you ever dream of being reunited with a lost pet? That's sort of how I feel as I stand staring at one of the vinyl bags. I want to play. I want to get into my Laa and muck about, to revisit the fun of being that character, of being all the best bits of me, of pretending the less enjoyable sides of my personality don't exist, but also being able to get away with murder. However, there is work to be done.

The auditions are taking place in a cavernous sound stage and the head honchos will be seated behind a table at the far end of the space. This means the actors will have to walk the full length of the studio before the audition even starts. I know from experience that this walk will be beyond terrifying. Imagine you are going for a job interview, but instead of just coming into the room, you are scrutinised over a twenty-metre distance as you make your way towards those who are judging you. I've always hated that walk. I am so glad it's not me making it today.

Most of the room is empty space. There is a table full of snacks with a tea urn and kettle on the right-hand side and the costumes are laid out on the floor to the left. They only arrived this morning so for the producers, the writer, the director and the other production staff, this is their first encounter with actual Teletubbies. They can't wait to see them, and I'm on hand to demonstrate the human/Teletubby interface.

I open the yellow box. There she is! My reaction is automatic. As soon as I get my hands on the mechanisms that operate the mouth and eyes, we're conversing. I can't help myself – the habit of playing with my alter ego rises to the surface, switching between voices as naturally as breathing. Laa starts it, of course.

'Where the bloody hell have you been?'

'Sorry, I—'

'Sorry? Sorry is not good enough. I've been in that sodding box for years. You didn't write, you never called, you missed our anniversaries . . .' I could go on, lost in my own little puppeteer's psychosis, but we must curtail the catch-up. It's time to stop larking about, be professional and bring Laa-Laa to life for everyone else in the room.

My body knows exactly where to go to get myself into the suit: how high I need to lift my legs, the angle of entry, where to hold onto the harness to bring it up around my waist, the exact dip of my shoulders needed to hitch the upper section into position. My physical memory is absolutely in charge. The wiggle I do to settle everything in place is probably the exact same wiggle I did for six years and more. The texture of the fur feels like home, the slight rub of the padding behind the knees a familiar discomfort, as is the weight – initially quite bearable but becoming heavier by the second. Then I lift the puppet head by its ears and when my arms are fully extended upwards, I duck my neck, dip my head under the cowl and slip into the skullcap, taking the mechanisms in my hands. Left for eyes, right for mouth. I am back: 'Eh Oh! Is y Laa Laa!'

Physically uncomfortable though it is, being back inside Laa gives me a deep-seated sense of security. This is something I know so completely I don't even have to think about it. I engage in a brief display of classic Teletubby puppeteering. The years apart melt away and I automatically know how to manipulate the controls to make the crowd warm to the character. Through the tiny gap of the mouth, I see the faces of my audience change. I watch the tilt of their heads as they lift their gaze to address the eyes of Laa-Laa, already captivated by the power of the puppet, allowing themselves to forget the human inside. I know the expression on their faces so well. No matter how much they tell themselves they are looking with professional eyes, I know they will be sucked into my reality. After only a few minutes – I don't want to get too sweaty – I lift the head off again, smiling at Laa's face the way you would at a sidekick, a mischievous accomplice or your best mate at school who always backs you up and joins your crazy schemes. I know what she has allowed me to get away with in the past and it makes me chuckle that we are still a formidable team. I turn back into my human self – puny in comparison to the size and dimensions of Laa-Laa – and leave the new bosses to study the workings of the puppet. My puppet.

It is decided that we will work with all the actors who are auditioning through the morning to see their set pieces, read some scripts, and try a little improvisation. Then we'll have a cull and those that remain can try on the costumes in the afternoon. Two candidates who make it through are Rebecca Hyland and Nick Kellington. I've worked with them before, helping them train for their roles as Upsy Daisy and Iggle Piggle in *In The Night Garden,* and now they are hoping to play Laa-Laa and Dipsy respectively. I'm glad to see them both. I couldn't think of better performers to take on the mantle of the characters John Simmit and I had created. They were well versed in the tone of Ragdoll's creations, familiar with the physical demands of this type of work and had proved themselves up to the job. Hard-working, good-natured, strong, funny and playful – what more could we want in a Teletubby?

In addition, I genuinely liked them. I liked the idea of Rebecca as Laa-Laa and I was very happy with this choice of who was going to 'be me'. Except that 'being me' wasn't really the job in hand as Rebecca would have to find her own Laa. Darrall Macqueen were very keen to stay faithful to the original Ragdoll version, but they also wanted to make their own mark on the show. The same would be true of the performers. A straight imitation of what had gone before was not what was required. It would be boring for them and a waste of their own individual skill and style.

The way I remember it, there was no question about which four of the performers that came to us that day were the right choice. The selection process could have developed into a long-winded nightmare, but there they were – immediately obvious. I don't even think there was much discussion around the decision, and certainly no argument. Rachelle Beinart had exactly the right mixture of feisty and vulnerable for Po, with a list of relevant credits as long as your arm, and it was a miracle that Tinky Winky's innocent eccentricity was personified so naturally by Jeremiah Krage. The four of them together looked like a pretty good line-up to me and I was excited to see how they would come across once inside the suits. The same designer who created our original costumes had been brought on board to make a whole new set of Teletubbies for the rebooted programme. It was going to take her some time to get them made, so the cast would be using our suits in the meantime – properly laundered, one would hope!

After lunch, Rebecca is primed to try out the yellow puppet, and the wardrobe department are on hand to learn, from me, the mechanics of the transformation. I help Rebecca into the body, then sit her down and feed the mechanisms for the head down the sleeves into her hands. Then I lower the puppet head onto her human one and fasten the back of the bodysuit. It's strange to be on the other end of the procedure and although I am trying to be as clear as possible in my demonstration, part of my brain is also browsing through a gallery of my past dressers and running through a montage of shared intimacies and in-jokes. When Rebecca is fully enclosed in my Laa-Laa, I stand back to look at her. This has never happened before. I've never seen someone else in my Teletubby. On set, we had put a director or two into a suit so that they could experience a little of the effort needed to obey their orders, but we'd always used Dipsy. I knew that members of the wardrobe department had also worn my suit in the course of their labours, but I'd never seen it. I used to joke, Judge Dredd style: 'I am the Laa!' The one, the only.

When people found out what I did for a living, they'd quite often ask, 'Were you just the body?'

'No,' I'd reply, 'I was everything: body, voice, soul.'

'Was it always you or were there other actors doing it too?'

'Just me. Only me. I am the Laa!' The one, the only.

And now I am not.

I wasn't prepared for the emotional impact of that. There was someone else in my Laa and this was how it was going to be from now on. It wasn't my job any more and she wasn't my Laa any more – it was time to let go. I was now an ex-Teletubby. I wasn't going to be the one making the crew laugh, joking around with my dresser, enjoying appearances on other TV shows, sharing the most surreal of experiences and calling it work, being paid to be funny and loving, being loved. I could no longer take it for granted that whenever I saw the image of Laa-Laa, it was me.

All sorts of things were wrapped up in this wave of emotion: getting older, not being able to deal with the physical stresses like I had eighteen years previously, not working in the television industry any more. Not being special. Not being the Talent. The sense of self-worth that the job had given me should have been immutable. It shouldn't have mattered that someone else was now doing my job – that's what happens in the grown-up world. But somehow it did matter. I felt less. I felt loss.

******

ARTISTES WITH STAMINA REQUIRED
for new children's television programme.
Unusual personalities and backgrounds especially welcome.
Ragdoll Productions

This was the advertisement in the *Stage* that caught my eye in September 1995. I had spent the previous fifteen years working as a performer, mostly dancing, mostly with my own dance company, mostly poor. Now I was about to turn thirty-three and it was time for a new chapter.

Age was catching up with me and with my dodgy knees in particular. All dancers at some point have to face up to the fact that their bodies are no longer capable of doing what they did when they were younger. The slope is now downwards. You can no longer improve. You will never become better at your job. You must come to terms with the truth that your glory days as a dancer are over. At this point, a part of you dies. The majority of you, however, is still alive and has a couple of alternatives. You can adjust how you dance, where you dance, when you dance, and carry on with a career that is adapted to the physical shifts you are experiencing, or you can quit. I chose the latter for reasons financial. Being brutally honest with myself, I didn't think I was worth paying money to watch any more. I'd never been particularly confident in my abilities as a dancer. I knew I relied heavily on performance skills, on musicality, on acting ability and on a certain emotional quality that managed to mask my less than perfect technique. Now what technique I had was becoming more difficult to maintain and I didn't think I'd be able to get away with this trick any more.

Also, I was fed up with being dirt poor.

I'd enjoyed a feast or famine existence – mostly famine – surviving courtesy of the Department of Health and Social Security for fifteen years. It's not that I was idle, far from it. I'd been creating dance theatre since I left college, running my own company, staging my own spectacles, touring and working with other choreographers. I was successful in every way except financially. If I was cast in a music video, landed a modelling job or nailed a short commercial contract, I could be pulling in a couple of hundred quid a day but because of the vast swathes of time when I had no paid work whatsoever, these funds fell into the bottomless pit of debt, making no impact on my day-to-day life. No, what my day-to-day life looked like was seven piles of three pound coins, lined up on my desk and representing one week's disposable income. Each morning I'd sit and toy with that day's allotment, the coins falling between my thumb and middle finger – thump, ding, ding, thump, ding, ding – as I pondered whether to eat or dance. A dancer should do class every day to maintain tiptop condition and at the time a professional dance class cost three pounds, leaving precisely nothing to spend on food. Sometimes friends were kind and fed me, sometimes I could snaffle the dregs at the end of the day from Lewisham's market stalls, sometimes I could eke out meagre supplies to last a couple of days. Mostly it was a compromise between my stomach and the rest of my body.

The level of poverty I was living in hadn't even registered when I was younger. Life threw miracles my way – I was doing what I loved with people I loved and I was grateful for that. Right up to the hilt, all the way home, with knobs on. But now I was in my thirties, my discontent persisted like a mewling kitten round my ankles.

Then one day, I made a decision. My sister laughed at me when I told her.

'I've decided I'm not going to be poor any more.'

'What are you going to do?'

'I don't know.'

'Well, what kind of a decision is that?'

'I don't know how; I've just decided I'm not going to be poor any more.'

'You can't just decide that. You have to do something.'

'Well, I will. I'm not going to just sit on my arse. I realise I have to give the universe the opportunity to help me.'

'To help you not be poor any more?'

'Yes. It will happen. I just don't know how.'

'Prrrfff!'

'The money will come.'

I said it to myself. All the time. Every day. It became my mantra. As I got on with my daily life I said silently to myself, over and over again, 'The money is coming. The money is coming', seeing in my mind's eye an endless stream of notes flying towards me as if magnetised.

I threw my heart and soul into my new decision. I went to the library every day to check employment opportunities in the papers and trade magazines. I trawled the notice boards of dance studios and art centres. I auditioned for roles big and small. I quaked with nerves through formal interviews. I applied to be a Christmas Elf at Harrods and Selfridges. I wrote glowing references for myself from the Tooth Fairy and the Easter Bunny, along with a damning one from the Bogeyman. I thought this was a touch of genius and showed my commitment to the role. The department stores thought I was insane.

Then one Thursday, from the back pages of the *Stage*, a new chapter beckoned. It was the line, 'Unusual personalities and backgrounds especially welcome' that caught my eye – what kind of an employer would put those words in their advertisement? The kind that might employ me, that's who!

I have no memory of what I sent them in response, but a couple of weeks later I came home to find an envelope from Ragdoll Productions waiting patiently on the mat. Good quality stationery as I recall. The letter told me I had been selected to audition and I was to be at The London Welsh Centre in Camden at 9.00am the following morning. The next morning! It was already 6.00pm. I'd spent all day at a hair studio being coiffured in preparation for a modelling job the following week. The vibe was 1960s pop-art and Bridget Riley monochrome. I was to wear black and white PVC boots with a matching belted mini dress that squeaked when I danced. My hair was cut in two layers, a short asymmetric bob dyed platinum blonde beneath a contrasting geometric shape dyed black on top. The style hadn't really worked. I looked less ready for swinging London and more ready to have them swinging from the gallows. You know the judge in a period courtroom drama who has to put a square of black cloth on top of his white wig before he passes the death sentence? That was me... 'And may God have mercy on your soul.'

I couldn't do anything about that – I had to figure out what I was going to do at tomorrow's audition. They wanted me to perform something suitable for three-year-old children, and a humorous piece for adults. Both were to be three minutes in length. I panicked and flapped and then did what any sensible person in my position would do – I went to my local pub and drank two glasses of wine (while fending off wisecracks about my ridiculous hair). The wine calmed my brain, and my brain gave me an idea. In a previous life, with my dance company Geographical Duvet, I had made a show about love named *What is This Thing Called?* which had followed the story of a couple through meeting, dating, wedding, birthing and falling apart. Company member Rachel and I had played the part of the couple's special bistro – yes, funny – and I had worn a large plywood disc around my waist covered in a red and white gingham cloth with a matching parasol on my head, as the bistro table. The cloth had perished long ago, but I had the plywood disc in my shed and with some refurbishment I could make it work as a table again. I could write a little song about being in love with a chair, a short tale of unrequited love.

I am a table.
I am in love with a chair.
But the chair.
Doesn't care.
For me.

Yes, it was coming together. I could address the children – the imaginary three-year-old audience – directly. 'Poor me, what shall I do?' That type of thing. Yes, I could make that work. Sad clown in table form. No-one else was going to do that. Stand out – that's what they say isn't it?

Twenty-five years on from its one and only performance, I can still remember the tune.

As soon as I got home, I searched the shed for my current plywood disc/future table, unprepared for the number of spiders and their webs. *Ick.* I was successful in my search. Indoors, I found a spider-free length of shiny orange cloth I'd previously worn as a sari and stapled it onto the wood to act as a tablecloth. I rehearsed the song and the scene in my kitchen until it was precisely three minutes in length – I take direction well – and committed it to memory. Done. 9.00pm. Then I turned my attention to the other task.

I rang my friend Robin – who knew all my best stories – and explained the situation to him. He replied confidently with: 'Why don't you tell them the one about the time your dad burned your arse on the carpet?'

'Do you think it's funny enough?'

'The way you tell it – yes.'

Great, I didn't even need to rehearse that one, I knew it so well. I ran through it a couple of times anyway for good measure, practised the table scene again, packed everything up and was soon ready to get an early night. I wanted as many hours as possible to toss and turn and fret and worry about the fact that I was tossing and turning and fretting and worrying instead of sleeping. Then the alarm went off.

I'm not sure if I mentioned that the plywood disc was as wide as I was tall and now had cloth stapled to it and ropes wrapped around it. What made it worse was the two trains and tube I had to catch to get across London – and at rush hour. It was a hoot!

I've always found people are much more helpful than expected when they see someone carrying a cumbersome item. Maybe it's the surprise entertainment value that predisposes them to lend a hand? At any rate, relying on the kindness of strangers, I managed to reach King's Cross tube station and wend my way down Gray's Inn Road, wavering from side to side as the plywood on my shoulder acted like a sail in the breeze.

What with wielding the disc and sharing a giggle with fellow Londoners, I had forgotten to be nervous until I was outside the door of The London Welsh Centre. I was early, but I wasn't going to loiter in the street with this thing. I entered shaking and sweating, but hoping there'd be some sort of foyer where I could wait. And a loo where I could wee.

I walked into a flurry of producers, all running around preparing the space, making coffee and handing each other lists. They had set up a horseshoe of around thirty chairs for the auditionees, facing a row of tables for the auditioners. This format was more akin to a drama workshop than an audition, but I rather liked that we were all in it together. I drifted about uncertainly near the doorway, with my giant plywood disc on my shoulder and my crazily contrasting hair. They definitely didn't need to ask if I was there for the audition.

I parked my table-top, took the penultimate chair on the right arm of the horseshoe and waited for the others to fill up. Then I watched the other chairs empty one by one as each of the hopefuls performed for the judges – mostly for longer than six minutes. Tch! Considering I was only sitting and watching, I expended an awful lot of energy. When somebody was really good, I momentarily forgot the context, sat back and enjoyed the show. Then when I snapped back into the room, it was with a suddenly accelerated heartbeat that took my breath away, quivered my body and flushed perspiration onto my brow and in various crevices. I'm never going to get this job, that person is much funnier than me, I thought. When somebody was really bad, I started to doubt whether I wanted this job anyway, then I'd have to admonish myself for being cocky, remember the good people, and the shaking and sweating would start again. A few hopefuls had interpreted, 'Unusual personalities and backgrounds' to mean 'downright strange'. They waggled badly made sock puppets and got confused about whether it was the puppet or themselves telling the story of the tramp in the frozen food section of Safeway, at some volume, in a bikini. Not really, I made up that last bit.

Hours later, it was my turn. Crazy Hair Girl. I got into my table and apologised for my hair. I felt like the strangest hopeful yet. I did my thing exactly how I'd planned, for good or bad and for precisely three minutes. Then I removed the table and said, 'I wasn't sure what to do for this "humorous piece for adults" bit, so I rang my friend Robin who said I should tell you about the time my dad burned my arse on the carpet.' An intake of breath and a glimmer of horror from my audience ensued – exactly as hoped for – and I began the story:

> An archetypal domestic scene: the lounge in the house I grew up in. I'm around nine years old. It's evening and I'm waiting up to see my dad before I go to bed. I've had a bath and I'm in my nightie, sitting on the floor leaning against an armchair watching telly. Mum is on the sofa, managing to watch and knit at the same time. I find the clicking of her needles comforting. Dad hates it. He's late. Mum sighs periodically. Her sighs say, 'He's in the bloody pub, isn't he? It's gone eight o'clock. Typical.' His car pulls up outside. Another sigh. The clicking continues as I listen to Dad come in, dump his bags, take off his coat and shoes, put on his slippers – not too drunkenly by the sound of things – and finally open the door to the lounge. His attention is instantly on me, 'There she is! There's my girl!' Yeah . . . he is a bit pissed.

He squats a little on his haunches, bending forward and reaching his arms out towards me, holding my gaze with his daft grin. He grabs my ankles and starts to run backwards and sideways, pulling me around the room. It could have been quite fun, but it wasn't because of the bare bum/cheap carpet interface. I am screaming my head off as the dragging and concurrent carpet burning persists. Mum doesn't look up from her knitting, 'Stop it Cyril, you're hurting her.'

Dad disagrees, 'No I'm not, she's enjoying it. Look.' He drags me with fresh vigour. He's having a great time. I try and persuade him that Mum is right, by clearly stating my case, 'Aaaaaaaaaaaaah!!!'

When my screaming turns to actual crying, he stops. He is more disappointed in me than apologetic – I am no fun – and he's insistent that the whole episode has been a jolly lark.

Oh! The sting of the TCP after the event, equally as eye-watering as the creation of the carpet burns. The compensation was being able to scratch and pick at the scabs on my bum cheeks without anyone telling me off for it, because I was the victim. Nuh Nuhnuh Nuh Nuh!

They laughed in all the right places, but these were professionals – just because they made laughing noises, it didn't necessarily mean they thought it was funny. Still, better than blank, silent stares.

One more person gave of themselves, but I was gazing into space hearing only the pounding of my blood and the ringing in my ears until the adrenaline eased off and it was time to drag my plywood disc and my spent self back to South East London.

This was the beginning of a long-drawn-out process. It was torturous, waiting for the expected letter of rejection after every follow-up audition. Those of us still in the running were asked back to improvise around various themes, to try out potential scenarios, to learn a little more about the mysterious *Teleteddies,* as the show was originally called. Then the big boss lady, the head honcho, Anne Wood, came in to explain to a group of around twenty of us what exactly it was she wanted to achieve with her new creative baby. And I fell in love.

Up until this point, I'd been treating the whole thing as I would any audition process: I might get the job, I might not get the job, just do my best, lap of the Gods. But everything changed when I listened to Anne explain the show. She talked about making an anti-*Power Rangers* for very small children, about creating something that made the viewing child feel the love, about how there was nothing on television specifically made for very young children, how she wanted to make that something, and make it with high production values. The more she talked, the more it became apparent that she had identified one hell of a niche. She continued with articulate passion, explaining the philosophy behind the show. She wanted it to speak to children directly rather than through an adult, to give them faith in their own ability to learn, to connect with the imaginative life of the child, to be innocent fun, full of love, and jam-packed to the brim with top quality integrity.

I was spellbound. I was hooked. I could see the future.

'Oh my God! This is going to be HUGE!' I really did think that.

Now I definitely wanted the job; now it meant something.

More auditions whittled the field down to a handful of hopefuls as Christmas loomed on the horizon like a matinée idol on a camel. During this agonising time, I described what little I knew about the show to a friend who said, 'It's like they made a job that had your outline and all you had to do was show up and fill it.' I didn't share her certainty. But suddenly there were only three of us in a rehearsal studio with Anne and Andy Davenport, the co-creator and writer. John Simmit was a Jamaican comedian from Birmingham whom Anne had had lined up for some months. John was solid. He cut quite an intimidating figure, if you didn't know he was a complete sweetie. This was something he enjoyed – played up even. But when he talked to his daughter on the phone, his whole demeanour changed, not just his voice, and he betrayed the kind-hearted, caring man he truly was – and still is. I believe this softer side was what drew Anne to him.

Then from the London auditions were me and Dave Thompson, another comedian, based in Lambeth. As flighty as John was rooted, Dave was an oddball and I liked him right off. His main claim to fame up to that point was being part of a cabaret act known for dancing naked, but for a couple of strategically placed balloons. This might not make him seem a good fit for children's television, but there was something quirky and unorthodox about Dave that reminded you of a certain kind of child.

At this point, there was no-one to play the smallest character. A couple had been tried but rejected, and the role was yet to be filled. Anne told us she was struggling to find someone with the right personality, someone who was devoid of pathos. I didn't know if she was trying other combinations of performers before choosing the final four, but there didn't seem to be anyone else around. It was starting to look like I was in with a chance. Dare I believe? Maybe not yet.

Anne was admirable. My hero. She was not a woman of great physical stature, but she had an undeniable presence. She'd worked in television for decades, having given us *Roland Rat*, *Pob's Programme* and *Tots TV* to name but a few, before punting everything she'd earned in the last fifteen years on this new show. That took some balls. *Teletubbies* was now the name of the show, as there was some sort of copyright issue with the original title, *Teleteddies*. It was a commission from the BBC, but Anne had also invested all she owned. I was small fry compared to her, but I recognised the same fervour, the same complete commitment and drive and the same dedication to the task at hand that I have experienced whenever I've been in the throes of a new creative project. Despite her air of authority, she had a tremendous sense of fun and play – and she was really good company.

Anne started her working life in teaching and that background goes some way to explaining her preternatural understanding of small children, but it doesn't explain it totally. Some people just have it. Maybe it's because they remember their own childhood more vividly. They seem to have a connection, as if an umbilical cord of awareness runs through the years enabling them to get right back in touch with the child's mind. Andy has it too, but in a less visceral way. His understanding came through a more obviously artistic filter as well as from the intellectual grounding from his studies of children's speech and communication. Lithe and handsome in an understated way, his gentle energy was a perfect foil to Anne's passionate bluster. I was fascinated by them both. More than anything I wanted to spend the next chapter of my life working for them and learning from their expertise.

During the years when I ran my own company, I had always strived to make dance accessible. It seemed to me paradoxical that though so many people loved to dance themselves as an informal recreational activity, performed dance wasn't that popular as a spectacle. Although, if you looked around at the theatrical dance available when I started out in the early eighties, it was pretty po-faced – no pun intended. When some long-suffering boyfriend or parent would come up to me after a show and say, 'I didn't think I liked dance, but I liked that' I would feel that my work was done. Although driven by the desire to make dance more accessible, I never specifically set out to reach children. Nevertheless, they enjoyed our shows and we'd even played some children's festivals. I realised that by working with Anne and Andy I could learn untold secrets about the workings of the child mind, and by gaining a better understanding of how to make meaning for children, maybe I would also learn more about humans in general.

On that final audition day, with just the three of us, we were shown sketchy pencil drawings of chubby little characters with televisions in their tummies and aerials on their heads, running over hillocks under the gaze of a magical windmill. After being sworn to secrecy we were sent away to count our chickens and though years in show business had taught me not to, I allowed myself to hope that this time I would get the lucky break, that the magical light would shine on me and the new chapter I was so desperate for would begin and free me from poverty and pain.

The romance in my memory tells me it was Christmas Eve when I got the phone call. Having waited for days, my hope had faded and I'd resolved to enjoy the seasonal festivities and then start 1996 with a fresh new outlook. I do remember that I was in bed, though awake – probably to keep warm – and it was Sue James, the series producer, who called to tell me that the job was mine. I was to be a Teletubby: I was to be Laa-Laa. I was to be employed – and yellow.

Best. Christmas present. Ever.

I later learned that Anne hadn't been sure about me at all. It was Andy who was my champion, absolutely sure. He told her, 'Oh yes! Crazy Hair Girl? We've got to have her!' Thanks Andy.

CHAPTER 2

SAY EH-OH!

1996. A new year and a new experience. I had been offered a contract for three years' work. Who knew such a thing existed? Being a fully paid-up member of the actors' union Equity, I rang them for some advice. They told me that as it wasn't an Equity contract – it had been drawn up independently by Ragdoll Productions – it was outside their jurisdiction and they could offer me no help. Zero. Zilch. Nada. Could they maybe give me an opinion? Some pointers? No, they could not. How disappointing. I didn't have an agent so it looked like I was on my own.

The contract included a 'Worldwide Buyout' clause, meaning if the programme was sold abroad and broadcast, anywhere other than the UK, we would be entitled to precisely zero repeat fees. This wasn't an unusual clause at the time, though in the good old days royalties would have been paid as a matter of course. American friends were amazed: 'That would never happen in the States, the Screen Actors Guild is way too powerful. No company could ever get away with not paying repeat fees in the US. If the show was being made here, you'd be making a fortune.' That may have been true, but if the show was being made in America, I wouldn't have got the job, so I didn't think I was in a position to complain.

It's surprising how often strangers ask me about my royalty

situation. I know! Some people have no shame. Mostly, they assume I receive money every time the programme is broadcast. They seem to think I sleep on a mattress of money.

'Must be nice getting that royalty cheque every month?'

'Honestly, do you think I'd be here if that were the case? If I got paid every time a *Teletubbies* episode was shown, I'd be on my tropical island right now thank you very much!'

I was in the middle of a pub pool tournament when this line of probing came up and I fronted it out – I was in a competitive frame of mind, obviously – asking the bloke outright, 'How much do you think I earn?'

'I don't know – £250,000?'

I laughed in his face.

Regardless of the royalty situation, the weekly wage for filming *Teletubbies* for three years amounted to more money than I had earned in my entire life thus far put together, and having been on the dole for fifteen years, I was very grateful for it. When I brought up the question of the buyout with the producers, their attitude was, 'This is the deal on the table. If you don't like it, you can say no, and we can employ the person in line behind you.'

Fair enough. I said yes. In a way it was a relief they were so intransigent, since I was completely out of my depth in terms of negotiation skills. I wasn't an idiot but until now I'd only dealt with simple contractual arrangements: the show is this much, or we have this much to pay for a day's work. The language was new to me too, 'in perpetuity' this and 'party of the first part' that. The only time I'd come across a tone this weighty and humourless was in a court of law, and I'd struggled to take that seriously. It wasn't just the contract. Nowadays, almost everyone knows what an NDA is, but I'd never come across a non-disclosure agreement before. It scared me, so I followed it to the letter. I didn't tell anyone anything. My lips were sealed.

'I can't say anything about it,' I'd tell my closest friends. 'I've had to sign a legal thing. If I told you, I would genuinely have to kill you. And then me.'

Obviously, I'm over that now.

It's impossible to over-stress how terrified I was of messing up. It seemed so unlikely that I'd been given this huge opportunity. It was extraordinary that taking the decision not to be poor any more had worked so well. I fully expected someone to take me aside and explain, 'I'm afraid there's been an error. It seems we've made a dreadful mistake. Please go back to your unstable, poverty-stricken existence and never bother us again.' Every week this didn't happen felt like a victory.

Initial rehearsals were soon underway, taking place in various studios around London. John, Dave and I were joined by Pui Fan Lee who was to play Po. Pui still tells a story about how when she was offered the part, she discussed whether or not to accept it with a friend who said, 'Just take it, it's regular income and no-one will watch it anyway.' Ha!

So there we were: two men, two women; two white, one Black, one Chinese; two comedians, one actor, one dancer – Tinky Winky, Dipsy, Laa-Laa, Po – in height order like a bar chart. Dave was to play Tinky Winky, the gentle giant of the Teletubbies. He'd been knocking about the stand-up circuit for years, but despite my having run a comedy club, I hadn't met him before. He cracked me up in rehearsals. When we were asked to do some homework imagining ourselves as a very specific three-year-old, different from our own memories of early childhood, he imagined himself as the child Buddha, which made me laugh a lot. But that would turn out to be Dave's issue – always going for the adult laugh. Ironically, he didn't seem able to transcend himself and focus on the viewing child. He was very lean and very lanky, with clumsily large feet and a smile that was searching for approval in constant nervous attendance around the edges of a mouth too full of something, not necessarily teeth. It was easy to imagine children relating to his awkward vulnerability. Later, it would become apparent that Dave didn't have the requisite skills to channel this quality to the advantage of the character. His interpretation tended to come off as anxious, especially through his seemingly uncertain legs.

John was a stark contrast. As a fellow stand-up, he and Dave had crossed comedic paths in the past. John not only toured nationwide, but also worked as a promoter, bringing Black comedians over from America and taking Black UK stand-ups over to the States. John was handsome, with natty dreads and a Barry White depth in his voice. He was also intrinsically strong, and rooted in his feet and hips where Dave skittered nervously over any surface. There was a tender, caring, careful individual behind the showmanship. He knew exactly what he wanted to do with Dipsy, what kind of a child was at the heart of his portrayal, and it showed the quality of the man that he wasn't afraid to draw on his own childhood truths. John was my buddy, and I think he felt quite protective towards me, despite my ribbing him incessantly. I used to tease him about his comedy gigs. Come Monday, he'd be filling me in on what he'd been up to over the weekend, knowing my background running cabaret clubs. I'd try and get a rise out of him: 'Are you funny yet?' He'd never give me a straight answer.

Years later, I went to see him perform at Up the Creek, a comedy club in Greenwich, and as we chatted before the gig, he said, 'Hey Laa, guess what? I am funny now. I got funny!'

'How did that happen?' I asked. I was being playful, but his answer was profound.

'After all these years, I realised that I didn't have to make the audience like me. I just had to make them laugh.'

This tells you more about John than anything else I could say.

In terms of physical type, Pui was closer to John than Dave. With a low centre of gravity, she was four feet and six inches of strength, and she had the personality to match, with intelligent mischief in her eyes and a contagious laugh that expressed itself through her whole body.

I was a little bit in awe of Pui. She was completely au fait with the whole TV thing and she seemed so confident. Like those kids at secondary school who just grasp it instantly, seeming to know where everything is and where to go. Pui was like that. I was still bumbling around, pretending. Hailing from Nottingham, she attended the Children's Television Workshop and had consequently worked in TV from a very early age. It turned out we had a few people in common from her days at The Albany Theatre in Deptford, and I knew fans of her one-woman show, *Short, Fat, Ugly and Chinese*. Pui was certainly Chinese and petite, but trim and rather beautiful. When I think of Pui, I think of her laughing. On set, I always relished a two-hander with Pui. I knew it would be a breeze because she was such a reliable performer, and hilarious with it.

We started our training with Johnny Hutch, an old school – also just plain old – circus legend who'd enjoyed television fame in the 1980s as the wee baldy-headed sidekick to Benny Hill. He was stern in a way I was familiar with from various borderline sadistic dance teachers. He put us through some fairly hardcore drills and taught us some classic acrobatic tricks to whip us into shape both physically and as a team. When we weren't working with Johnny, we were with Nicky Hinkley, our choreographer. In addition to scripted sketches, the Tubbies would perform a selection of dances to be periodically inserted into the show. While Andy completed the first batch of scripts, our energies would be spent learning the Tubby dances. What a piece of good luck. Focusing on the physical aspect first put me firmly within my comfort zone and would give me a couple of months to let my nerves subside and the actuality of the situation sink in. A plan that was severely disrupted by my having to be unexpectedly whisked into hospital!

Working with Johnny in a studio in Fulham one day, I became increasingly aware of a swelling in my crotch. Something wasn't right. Johnny was uninterested and, as we still had an hour of rehearsal left, he brushed it aside as a swollen gland and therefore trivial. When I got back to New Cross, I had an egg between my legs. I waddled straight to the doctor, who immediately sent me to Lewisham Hospital.

'Now. Go now. Get in a cab and get there as quickly as you can. I will phone ahead. It's urgent because if the swelling bursts there's a high risk of death.' Oh, not so trivial then.

At the hospital, my operation time came round fast. I was in. I was out. I was awake. I was asleep. I had no idea what was being done to me.

I woke up the next morning and found I couldn't move my legs. Oh! This was it. This was my destiny unravelling. Something had gone wrong. I couldn't walk and now I was going to lose my job. It was all over. A nurse spotted my upper body panicking and came to explain that during the operation they had to give me an epidural, and that's why I couldn't move my legs. Phew! Once I could walk again, they gave me a crateful of industrial-strength painkillers and told me to go home and lie down for a week. A whole week? If the bosses liked to be tough on unforeseen absenteeism, then job loss was still possible.

Once safely wrapped in blankets on my couch, I rang Ragdoll and explained my situation, with the facial expression you might pull if you were anticipating being hit round the head or having an ice cube dropped down your back. They were very understanding and wanted only for me to make a full recovery and come back to what was still my job. Hoorah! The following week, I was back in the studio and Johnny was wonderfully dismissive. 'Mmm. Swollen gland. Like I said.' A Bartholin's Gland Abscess to be specific, and what he didn't know was that the operation I had undergone was called a Marsupialisation, because they had to make a little pouch to remove the egg of gunk. Nice. I was a marsupial now. This did not compromise my ability to also be a Teletubby.

Healing nicely, I could turn my attention to the next task. I needed to get inside the head of a three-year-old. Not literally. Anne encouraged us to spend time with small children in order to familiarise ourselves with our audience. I lived next to a park so had ample opportunity to observe children playing. I wrote to the local day nursery, who kindly allowed me to sit quietly in the corner and watch the children interact. At the time, I'd had very little to do with kids of any age. I understood the wisdom of reacquainting myself with their ways, but I was uneasy – nervous even – in their company. I was making myself do the research because that's what the job entailed, but I had no real enthusiasm for it. At first. Once I started properly observing the children, really watching and trying to understand them, I became fascinated.

One day, a group of around a dozen giggling toddlers were holding plastic bricks, banging them against one another and yelling, 'Cheese!' at the tops of their voices. It took me an embarrassingly long time to figure out that what they were doing was playing 'Cheers!' The penny dropped: kids were really funny! I soon commandeered my mates' toddlers, especially my friend Smiler's three-year-old daughter Georgia. She was a proper little character, feisty but charming, eager to please but with her own agenda. Everything I learned about her went into my notebook, along with notes about the children in the park, in the playground, at the nursery, in the library and the swimming pool, on television, in books and in my own memory. These days I'd probably be pulled in for questioning. I processed all my observations through the filter of what Anne and Andy were trying to do with the show and came up with a list of characteristics, the quirks of personality that made Laa, Laa and that would define her always. My 'List of Laa' covered two sides of A4 and included:

- Cares deeply about the wellbeing of the other Teletubbies and hates anyone to be unhappy or in pain
- Can become totally engrossed in a single activity to the exclusion of all else
- Loves to show off (because it amuses the others)

Honestly, it was barely acting. Anne never forgot this list. Whenever I needed reassurance, she'd remind me that I'd never wavered from it, not once. Not once in six years. I'm proud of that. If you're going to create a character that people, especially children, can relate to, it helps to be consistent.

The four of us were lucky to have been given so much freedom to develop our characters – in other hands we'd have been given our instructions and told to get on with it. We'd have been expected to do as we were told and nothing else. I took the responsibility seriously. I believed our audience of small children deserved my best efforts, and I was learning daily how best to make meaning for them. I learned how perceptive children were and how they needed clearly defined personalities to latch onto. Anne was especially concerned about Dipsy and Laa-Laa. Tinky Winky and Po, being the largest and smallest respectively, would pick up favouritism from children who related to their stature even before they layered on any traits, quirks or foibles, but how would we middle two distinguish ourselves? There was talk about us emphasising the fact that we were best friends, and early scripts rather laboured that point with lots of handholding between the two of us and so forth. However, early tests showed that the children were perfectly able to pick up on our individual identities and didn't need this additional forced pairing. Although it did give rise to the birth of the 'Citrus Posse' (named for the two of us in green and yellow suits) in every way superior to the 'Forest Fruits' (in red and purple). John was the one to name our rival gangs and it became a running gag between us that lasted the full six years.

Back in the studio, we had new trainers on our feet but the same old trainers on our backs. We were learning and rehearsing our repertoire of dances for the first season. They weren't complicated, and as this was my skill set I found the work fairly easy. John and Pui were drawing on their physical strength and ability to co-ordinate, but Dave struggled to retain the information and hit the beat. My struggle was keeping my big trap shut. I was a choreographer and couldn't help but have my own ideas about our movements. I knew it would be inappropriate and annoying for me to chip in, so I zipped it. Nicky's way of working was different from my own and the pace was much slower. I understood that it needed to be – we were not a company of dancers – but it was still an adjustment. I was impatient. I didn't want another tea break. I just wanted to get on with it.

It was decided that mine would be the first costume to trial – maybe that would slow me down a bit. I couldn't wait. I was excited and I couldn't deny that my ego was enjoying being the Chosen One. If it hadn't had been me, I'd have wondered why – what had I done wrong? Rationally I realised that it was probably just chance or based on something like which material arrived first, but rationality isn't the order of the day when it comes to performer insecurities.

The suit would be arriving bit by bit as the different elements were completed. Today, it was the body armour and feet. I was immediately struck by how beautifully it was made. The foam exoskeleton was sculpted with care, and the shoulder and hip joints reminded me of a teddy bear. Each unit of foam was covered with yellow Lycra, perforated Lycra was stitched over the joints and the interior was lined with white terry towelling. The stitching was immaculate. The whole thing hung on a sort of belt and rucksack harness arrangement – and then there was the bum.

The intention was for the Teletubbies to look like toddlers, to encourage the toddlers watching to identify with the characters. We needed our audience to relate to us and to see that we were experiencing life in a comparable way. Our physical interactions with the world needed to be as similar as possible to that of the child watching, and the cumbersome nature of the costumes meant that this would happen naturally. To achieve the look of full nappies and the subsequent waddly walk, a large saddle arrangement sat between the legs, protruding to the rear and giving the desired effect. You'd perch on your saddle when sitting down, which lifted you about a foot off the floor, and then you'd forget how large it was when you were standing up and bang into everything. Trainer-shod feet slipped into massive foam overshoes – covered with the same yellow Lycra in the same careful stitching – which attached to the foam legs with elastic. The hands were not yet ready.

It wasn't too bad. It wasn't as restrictive as I thought it was going to be, and not too physically taxing to manoeuvre. Hey, this was going to be okay. We ran through a couple of dances and very little had to be adapted to accommodate the new Tubby suit. I just needed a bit more room. After twenty minutes, I was exhausted. Maybe this was not going to be so easy after all. I realised I had to get used to how much space I needed – especially to the rear – and that I couldn't see my own feet because of the size of my stomach. It was surprising what a difference that made. You wouldn't think you look at your feet much in the general run of life, but it's more than you might imagine.

Anyway, this was not the general run of life. It was very peculiar to have your feet invisible to you, especially when you were required to hit very specific marks. What fun. A whole new learning curve.

I am a childish person – a positive boon in my new employment – and I couldn't help my infantile reactions when it came to divvying up the signifiers for our characters. I was obsessed with red at the time and a little disappointed that my designated colour was yellow – it wasn't a favourite. But hey, at least if I was wearing it, I wouldn't have to look at it. I did a little reading to help myself learn to love it and I found research that showed in Europe, Canada and the US, people associate the colour with amusement, gentleness, humour and spontaneity while in China, yellow is the colour of happiness, glory, harmony and wisdom. Now all I had to do was put aside the duplicity and cowardice that most other cultures seemed to agree were inherently yellow, and I'd be fine.

Then there were the aerial shapes. The triangle, the prong, the circle and the ... what even was that? A wiggly squiggle? It couldn't possibly matter which one was mine, but I loved the wiggly squiggle – it made me laugh. I tried to pretend I didn't have a preference, but I did. I told myself that out of the four on offer, it fitted my 'List of Laa' the best, but really it was just arbitrary desire. Thankfully, I was assigned the wiggly squiggle – I didn't even have to ask. Happy toddler!

We were also to be designated 'Favourite Things', special toys that belonged to our characters: Bag, Hat, Ball, Scooter. We had not yet seen these objects in three dimensions – only as pencil sketches – but obviously it was still easy for me to have an opinion. I wasn't excited by the bag, even though it was red, and I could imagine it being an annoying extra weight to carry around. Dave was welcome to that. Similarly with the hat. I loved the Friesian cow pattern, but I could imagine it being a pain to manipulate. Poor John, I think he got the short straw there: 'Here's some more weight for you to carry around on the massive puppet head balanced on your human neck'. I confess that I felt a twinge of envy when Po got the scooter as I could imagine that being the most fun. Later however, watching Pui push it up the hills, I felt very glad that the scooter was not my Favourite Thing. No, I was to have the ball. An orange ball. Nice. It wasn't actually a ball, but a weather balloon. Light. Yes, I was very happy with that. Laa-Laa's ball, Laa-Laa's ball, Laa-Laa's favourite thing of all.

Then came the issue of the heads. The four of us were to have plaster-cast mouldings of our heads taken, so that the skullcaps could be custom-made for a snug fit. This process involved having your whole head covered in plaster of paris, all the way down the neck to the torso. There's something primal about having your face covered – the body doesn't like it. Squishing my hair into an industrial swimming cap and being wrapped in cling film was uncomfortable but bearable; the metal headrest sticking out of the chair behind my neck was disconcerting, even when it was explained to me that a whole head of plaster was surprisingly heavy, so if I needed support, it would be there; the straws up my nose were positively unpleasant and this was when the fear kicked in. It didn't matter how many times I told myself that this was perfectly fine, completely safe, and hundreds if not thousands of people had been through this procedure without incident, it didn't help. I told myself to get a grip, it wasn't a medical operation, I wasn't having a crotch egg removed. But it was horrible. Not only was the plaster heavy, it was also surprisingly hot. I guessed that was something we were going to have to get used to. I can't remember exactly how long I had to sit there while the plaster went off – half a lifetime maybe – but I spent the whole duration talking myself down from the hysteria I felt rising. Then, when somebody finally yelled at me that I was cooked and release was imminent, I heard the terrifying sound of a tiny saw being used very, very close to my actual brain. Breathe, just breathe. Throughout those early days, we had a B-reel film crew periodically following us around filming behind the scenes footage, and the first thing I saw when I was freed from my plaster casing was the lens of a camera shoved in my face, capturing me at my best – clammy and wan, with swathes of cling film sliding off my sweaty head.

When confronted with the casts later on in Teletubbyland, the stress on our faces was easy to read. We were all bald and grumpy. Except for John. His cast was only partial: everything from the cheekbones down was missing. He had refused point-blank to have the lower part of his face covered so he could be sure of breathing – sensible fellow. At least the plaster casts were of use to our wardrobe department, for storing and working on the puppet heads, because the whole 'bespoke fit' business was a joke. We went through the plaster ordeal twice and I don't remember ever having a skullcap that fitted my head properly. Our wardrobe team always had to insert little bits of foam to compensate for the lack of the promised snug fit.

Looking back now, it's difficult to comprehend how uncharted this territory was for everyone involved. Nothing quite like *Teletubbies* had been attempted before. Aside from the physical aspects, we had to get our heads round the strong philosophy behind the programme. All that Anne had spoken about at that early audition underpinned every aspect of the show. I had never seen people take children's fun so seriously. The language was wonderful, new and strange:

'They are technological space babies.'

'They live in the Tubbytronic Superdome.'

'They have a magical vacuum called Noo-Noo.'

Of course they do.

And I couldn't tell anyone about any of it. Well, okay, I did show my parents some footage of our dance rehearsals, just to prove I wasn't lying about the job. I don't think they were very impressed. My dad asked, 'What gimmick will you employ to make sure you're everyone's favourite?'

No-one could be everyone's favourite, I thought – that's not how these things work. But I told him, 'I thought I'd just try and be the best.'

CHAPTER 3

SPIRIT OF YELLOW

Winter was gradually giving in to the promise of Spring and we were in a minibus driving up the M40, going to Stratford-upon-Avon. No longer would we be confined to featureless function rooms in the capital – this was the main event. We were off to the mothership, to our new home, to our first glimpse of Teletubbyland – the magical picture-book perfection of the English countryside where, for reasons no-one knew, the Teletubbies resided.

We were taken over the hills and far away, which was approximately eight miles south of the town. We drove off the A road onto the B road, off the B road onto the road to a farm, off the farm road onto a dirt track, off the dirt track and into a field. In this field was a large muddy hole and a couple of JCBs busily making it larger. Not picture-book perfection just yet then. It was an exposed site, but well away from public gaze. Ragdoll had already built a little cottage in a wooded glade on the same farm, where they had filmed *Tots TV*. This time the farmer would be playing host to some altogether larger puppets.

Once we'd parked at the edge of the field on a small patch of what little grass remained in the sea of mud, the van driver came to help us out. The boys descended first, rejecting any assistance. When it was my turn, I took the driver's steadying hand out of politeness while cracking a joke that made him let out a single guffaw and exclaim, 'Oh! We've got ourselves a comedian, have we?' I threw a glance that said, 'Hear that?' at the two professional comedians who had failed to be sufficiently entertaining in the eyes of our chauffeur. Yes, that is how it's going to be, boys.

Anne and Andy were with us on that first day and it was obvious they shared a clear vision of the finished landscape. They excitedly described the new world they were creating, tripping over each other's words and finishing one another's sentences.

'The dip will go out to there . . .'

' . . . and the mud will be used to form little hillocks all along there, you know like at Burton Dassett. And the windmill will be there, and paths . . .'

' . . . will go all the way around there and there with a big entrance slope just there . . .'

' . . . and the dome in the middle down there, obviously, with trees planted there and there.'

'And also over there.'

We obediently moved our heads in the directions indicated and nodded as if we too could see the picture they were painting. I followed as best I could. Even though I wasn't able to fully visualise the concept at this juncture, I'd be seeing it in actuality soon enough and that steadied the panic. It was all out of my hands and right then I had no actual responsibility, so I thought I may just as well sit back and enjoy the ride. The biggest things I had to concern myself with were that my cheap shoes weren't up to the mud and I was distracted by trying to stay vertical on the slippery hillside – plus, there was a powerful and freezing wind. To escape the chill, we were taken to a local pub for lunch and told that Ragdoll would be footing the bill. Hoorah!

We dined on the company fairly often during those first few weeks in Stratford, which was a whole new world for me. I had been hungry for approximately fifteen years, so every time I had the opportunity for a slap-up meal at someone else's expense, I ate as much as I possibly could. It wasn't even a conscious decision – I'd just got so used to not knowing where the next meal was coming from that it was instinctive to make the most of any opportunity to fill up. It took a long time for this to change, for me to come to the realisation that I didn't have to consume every meal as if there was no tomorrow. There would be a tomorrow, and it would have a catering truck in it.

After lunch, we went to the Ragdoll office in the middle of town to be overwhelmed by meeting new people with mysterious roles behind the scenes. I tried – and failed – to retain the information of whose face went with which name and job description, and what that job description actually meant. Then we were taken to visit the Ragdoll Shop in the high street. It was peopled with characters from all the company's shows and there was an actual replica of *Rosie and Jim*'s boat. It wasn't your average toy shop, because the primary function was not to sell things – although it did – but to be a place for children and their families to come and play. The play areas in the shop allowed the programme-makers to watch unobtrusively how children connected with various shows and characters. What a clever idea. I couldn't wait until there was a *Teletubbies* section and we could visit ourselves, incognito, to see how the children related to us.

Next, an excited production assistant took us to view a new-build property in a nearby cul-de-sac. The idea was that the four of us would live in this house during the week when we were filming – paid for by the company – and then be free to return to our actual homes each weekend. The house was in the centre of Stratford and had been built with family occupancy in mind:

one large master bedroom, one ample guest room and two small rooms for the kids, who'd only need a single bed. Which of us would be content with being the kids? We took the tour, nodded politely, smiled, tried to read one another's minds and said all the right words. I did my best to hide the panic rising inside me. It was only held in check by the desire to remain positive and not come across as one of those ungrateful actor types.

That night we stayed in one of the best hotels in Stratford.

'Don't get used to it – it's a one-off treat,' Anne said firmly but with a smile. It made me like her even more.

That evening, Pui broached the subject as we shared a nightcap in her bedroom.

'I'm not sure about the house.'

Phew! Thank goodness.

I was terrified that it was only me who had reservations. I was filled with dread at the thought of the four of us working together all day, in a field in the middle of nowhere, and then coming home to spend our downtime in one another's company too. I really liked them all, but it was obvious the work was going to be intense. We would get tired and irritable – or at least I knew I would. Twenty-four hours together was a bad idea, especially if you drew the short straw and got one of the small rooms. It was such a relief that Pui felt the same way. The boys agreed, but it was Pui and I who put on our kid gloves to explain how we felt. We didn't want to be difficult – we were grateful, truly we were – but for the good of the show, we felt it might be a better idea for us to maintain some independence outside of work hours. It didn't seem unreasonable, and we hoped that anyone putting themselves in our position would understand our point of view.

Luckily, Ragdoll did understand and promised that alternative arrangements would be made. Nevertheless, I worried that it was a blot on our copybook, a point marked against the difficult 'Talent'.

Rehearsals continued through the early part of 1996, and we were now splitting our time between London and Stratford-upon-Avon, where we stayed in modest hotel accommodation. We were immediately aware that this was better – much better – than living in the same house.

All four of us had been working in our skeleton bodysuits for a while, so it was time to progress. We were summoned to the designer's house in West Norwood for the next stage: meeting the baby-gro that was to become our outer skin. Niki Lyons had a large house, but it wasn't large enough to accommodate four enormous furry space toddlers at once, so our appointment times were staggered. John had been seen before me and when I passed him on the stairs on his way out, he was soaking wet with sweat. 'You remember how we used to be able to move?' he said, before falling out the door. He was right. At the time, the fabric used for the Teletubbies' outer layer was revolutionary: four-way stretch fun-fur. It was made in America and shipped over to the UK already dyed, to be stitched together by Niki's team.

As I went into the workroom, sewing assistants who would later become our dressers were pulling a yolk-coloured stretchy fur over a foamy fat suit. It looked like a lot of effort. John's words rang in my head as I made sense of what I was witnessing. Once inside the newly fur-clad costume, I understood what he meant. There was now four-way resistance every time I tried to move. In addition, the welcome airiness of the perforated Lycra over the joints was now rendered obsolete. No air could penetrate that fur. This was a whole new level of hot and uncomfortable. Mitten paws/hands were poppered onto the arms, and the now fur-covered feet were similarly attached to the legs. I was sealed in from the neck down. This was going to be tougher than I had first imagined. For the first time, a thought entered into my head which would be a recurring mantra for the next few months: I am going to die. It wasn't an existential revelation. As a puny asthmatic – an affliction I shared with my Citrus Posse buddy – I was seriously worried about my ability to function in this thing.

My boyfriend at the time had come along for the ride, so we could have a walk in Dulwich Park on the way home and make a day of it. He had been sequestered downstairs so as not to be exposed to any top-secret costumery, but on our way out an assistant handed a large black plastic moulding to the designer.

'Look,' she indicated to me, 'this is what the face will look like. Not black plastic, obviously – it'll be covered with flesh-coloured fabric and painted up with facial features.'

'What size will the real one be?' asked my boyfriend.

'This is the real one.'

It was huge.

I was going to die.

As the costumes neared completion, we were spending more time in Stratford-upon-Avon and Anne had lined up a cornucopia of experts to help us fulfil our contractual obligations. We spent a day with the founder of Clown Doctors: performers who visit and play with children in long-term hospital care. She schooled us in non-verbal communication and physical comedy, as well as workshopping us in slapstick, pantomime and mask. We worked with professional clown Angela de Castro to hone our funny. To help us develop vocal strength and character, we learnt to open our throats and chant in a Mongolian fashion, which was much more fun than it sounds. Crucially, we worked on our puppeteering skills with master puppeteer Robin Stevens – a long-term Ragdollie who played Pob in *Pob's Programme*, Tom in *Tot's TV* and Jim in *Rosie and Jim*.

At last the heads were sufficiently ready for us to work with, although the intricacies of their facial paintwork – their make-up if you will – had not been completed. Robin worked with us two at a time. Pui and I sat in front of a large mirror with our puppet heads on our laps. In our hands were two controls, very much like the brake mechanisms on a bicycle, one to blink the eyes and one to open and close the mouth. All high-tech stuff. By working with a mirror, we could see the effect that our puppeteering had for the viewer. First, we needed to decide which hand would operate which feature. I asked the question, 'How often should we blink? Should we co-ordinate it with our own blinking to look natural?'

The answer Robin gave sounded obvious once he said it: 'No, that's impossible if you're speaking at the same time. You should blink whenever you think of it – it's what gives the puppet face life when it's in repose. Ideally it should become like a background noise, an instinctive, automatic thing that you don't even have to think about, like an involuntary muscle movement. It's important that you don't stop whenever you have to speak. Just keep blinking.'

I was glad I'd started taking drumming lessons the previous year, so had been practising the kind of pat-head-rub-tummy co-ordination skills I now needed. As the blink had to be constant, it made sense for my left hand to do that job, while my more dextrous right hand – I am right-handed – operated the mouth, which required more detail.

Working with a mirror allowed us to closely study how human mouths actually move when speaking. It's more complex than you might suppose – not just a matter of opening on the vowel sounds and closing for the consonants. For example, many words have a 'bounce': the lips don't close and remain closed, they rebound a little at the end of the word. Try it – stand in front of the mirror and say the word 'bounce'. Do you see? So, when puppeteering such a word, there's the main opening of the mouth and then a small rebound movement at the end. Details such as this made the articulation of the puppet more believable and made a nerdy dance performer thrill at learning a new skill.

I worked hard at the puppeteering. I loved the challenge of trying to be as accurate as possible. I also learned that almost nothing is funnier than standing completely still looking straight to camera and blinking. You can make those blinks say a lot. Operating the mechanics of the puppet soon became an automatic reflex. Once, when I was taking a nap on my couch at home, I woke myself up by talking in my sleep. As I came to, I realised that my right hand was moving in time with my mouth, as if I was puppeteering myself, and my left hand was blinking. I wasn't even dreaming about *Teletubbies*.

The voices were a whole other issue and were set to plague us for months to come. I could understand Anne and Andy's consternation – it was crucial that we found voices with which the viewing audience could identify and that they would warm to. We were encouraged to err towards a higher pitch – research shows younger children respond better to the top end of the human range – but to avoid becoming too squeaky or grating. We needed to identify a consistent Teletubby sound, but to also develop four voices that were sufficiently individual not to be confused with one another. This was also the area where we received the least direction as the producers were keen for us to settle on a sound that felt true to our character development. Consequently, whenever the six of us were together, the question of how we were getting on with 'finding our voices' would always come up.

One evening we were all in a local Indian restaurant for dinner after a late rehearsal, seated at the only occupied table in the upstairs section. Anne had us stand up in the middle of the room, one at a time, to demonstrate how far we'd got with 'finding our voices' as the staff manoeuvred around us laying out poppadoms and pickles. The nonchalance of the waiters when confronted with this display led me to believe they were used to the crazy television lady, as were most of Stratford's eateries.

We were also asked to create an identifying theme tune for each Teletubby. These musical signatures were to be an integral part of the programme, so a great deal of care needed to be taken with getting them right. I'd rather lucked out with being called Laa-Laa – no great taxing of my creative brain necessary as far as lyrics were concerned. However, I wasn't sure whether they'd go for my idea to keep the tune random and improvised, to reflect how she was feeling at any given time – though she was usually feeling delighted with everything. I needn't have worried; I was free to make it as bonkers as I fancied. Laa-Laa was free to scat her way over Tubbyland, reflecting the highs and lows of the landscape in her vocalisations.

Anne wanted John to draw on his Jamaican heritage, so he incorporated a little reggae groove – that's where, 'Bubbadum Bubbadum Bub-badum' comes from, *not* inspired by the poppadoms at the Indian restaurant – and John extended Dipsy's repertoire with the unforgettable 'Hat' song. Altogether now . . .

Because Po was going to be a dynamic personality, and she had the scooter, Pui suggested 'fast' and 'slow' would be appropriate words for her song, and she wanted to say them in Cantonese, 'Faai-di, faai-di, faai-di. Maan, maan, maan.' This led to all sorts of controversy further down the line from those who claimed she was saying 'faggot' or 'fuck it' or other phrases offensive to Western ears.

I don't remember whether Dave invented Tinky Winky's song, 'Pinkle Winkle Tinky Winky, Pinkle Wiiiiiinkle Tinky Wiiiiiinky', or if that came later from Mark Heenehan who voiced the character. The bosses weren't very happy with the vocal characterisation Dave was offering up. Pui and I wondered if all the drama about the voices was really aimed at him, but in not wanting to single Dave out for negative attention, the producers chose to keep on at all four of us. We shall never know whether this theory was correct.

Laa-Laa's singing was a really important element of her character. As a child, I loved to sing and dance and threw myself into any performance or creative endeavour with gusto, taking my efforts with a level of seriousness that probably only added to the overall comic impression. I thought bringing this characteristic to Laa would be funny for the viewing children and for their parents too. Later on when we were in the swing of filming, it was my favourite thing to read in the script, 'Laa-Laa sings a song'. Laa-Laa would sing for all sorts of reasons, for example to heal Po's poorly tummy or to coax the ball out the tree or to solve any random conundrum. I knew I could let rip in any way that felt appropriate – by which I mean funny – and I'd leap at the opportunity to ham it up as much as possible, bringing operatic intent to deliberately flimsy content. *Nowhere to Sit* was a classic example and if *Laa-Laa's Greatest Hits* existed, that song would definitely be featured. In an early script, 'The Chair', Andy indicated that Laa-Laa should express her frustration with some kind of vocalisation, possibly a child-friendly expletive. I thought long and hard, then I remembered the children in the nursery all those months ago, saying 'Cheese!' instead of 'Cheers', and came up with, 'Bibbley Cheese!'. It doesn't feature in many scripts, but it did catch on among certain members of the crew.

The decisions around how the Teletubbies spoke were some of the most collaborative in those early days. Andy, being qualified in Speech Sciences, drew on extensive knowledge and research as well as his own unfailing instinct. Together with Anne, he had prepared a list of defined words and phrases that the Teletubbies would say. The total was fewer than thirty, including our names. The premise was to keep things very simple, to have a similar range of vocabulary to the children who would be our audience and not to waver from this. The only exceptions were words we repeated after hearing them from the narrator or the voice trumpets. Given these restrictions, we had to make sure that our definitive vocabulary list would suffice for any given situation that might arise. It was fascinating to pare down human communication to the bare minimum – to the very least we needed.

My contributions were 'Ee-Arr' as a well-used shortening of 'here you are', 'Nice' as Laa-Laa's go-to phrase of approval, and 'Please' and 'Thank you' – being polite was on the 'List of Laa' after all. Anne's and Andy's knowledge, their level of care, their attention to detail and all-consuming integrity was such that any time either of them accepted one of my ideas, I felt as if I'd been given a gold star at school. They were thorough in their methodology, clear in their intent, and totally focused on the viewing child. I was just Crazy Hair Girl from New Cross.

While we were developing our characters, concrete foundations for what was to become the Tubbytronic Superdome were being laid in our field. A local farmer complained to the council that someone was building an alien landing-pad south of Stratford-upon-Avon. In a way, he was absolutely right. Were we aliens? Well, if you wanted, you could argue that the Tubbytronic Superdome was in fact a crashed spaceship over which grass and flowers had grown. All we Tubbies really cared about was that it was our home. We never offered any backstory about where the Teletubbies came from, why they lived out in the English countryside or how they got there. These things wouldn't be important to the children – they'd be more interested in what was going on with the Tubbies in the here and now. Only grown-ups would bother themselves with that kind of boring detail. As the set started to take shape, Wembley turf was laid over the moulded mud, steelworks were erected to support the dome and the groundworks for the windmill – which needed to be able to hinge in and out of view so as not to be a permanent landmark – were put in place. The Teletubbies were getting closer to taking up permanent residence.

As the set moved nearer to completion, so did the costumes and eventually the moment of unveiling arrived. Ragdoll had taken over the United Reformed Church Hall, all dark wood and gothic detailing, and most of the adjoining car park was filled with our trucks, busses and cars. Within the hall a flurry of costumiers and dressers were making final adjustments and feeling their way to some kind of modus operandi that we could implement over the coming months.

My dresser was the wardrobe mistress, Beth Ferdinando, henceforth 'Aunty Beth' – small, bright and perfectly formed with an easy laugh belying a flinty Yorkshire edge. Aunty Beth wasn't to be messed with, but she was playful too. There's a curious transition phase in this kind of character work between being your everyday self and becoming the personality you are paid to inhabit. The fun is in the clash of the puppet's voice, physicality and quality with the everyday speech patterns of your human self – including the swearing. It was a juxtaposition we all played on for laughs, and Beth and I developed our own series of running gags. For example, the puppet feet were built around a pair of trainers and when she put them on me, the tongue of the trainer would get ruckled up inside and need straightening out. The words, 'Tongue me, baby,' coming from Laa-Laa would usually raise a smile.

But all that was yet to come. Today was the first time that the four of us would be in costume together, adding a ridiculous amount of dazzling colour to a dingy church hall. This was the moment of truth for Anne and Andy. All that time and money and effort, all those people relying on their crazy idea becoming a successful reality – now we would find out if it had. They stood motionless, arms folded, looking at the four of us fully Tubbed-up. We were the stuff of their combined imaginations made flesh, or fun-fur anyway. I desperately wanted to make it work for them. I wanted them to be happy, to be pleased with what they had wrought, but most of all I wanted to make them smile. I thought they were smiling, but it was difficult to tell from inside the suit. I was trying to look out of the mouth but I couldn't really see anything. I was already dripping with sweat and the weight of the head on my neck was excruciating. My shoulders ached. There was that thought again: I am going to die.

'Can you fall over?' they shouted at us.

I gingerly tried to lower myself to the floor. My massive bum hit first, which threw me off-balance backwards and then the weight of the head took over and I was down, flat on my back, my legs waggling in the air. I could hear Anne and Andy falling about laughing.

'It's wonderful.'

'It's hilarious.'

'Oh, excellent, it is going to be funny.'

'Thank you, now you can get back up again.'

Nothing.

The saddle between my legs meant my legs were forced upwards and I couldn't touch the floor with my feet. The weight of the head was such that lifting it up from the ground was out of the question. As I tried to roll to the side, the ears were so huge that I couldn't manoeuvre myself over. I was stuck. At least I was not alone in this conundrum – all four of us were poleaxed. Anne and Andy stopped laughing. This was a disaster. Falling over and getting back up again was a mainstay of the show and it would literally die on its arse if that couldn't be achieved. The dressers helped us back to our feet and I was starting to realise how dependent on Aunty Beth I was about to become. However, the Tubbies would not be beaten. We would persist and crack this thing. We tried again. And again. Eventually, we figured out how to stand up unaided.

Unsurprisingly, it was more or less the same technique that toddlers use when they figure out how to get to a standing position. We rocked from side to side to build up momentum, then flung ourselves over in one direction. It took a great deal of effort, not least in order to overcome the giant ears – one problem toddlers don't have. As part of the same motion, we had to kick our feet to keep the momentum going, while simultaneously reaching out the uppermost arm in order to roll onto our fronts. Despite having a huge belly in the way, we then brought our knees up, leaned onto our hands and somehow found a way to get the soles of our feet in touch with the floor. From this position, there was another big effort to push back and heave ourselves to a standing position, supporting our giant heads as we did so. Initially this whole process took a long time – too long. After a week or two of practice we were proficient toddlers, and eventually it became speedy second nature.

After that first thirty minutes or so, fully exerting myself while hermetically sealed in four stones of fun-fur, my big fear started to seem like a real possibility. Maybe I actually was going to die. Though I now had first-hand experience of exactly how physically tough this job was going to be, I still had to factor in the hills, the dancing, my asthma, hay fever. Good God – I didn't even know if I was capable of getting up at 6.30am for five days on the trot. I was a theatre performer – everything happened in the evenings! Then Anne said, 'Oh, by the way, the rabbits arrive next week . . .'

The what now? So we learnt that yes, we would be sharing Teletubbyland with five Flemish Giant rabbits – a breed that can grow up to 22lbs.

'I hope no-one's allergic!'

I was allergic. I'd been allergic to all things furry for as long as I could remember, and rabbits were very furry, especially giant ones. Eeek! I was such a wimp. I hated myself.

This was the straw that broke my drama-queen camel's back. I was having a freak out, suddenly everything just seemed a bit Aaaaaargh! I needed to calm myself down, to get over myself, to have a word with myself. So I did. What was my deepest concern? It was being unable to breathe. It was my asthma preventing me from being able to do this job. What was the chief driver of this fear? Being enclosed in that thing, with only the tiny gap that constituted the mouth giving me access to any air. Was it the head that was freaking me out? Mostly, yes. Okay then, I thought, I need to find a way to cope, so let's spend some more time in the head.

When I wasn't needed at rehearsal, I'd lie on my back with my human head in the puppet head – deep breathing – and try to dismiss the reality of existing in a claustrophobic black bowl, thinking instead about what the audience would see. Aha! They would see yellow. I drew on my colour-based research and decided to make a better, more positive mantra than 'I'm going to die'. I chose 'Spirit of Yellow'. I imagined the sunny yellow of Laa permeating the puppet and filling me with each breath. With every inhalation, I became the embodiment of all that happiness, humour and harmony; rather than focusing on being a terrified wimp, I exuded that happiness, humour and harmony back into the world.

In our training, Anne had talked to us about focusing on a particular child watching the television. She encouraged us not to think about a generic audience of children, but to focus on just one. She wanted us to have a clear idea of that child, to speak to just them, to communicate with just them, only them and directly – perhaps we could try thinking of a specific child we know. I thought of Georgia, of course. It was excellent advice which, alongside my new 'Spirit of Yellow' mantra, gave me what I needed to overcome the unpleasant human experience of being inside the puppet.

I might still be going to die, but at least I'd die a whole lot happier.

CHAPTER 4

TELETUBBIES COME TO PLAY

No matter that the set wasn't quite finished, no matter that the 'backstage' area looked like Glastonbury on a bad year, no matter that the level of uncertainty vastly outweighed anyone's knowledge of how to make this madness work: if we didn't start filming now, we were never going to get the first season in the can. It was April, and inevitably everything was behind already. Poor Anne smiled the smile of a woman on the edge: equal parts excitement and terror. She was not alone.

Although the majority of *Teletubbies* was filmed on the real set, in the real countryside, some elements of the title sequence needed to be filmed on a blue screen. For this we decamped to a huge sound stage on the outskirts of London. These special effects were also material we could get done while they finished building the set.

One of the required components involved each of us jumping into and out of the top of the dome. To achieve this, two setups had been built: one a blue trampoline in front of a blue screen and the other a giant moulding to match the curve of the top of the dome with a massive pile of crash mats and cardboard beneath. It was a would-be stunt person's paradise. There were blokes everywhere, marching around sorting lights and cables and camera angles and so forth – it looked like a proper film set and I was doubly excited.

It would have been more usual to use a green screen, but the colour of Dipsy meant that if we used green, he'd just be a floating face! There was still a keying issue with Tinky Winky's purple on the blue, but it was the lesser of two evils. To clarify, keying is the technical term for making sure the outline between the action and the background is clean and clear and doesn't have a fuzzy halo, which used to happen in the early days of this process.

John was first up on the trampoline and he really struggled. Aunty Beth had been a trampolining champ in her youth, so she was yelling instructions from the side-lines as John persisted. He couldn't seem to get enough height for a clear shot. I was genuinely concerned for his wellbeing – perhaps it wasn't me who was going to die after all. After many takes, a clean shot was achieved and John was freed from his torture. He had sweat dripping everywhere and was the wettest human being I had ever seen. Now it was my turn.

I was apprehensive after seeing John struggle, but my dance training stood me in good stead and thankfully I didn't suffer the same lengthy torment. Actually, it was pretty good fun – don't tell John – despite the disconcerting sensation of not being able to see whether my feet would land on or off the trampoline. Once the Forest Fruits had done their bit, we all went over to the other setup.

This was more like it – we were to trot up a sizeable slope and fling ourselves off the back onto the crashmats. It was possible to throw your arms in the air in a way that stabilised the head but looked as if it was 'like you just don't care'. I wanted to do this over and over, like a kid at the funfair. But no, once it was shot and in the can, the day's adventures were over. Bibbley Cheese!

Then, just as filming had finished for the day and the four of us were milling around while everything was packed away, a wave of excitement washed over the room. The composer had arrived with the first draft of the theme song and it was to be played to everyone over the studio sound system. I was having an argument with a producer about some expenses I was owed. 'For God's sake Nikky, it's only eighteen quid.' He had been in television forever, whereas not so long ago, that was six days' money for me. Then the music started up and nothing else was important.

The song was brilliant. The beat sounded exactly how we looked, with our comic full-nappy waddle, and the instrumentation chuckled along in such a way that it was impossible not to smile. I pictured a room full of toddlers dancing and singing, joining in with the song and having the time of their lives. The same feeling rose in me that I'd felt that first time Anne talked about what she was trying to do with *Teletubbies*. Oh my God, I thought, I'm involved in a work of absolute genius.

With the studio-based material completed, it was time to settle into the routine of filming in Teletubbyland. Let me take you on my journey to work. My call time was always 8.00am, bright and early, on a Monday morning. I did not drive. I'd had no reason to drive during the decade or so I'd been living in London, where there was public transport. Public transport was not really a thing in mid-1990s rural Warwickshire. There were no trains from London to Stratford-upon-Avon on a Sunday. Luckily, Dave lived in Lambeth, which was a mere number 53 bus ride away, and he kindly agreed to give me a lift on Sunday evenings. We drove up the M40 – the road which would become our new best friend – to Mickleton in the North Cotswolds where three Tubbies and half the crew would be housed in The Three Ways Hotel, every week until the clocks went back. It didn't take long for everyone to decide which room they liked best. My choice was up in the eaves, out of the way, and it overlooked the bus-stop where local youths liked to gather and check out a moped or some such.

My routine on arrival, at around 10.00pm, was a swift pint then straight to bed. It was years since I'd had a regular job that entailed getting up early every day and I couldn't help but doubt my ability to do it – to do any of this job – so I took it very seriously and was extremely disciplined and well behaved. As Dave took forever to get ready and I was – and still am – a fiercely punctual individual, Pui gave me a lift to work every day in her little red Micra. The route took us over the rise of Meon Hill, where we could snatch a peek of the Malvern Hills if we were lucky, through archetypal rolling English countryside and the chocolate-box village of Admington. We passed 'Man of Many Dogs' – a regular-as-clockwork local dog-walker with whom we exchanged cheery greetings – and went around an old barrow that shared its field with hawthorn and sheep, before winding round three horse corner, and straight over a cattle grid to arrive at Sweet Knowle Farm.

The farm was quite a large settlement. There was a charming gatehouse occupied by old Mrs Hardiman, an imposing main building where the farmers Rex and Rosemary lived and from where they ran the farm, a row of workers' cottages and then Avon Aquatics – an emporium of everything needed to keep fish in a house or a garden, including the fish. If you walked down the track from behind a selection of farm outbuildings and a landmark silo, you'd find the home of the Teletubbies and all those that facilitated their existence.

First, on your right, was the rabbit enclosure – home to five *mahoosive* occupants to welcome you to Teletubbyland. Next to that was a Portakabin for visitors to arrive at and wait, before being escorted onto the set proper, which was directly ahead. On the left was a battered old caravan, wherein resided the genius of Andy Davenport who, when not writing, writing and writing, would watch everything being filmed on his monitor so that he could come rushing out to correct us when we strayed from his vision. Past the caravan took you to the top of the slope down to the dome. The slope itself was Astroturf, but the banks that surrounded the dip – in which the dome sat in all its glory – were covered in hallowed Wembley turf. On the front side, at least. The back side, which would eventually grass over nicely, was currently mud. Everywhere that wouldn't be seen by the camera – and some places that would – was currently mud.

If you turned right before you got to the slope, you'd find yourself walking down a street of Portakabins. On your left, built into the earthen bank, was the gallery: a subterranean control room from where director, production assistant, vision mixer, and other puppet-masters issued their instructions. Next door was the art department – home to flowers, toast, custard, scenery, props and the marvellous people who made them. Then there was the wardrobe department and drying room. Although it was possible to wash the outer baby-gro, the padded suit was not so easily absolved of its occupant's sweat. Praise be for ample applications of Febreze and an overnight stay in the drying room after each day's filming.

At the end of the Portakabin street, you'd find the Talent. We had a super-sized Portakabin with a central lounge area where the daily read-throughs took place, and a changing room at either end. We were perfectly positioned for nosey-neighbouring down the strip, and there was a handy sliding window which I opened as a Chewits shop during the afternoon tea break, handing out sweets to anyone who needed a sugar hit to get them through the last quarter of the eleven-hour day.

On the other side of the street was the kitchen and canteen, the office, and the toilets facing the boys' dressing room. In his downtime, John was a hygiene sentinel, sitting in his armchair like an old man, cussing those that came out of the gents without washing their hands. At least we knew whose mitts to avoid. While I'm on the subject of sanitation, we soon realised that a production unit of around forty-five people created a fair amount of waste, and that had to go somewhere, right?

Once a week, the dreaded Shit Wagon would arrive and pump the accumulated wee and poo out of the septic tank and into a lorry to take it away – far, far away to somewhere we didn't need to worry our pretty little heads about. This process stank. No words are sufficient to do justice to the force of this odour. Imagine the worst smell of excrement you have ever smelled and add a metaphorical nought. Or two. You could run, but you couldn't hide. It didn't matter where you were on site, the stench would reach you and make you heave. We learned the hard way how important it was not to leave the puppet head outside with the neck hole facing the prevailing wind. Taking all this into account, it's amazing how cheery the Shit Wagon driver was. I don't think it would be an exaggeration to say he loved his job.

One of the most common questions I get asked – even now – is how *Teletubbies* was filmed. Was it in a studio? Was it done with green screen? Did we rely on CGI? When I tell them that it was all real, that Teletubbyland actually existed, I feel a little thrill – akin to those early days when everything was new and extraordinary and exciting. I'm so proud of the people who made it exist in real life, who put in all those man-hours and all that effort to make a child's fantasy world into reality.

One sunny summer weekend, I took my family to have a look at the place and it immediately worked its magic on all of them. My aged Nan positively frolicked around with delight – Teletubbyland just had that effect on people. I couldn't have imagined a more wonderful workplace. I loved it so much that I remember asking if I could live in the dome when filming was over. Unfortunately, it had been a proviso of the planning permission that after filming the site would be flooded and put back to nature – plus the structure wasn't really sound enough to last indefinitely into the future. Then there was the poo problem.

Never mind – if I couldn't actually live in Teletubbyland then at least it would be my pretend home for the next three years. By this stage, it was gradually filling up with furniture. Huge bubble-wrapped packages were manhandled into the dome as designers and fabricators gathered, eagerly awaiting the nod of approval from Anne. She had a reputation for being fierce, but though I could see the steel behind her eyes, I struggled to understand this reputation – until the day the toast machine arrived. The four of us had not been included in any design conversations and when this new addition was unveiled, all we saw was another astonishingly giant object, more or less in keeping with the other astonishingly giant objects in the dome. It was triangular, like a huge Dairylea cheese segment with its point upwards. In the eyes of Anne, what it actually was, was wrong. It was wrong in all sorts of ways: it was not what they discussed, it was the wrong colour, it was the wrong shape, there was nothing for the children to countdown, it was ugly, it was lacking in fun and playfulness, and besides all of that – how was a circular piece of toast meant to fit within a pointy slot? As we listened to her rage about this, I made a mental note to stay on the right side of Anne. I was glad my job was to be funny – at least I knew what that was. The poor production designers were having to create enormous furnishings and appliances, the likes of which had never been seen before.

You know how it is when you go to a primary school and sit at a desk or use a teeny tiny toilet and it makes you feel like a giant? The Tubbytronic Superdome was the exact opposite of that. Sitting at the Tubby Table without my costume on made me feel like I was four again – which was handy in this circumstance.

Then there were the beds. In our human forms, all four of us could get in the biggest one at once, and each of them was pretty sizeable. What a treat it was to have a job with a really comfy bed on site. In costume, the beds were less comfy. The problem was that each bed had a hood at the head end, rather like you would get on an old-fashioned pram. We couldn't lie straight back because the aerial and the top of our heads would get jammed against the hood, scrunching our human head forward and, more importantly, looking terrible on camera. I think we all developed our own techniques to solve the problem. Mine was to crawl forwards onto the bed, ducking my head right down to ensure the aerial got under the hood, then flipping over onto my back and wriggling like a stranded tortoise until in position, at the same time manoeuvring the blanket to lie beautifully over my legs and tummy. Camera trickery and many tucking-in dressers helped with that last stage of the process. Like almost all of our props, the beds were much more fun for us as humans than they were when we were encased in fur with a huge bum and a giant head.

Getting used to being in the giant head was a real challenge. In case you've ever wondered, this is what it was like from the inside. Our human heads sat within a skullcap with struts coming out of it, connecting it to the exterior puppet head. The position was such that our human eyes were level with the puppet's mouth. In front of our eyes was an assemblage of metal: the hinge mechanism which opened and closed the mouth. It was a little disconcerting to have sharp metal bars directly opposite our vulnerable little noses, and at first I was terrified that at some point I would fall over forwards and impale myself on my own mouth. Yes, I was still noting the myriad ways in which it was possible for me to die doing this job. When, inevitably, I did fall over forwards, I pulled the face of dread and waited for impact... but no. The skullcap was a tight enough fit to hold my head in place, and although the impact squished my puppet nose – not a good look – my exoskeleton was strong enough to protect me, helped by my huge stomach. So I was in the extraordinary position of being suspended face down within my puppet like an element in a lightbulb. Strangely comfy.

From the camera's point of view, if you shone massive lights at a puppet head with a mouthful of metal, that metal was going to catch the light and glint it back, so the gape of the mouth had to be covered in black gauze to prevent this from happening. Therefore, once sealed in the suit, our only visual connection with the outside world was past a load of metal and through the tiny holes in the gauze. I had been worried about whether I would be able to wear my glasses inside the head and, if not, whether I would have sufficient vision. As it turned out, I could see so little anyhow that it didn't really matter if what I was seeing was in focus. At the beginning of every season of filming, I would have to 'get my eye in' afresh. I'd struggle for a few days, and then my brain would remember how to adjust the focal length to blur out the obstacles in the foreground, to see past them to the camera and the other giant, partially blind, brightly coloured blobs.

To give you some idea of the size of the head, if I reached my arms out to my sides as far as I could and then bent my hands upwards, that's where my ears were. If I reached my arms forward on a diagonal as far as I was able and did the same, I could just about put my hands over my eyes. That's one big head.

You may be wondering why the head, and everything else for that matter, had to be so enormous. It's a fair question, and it hinges on the problem of employing fully-grown adults to play what are, essentially, toddlers. I don't need to explain to you that grown-ups are – or should be – a different shape to toddlers. The proportions aren't the same. Beyond this, the intention was to exaggerate the toddler characteristics – to have even bigger nappy bums than an actual child would, to have fatter tummies, to overemphasise the disproportionate size of the head. The ears were just for fun. In short, to get the ratio right and in order to look like a toddler, the whole puppet had to be huge.

If you want a toddler to identify with a character, the toddler must believe that the character is the same size as them. Therefore, if you want giant puppets to look small, everything they interact with has to be doubly ginormous. It's all very clever. The rabbits were perhaps the smartest move. Most small children know the approximate size of a rabbit, so if you bring in unfeasibly large rabbits, the children will automatically make the presumption and do the maths for you. Our giant rabbits also confused the local population. If a fiercely punctual person such as myself got to work early and decided to walk down the dirt track rather than wait for the minibus shuttle, they might well come across a delegation of normal-sized wild rabbits lined up outside our giant rabbits' hutch. Marvelling. 'See, I told you they were real. Bow down, bow down, they are as gods to us!'

With the physical proportions of Teletubbyland designed to give the impression that the Teletubbies were the same size as toddlers, it was also necessary to set up social norms and conventions that chimed with the lived experience of most children under three. The main symbols and conventions were introduced in the title sequence so that their function was readily understood when they made an appearance in the body of the show. Once the societal customs had been established, the viewers' attention would be more readily drawn to any element of change or surprise. This framework also gave us something to rail against in the same way that toddlers do. Dotted around Teletubbyland, indoors and out, were mysterious trapdoors that covered cylindrical holes about three feet deep. These existed to house the voice trumpets. Whenever a script called for their enigmatic voice of authority, they'd rise up periscope-like with a farty noise that rather undermined that authority. Despite bossing us Teletubbies around, they kept an element of fun – a sense that it was all a game – and if we got fed up of being told 'Up the hill. Down the hill' too many times, we could run away without fear of punishment. A Teletubby was never in trouble with the law, no matter how much we revolted. More often, the voice trumpets were the instigators of the game.

There was a similar relationship with the narrator. When a 'something' appeared in Teletubbyland – a butterfly or a puddle – the standard response from a Tubby was 'Whassat?'. Always. We knew nothing. We never knew what the 'something' was. We were much less smart than the viewing child. This was very important. For example:

In the episode where a chair appeared beside Laa-Laa, she asked, baffled, 'Whassat?' and I could imagine the child at home shouting at the television as vehemently as we might yell at the news, 'Chair! It's a CHAIR!'

After leaving a pause for this response to happen in sitting rooms all over the land, the narrator then stated, factually, 'It was a chair.'

'Oooo. Chair.' Laa-Laa repeated, trying out the word like it was a new food.

At home, the viewing child would think it hilarious that Laa-Laa didn't know what a chair was. On top of the laughter, this built confidence in the children. They were pleased that they knew something the character didn't, which was then verified for them by the narrator. The narrator never conversed with the Teletubbies as such, but they knew that his purpose was to tell them what was going on – all they had to do was wait, blinking. Mostly the tone was more the unfolding of the game than the issuing of instructions. The narrator would occasionally voice what the child at home might want to say or would become complicit with the child in observing the play. 'Naughty Noo-Noo!' for example. Although again, it was perfectly clear that Noo-Noo wasn't really in trouble – it was all part of the fun.

Teletubbies lived without danger in an adult-free world. Nothing really troubled them. When the chair disappeared, it was merely, 'All gone!' It was nothing for us to be sad or disappointed about – although we might play act these emotions for fun – it merely meant that particular game was over, and soon it'd be time for something else. Children are good at this – when a thing's done, it's done. The narrator never explained what was going on to the child at home in a teacherly way. When he explained, he was almost thinking aloud for the child to hear. This setup made perfect sense to children, but a lot of adults struggled without implicit explanation, without the reassuring voice letting mums and dads know what was happening and why. No wonder adults were blind-sided – they were left out of the game.

The real dictator in Teletubbyland was the windmill, and it too was introduced in the opening sequence. The windmill was always to be obeyed as it signalled the end of one adventure and the beginning of another. Someone – a grown-up – once asked me why the Teletubbies say 'Uh-oh!' when the windmill spins. Is it because they're scared of it? I was a little disappointed. I'd hoped it was apparent from the whole series that the Teletubbies have no reason to be scared of anything, ever. They can play at being afraid and run away, but it's only ever a game. Nothing has ever happened to them to teach them fear. But everyone brings their own perspective, and you don't know what goes on in a person's childhood that colours their interpretation. But no, the answer was no – they were not scared. The 'Uh-oh!' was the kind of uh-oh you might make when you're about to be tickled, or you're playing out a pretend drama of some sort. Play is the key word, and we nailed our colours to the mast from the off: 'Over the hills and far away, Teletubbies come to play'. There it was. There could be no doubt. There were the expectations managed, right there: nothing untoward or stressful is going to happen – everything is a game, you're safe, it's play, off we go!

It was very important within the show to have established signals that a change was about to come, that something had ended and a new something was about to begin. It meant there would be no nasty surprises. There was a secure framework in which to operate without any of the viewers' attention being wasted on it: all the attention could be put on the new information, the bit we really wanted our audience to focus on. The overall upshot was that there'd be a balance between the predictable and secure on one hand, and the novel and exciting on the other. The playful nature of the show kicked in right from the start. During the title sequence, the viewer was introduced to all the major players and to a banging theme tune, with a few tummy jingles and bottom parps thrown in for good measure, all rounded off with a big hug. The big hug was a symbol of the other key word: love. What's not to love in Teletubbyland?

Existing invisibly behind a show that looked on the surface like four furry space babies larking about in the countryside was a significant amount of deep theory. Now all we had to do was turn theory into reality – it was time to start filming actual episodes.

It was the early days of the British summer, and after working up to it since January, the big day finally arrived. The first ever *Teletubbies* sketch material was to be committed to celluloid – well, videotape. The sketch was called 'Watering Can' and was a solo piece for Laa-Laa, to be shot on the slope with the tidiest – least muddy – looking grass, which had been decorated with clumps of exquisitely made individual ceramic flowers.

I was dressed in the puppet body, minus the feet, and walked round onto set. By the time I reached the location, I was exhausted already. My dresser, Aunty Beth, was head of wardrobe, so whatever the two of us learnt from this first experience would form the basis of operations for all four dresser/innard pairings. The first lesson was that it would be a better idea to get dressed on the set, eliminating the tiring walk. If we were going to protect our precious costumes from the damp and occasionally muddy grass, we were going to need a lot of tarpaulin.

I stood, sweating patiently, while Aunty Beth did up the press-studs to attach feet to legs, hands to arms and neck to body. It took ages. Finally I was walked into position and I had a good look around to get my bearings and suss out where the flowers were. The geography had to be more or less memorised as it was impossible to see your feet and pretty damn hard to see anything else. Look out rabbits! Now, where is the camera?

We had two cameras and therefore two camera operators, plus an assist and a soundman. Then the lighting director and sundry sparks – electricians – pushing huge lights around the hills. The first AD – assistant director – had a pivotal liaison role. He stood out on the hills taking instructions, via an earpiece, from the director who was watching everything through monitors in his bunker. The instructions were, in turn, passed onto me. The art department put the final touches to the flowers and handed me the watering can so that I could practise holding it. It was a normal human-sized watering can, which was tricky to manipulate with my decidedly unhuman-sized paws.

Interacting with physical objects once Tubbed-up held many challenges. Firstly, our actual hands were busy operating the eye and mouth mechanisms. It would look creepy if we stopped blinking every time we picked something up, and we had to be able to deliver our lines while holding an object. Consequently, using the pads of our thumbs to hold whatever it was became the order of the day. We could squeeze the object between our carpal bones to pick it up – just – which would leave our fingers free for blinking and speaking. Squeeze is the operative word. There was so much padding to the front of the suit that getting our hands together meant exerting effort to force the padding out of the way. In short, the costume had a default position in which it liked to be: standing, arms by sides. To move it out of this configuration, to lift our arms in any direction, meant working against resistance. No wonder we'd been put through that physical boot camp.

So, back to that first day and we were going for a take, the very first *Teletubbies* take, and it was all down to me. Oh, how I wanted it to be good. I really wanted everyone to be thrilled. Everyone. The script was based on 'Mary, Mary, Quite Contrary' and involved me taking the watering can around various clumps of flowers who were asking to be watered, and watering them while a voice trumpet sang the nursery rhyme. I felt ready. I had all my research, all Anne's wise words, all my knowledge of non-verbal communication, and my magic Spirit of Yellow mantra. I remembered to focus on that one child who would ultimately be sat in front of the television, watching the show. I thought about Georgia and what she needed from me for the sequence to have meaning. I thought about making her feel the love. Off I went. Off Laa-Laa went.

In actuality, the dichotomy between the exterior puppet and the human innard was pronounced. What the crew were seeing was a giant yellow furry character going about her business, sweetly but clumsily trying to water the flowers, much as a small child would. In its own way, it was utterly adorable. Within that charming baby-giant, however, was a small woman blinking sweat out of her eyes, trying not to stand on any flowers or rabbits, desperately wrestling with the watering can. My internal dialogue went a lot like this: Get some water out, make sure not to spill any on the costume and – oops, I think I got some on my feet . . . Ah well, no way of knowing – try to judge the amount of water so I don't run out. My arms are *aching*. Remember to blink. Where's the camera? Ahhh, my legs. What? Where am I going now? Up the hill again. Draw the child's focus. Breathe. When will it be over? Have I ever been this hot? Ahhh, my legs. Blink. Am I getting it right? Okay. Put the can down. Oh that's good. Windmill. Exit. Cut.

That was it. Voila. After a few close-ups, the very first *Teletubbies* sketch was done.

I stood patiently while Aunty Beth unpopped all the poppers. It was so good when my wrists got some air, but nothing compared to the oxygen rush of getting out of the head. Phew-wee! Then the shoes came off, and I schleped back to wardrobe, still in my suit. There was no way I wanted that adopted as a system – I would be lobbying for us to get in and out of suits on set in the future.

In general the whole thing was a success, and I didn't die. People rushed to me as soon as they saw me returning from the set. How was it? Well done! Tell us all. I was the centre of attention, which is, after all, why I did this. As many people as possible clustered into the gallery to watch it back on the monitor. It was okay, maybe even good. At any rate, Anne and Andy were pleased and the rest of us were already learning about how to capture what lived in their imagination and make it real for the children.

After our first day of on-set filming, the four of us were wrapped while the grown-ups discussed the lessons of the afternoon. John was also a non-driver so was taken by chauffeur-driven car – how he loved that! – to Stratford, to get the train to Birmingham. He didn't travel back every night, but he had a young family and liked to be present when he had the energy to make the journey. Even when he stayed over, he preferred to be in Stratford at the hotel where most of the crew were sequestered rather than out in the countryside with the rest of the cast. I couldn't really understand this at first. Why didn't he want to take the opportunity to get out of the city and into a rural Cotswold idyll? I put it down to the fact that he was an out-and-out townie. Then I caught a glimpse of what may have been an underlying reason for John's decision when I invited my Rastafarian boyfriend, Elton, to spend a weekend in Mickleton with me. He immediately became the most interesting thing that had happened to the youth in the bus stop – so much more exciting than the moped – and they shamelessly vied for his attention, competing to have the closest friendship with the 'mysterious' stranger. When we went to the local pub for a pint, Elton had his change in his hand, looking to see if he had enough money for another round, when the elderly landlady asked, 'Are you still getting used to the money, dear?' He had been in England for forty-odd years. Stratford wasn't much more multi-cultural at the time, but I could see how John might want to avoid being so much on display in his downtime, especially when that was his job during the day.

Pui and I were keen to make the most of our time out of the metropolis, and during those early days when our schedule was more erratic and we had more time and energy to do so, we would take little jaunts through the surrounding countryside. We explored chocolate-box villages with quaint names like Darlingscott, we drove down secluded gated roads with grass growing in the middle, we climbed up onto the northernmost ridge of the Cotswolds from where, on a clear day, you could see over to Wales in the west and Coventry in the north. We took deep long breaths of the shockingly fresh air until it choked our urban lungs. We revelled in our good fortune. These were the halcyon days when we Tubs could sit in the hotel garden after work and chat over a glass or two. I took to walking through the churchyard and up onto the ridge in the low-sun sultry evenings, kindling a love affair that would eventually see me making a permanent home at the base of the self-same ridge. This idyllic lifestyle was short-lived because once filming began in earnest, the priority was to be tucked up in bed as soon as possible.

With the prototype 'Watering Can' sketch in the can, it made sense to move on to filming the dances. We'd been rehearsing them in London, so they were fresh in our minds. As yet, no-one had figured out how the voice recording was going to work, so these were sequences without dialogue we could get along with until they had. Today it was all four of us filming together for the first time and we were on one of the paths that run up the hills flanking the dome, getting ready to film the 'Stamping and Stepping Dance'.

This time, we had changed into our costumes in the dome – using our beds as a base – so we had less distance to travel to our starting positions. Each of our dressers were now fully equipped with a small plastic stool that doubled as a carrying case for their tools of maintenance. These were the perfect height for us to sit on between takes, thereby avoiding a muddy bum. The dressers all wore builder's utility belts which held, among other things, a dog comb for fluffing up any flat or holey bits of the costume and a completely ineffectual fan. Once it became apparent that hand-held fans were of limited use, two gigantic, free-standing, wind-machine type fans were purchased and we'd jockey for prime position in front of them to cool down. Writing this now, I wonder why they didn't buy four!

The final necessities were a towel for wiping away our sweat and a plastic drinks bottle of the sort that are ubiquitous now, but which at the time were really only used by cyclists, and which always put me in mind of lambs at feeding time whenever my dresser offered it in front of my mouth. We couldn't open the drinks bottles with our massive paws, and even if we could, holding the bottles would be tricky, and the possibility of spillage onto the costume would be high, so we were fed water like the helpless souls we were.

As I've mentioned before, the Teletubby baby-gro was made out of a revolutionary fabric. Four-way stretch fun-fur had only just been developed, and as such could be a little inconsistent. The dyes had also been especially mixed for us – Laa-Laa's Pantone colour is 115-T – and each colour had a slightly different effect on the nap of the fur. These colours also had to be matched with thread and plastic Kimble tags – those short lengths of plastic that fasten price tags to clothes and are horribly annoying to remove. A Kimble gun was a Teletubby dresser's best friend: it hid a thousand sins.

Filming was a whole other ball game when all four of us were involved. If you were too efficient at getting suited up, and one of your compadres had some kind of problem, then you were sat there, using up your oxygen and working up a sweat, before the proper labours had even started. Then there was the issue of the space we took up, and the fact we could barely see. It would have been out and out hilarious if it wasn't for the fact that all our livelihoods and bucket-loads of license payers' pounds were riding on us making it work. We also had to overcome the additional challenge of our first quartet scene happening on a narrow sloping path, which made for lots of 'excuse me', 'sorry, excuse me', and trying not to topple over.

The camera crew were no less awkwardly positioned. The wide-shot, the close-up camera, the assist, and the first AD were perched on the side of the dome in an ungainly cluster. Jeff, the Geordie on the wide, called out to Aunty Beth, 'Can you ask the yellow one to move to her left a bit?'

My reply was instant, withering and totally in character, 'De lello one?!! De lello one?!! Can I ask de norven one to show some mannez? I hab a name fanku bery much. Iz Laa-Laa, buh YOU, you can call me MS Laa!'

Everyone collapsed in laughter and this became my raison d'être. It was a truly good day when I could make the crew laugh.

I had set the tone for off-camera Laa-Laa and it was a game I played throughout the entire six years of filming. I still have friends from the old days who will greet me, 'Ah! Ms Laa!'

Our choreographer was putting in the miles, running backwards and forwards between watching various takes with the director in the gallery and coaching us through the dance on the hillside. The four Tubbies had entered an almost transcendental state of effort. By the end of the dance I felt like I was moving up the slope, but I didn't seem to be going anywhere. Dave – who had always been the weakest dancer – struggled most of all, but the consensus from the gallery was that it looked quite cute when he got it wrong all the time, because little children weren't always on the beat either. The difficulty with our eye-lines was a more serious problem. It was essential that we could all find the lens and look directly down it because the lens was the window to the child at home, and the child at home needed to feel that we were looking directly at them, not squinting off to the left for some reason.

I would defy anyone to easily find a camera lens that is twenty-five yards away, next to another camera, in a cluster of people, while you're dancing. Given our additional visual impairment, it was nigh-on impossible. Later on, some bright spark in the camera crew fashioned two wooden boards, one fluorescent orange with the number one on it, and one fluorescent yellow with the number two.

'Look at camera one!' meant 'Find orange.'

'Now camera two!' translated as 'Find yellow.'

Old school but completely effective.

Even though we didn't have the camera boards on that first day and despite all the other challenges involved, we managed to complete the dance and get our first four-Teletubby sequence in the can.

Afterwards, everything ached. I was soaking wet, exhausted

after only a few hours, desperate to breathe some fresh air and incredibly thirsty. Because no-one had attempted anything like this before, because no-one had ever asked performers to do this exact thing, Ragdoll had taken the precaution of engaging a paramedic – just in case they did actually kill us. Fancy that! After all the time thinking that I was being namby-pamby and paranoid, I felt justified that it turned out the production company were also worrying about whether humans could do this Teletubby stuff and survive.

The paramedic was a jolly rotund fellow who looked more like a butcher. He couldn't believe his luck that he was being paid to stand in the sun in the middle of the English countryside watching TV characters messing about. We knew he'd only be around for a couple of weeks – long enough for the producers to establish that they could ask us to do all this without it killing us – so we wanted to make the most of him. He had a seemingly endless supply of Dioralyte and became our rehydration dealer. You know how disgusting that stuff usually tastes? Let me tell you – when you really need it, it's absolutely delicious.

The paramedic was a prudent move though. If, in the future, we got too whiny about how hard the work was, the producers could refer back to him: 'Remember that paramedic we had? Well he seemed to think you'd be okay, and he's a medical professional.'

Nowadays, there are strict rules about suit work. A performer who is completely sealed inside a costume can be so for a maximum of twenty minutes before being allowed a break to – at the very least – get some air. Working on the reboot of the show, I was amazed at the vigilance of their first AD in this regard. It was wonderful to behold. We originals weren't quite so lucky.

As time passed and we got used to the job, we developed our own methods for ensuring regular air breaks – one out, all out! – but in the first year we spent hours in those things. Partly out of dedication to the task – because we knew we were behind our schedule – and partly because we were terrified of losing our jobs. We were regularly reminded of how easy it would be to replace us. One day I was in my costume for the entire afternoon. By around six o'clock I had had enough and passed out – I'm not even sure myself whether it was a genuine faint or if I'd just decided to call it a day.

In less extreme instances, I had a special technique to overcome fatigue: I'd remember the child, the one child who would be watching the show and who deserved my best efforts. Without judgement, Anne encouraged us to consider the child who had been sat in front of the television while their parents got on with a mountain of other responsibilities. This one child was to be the focus. We should deliver our performances to that one child as if they were the only audience member in the world – because to them, they were. We should deliver our performances not to an audience of millions but to the individual. The individual who would be transfixed by us, who would absorb whatever it was we shared with them, who would be inspired to emotion by what they watched and heard. Wouldn't it be nice if they were inspired to feel love – to feel loved in return? That's what I tried to do.

We had our first taste of what we'd signed up for during the filming of that initial dance. It was tough but we could do it, and in a weird way, it was quite fun. It was something of a relief to us all to get properly started. Later on, watching back the rushes, I was convinced that we'd have to re-film 'The Stamping and Stepping Dance' further down the line when the teething problems had been ironed out. I was not convinced that Tinky Winky being out of time was cute. The dancer in me thought it looked messy. Also, my aerial was squiffy. We did not, however, film this again. It exists in its ropey old first-attempt entirety, right there in the programme and on YouTube. For some reason, people are very fond of setting this particular dance to other music, as seen in various online mash-up clips. Many versions exist – the most popular is Ed Sheeran's 'The Shape of You' – so maybe I was wrong about the messiness.

The most important thing was that we had all proved to ourselves that it could be done. This thing was really going to get made. We just had to hurry up!

Other than the fact we were behind schedule, the problematic elephant in the room was still the sound. There was the practical consideration of how to communicate with the human innards while they were sealed in their puppets, and who needed to hear who, and how. Then there was how to record the soundtrack that would be used for the actual broadcast.

The first issue had been tackled by yelling at us through a megaphone during that initial dance sequence, but it was clear something more subtle was needed. It was decided that we'd have earpieces and microphones within the heads. We had no problem with that, but both would require a power pack. There was nowhere else for these to go except the head, which really didn't need the extra weight. Ah. We desperately wanted to find somewhere else for this added load to go. We tried wearing them like necklaces but they strangled us and came unplugged every time we fell over. We tried attaching pockets to the insides of our suits but the packs would fall out and become lost within the darkest, wettest corners of the suit, and the same thing happened when we tried fixing them to the harnesses that attached the suits to our bodies. I guess it was inevitable from the start that they were going to have to go in the head.

With much trial and error and Velcro, we all found places for the power packs to be attached which maintained balance and gave the sound guy a fighting chance to reach in and change batteries when needed. I can't tell you how curious a sensation it was to be so physically isolated from everyone else but to still hear them as if their mouth was right next to your ear. At first, everyone thought it would be beneficial for the Tubbies to be able to communicate with each other whenever we were inside our puppet heads. Everyone was wrong.

What we imagined was a party line enabling us to give one another helpful guidance and warning:

'Approaching to your left, Mr Winky.'

'Thank you so much, Ms Laa. Dipsy, please be advised I will now be stepping to my right.'

What actually happened was that either no-one spoke at all, or everyone spoke at once. Plus the sound of one another's puffing and panting, and the mechanisms bashing around. All of this drowned out the voice of the first AD who was trying to give us actual useful instruction. No. Unless we were speaking script, we would be heard only by the sound guy, Pete Lee, and the gallery. With the flick of a switch, Pete was able to control whether we could hear each other, but we always had the first AD in our ears. How much this was likely to drive you insane depended very much on the sensitivity of the individual involved. We had a parade of firsts over the years – probably into double figures. Some we loved and some we . . . didn't love. There are one or two voices from those days that I would actively cross the street to avoid. To be fair, being our first AD was a difficult job. They, in turn, had the voice of the director in their ear, so they were living a variant of the same hell. The skilled ones didn't pass that on or let it show.

The greater sound problem was how to record the Teletubby vocal tracks. It was perfectly possible to make a live recording, but the issue was that along with our voices, the sound of mechanisms clunking around in the heads was also recorded. As was the huffing and puffing of puny humans lugging many kilos of costumes up and down hills. The first idea was that the live recording would be used as a guide track, and then we would record a clean track at the end of the day. This couldn't happen on set because the crew would be busily – and noisily – striking cameras, lights and props, so we all huddled together round the back of the Portakabins, in the mud, redoing our lines in the correct ambience. Unless the farmer was out on his tractor, or the sheep wandered over, or a plane flew by on its way to the nearby airfield. It was also the end of the day and everyone was knackered. No, this wasn't going to work at all.

Frankly, I was worried. I was picking up on a development I didn't like the sound of. A rumour was circulating that the issue of the voices might be taken out of our hands – or mouths. I managed to corner Anne in the dome one teatime and expressed my concerns. She brushed me aside, her mind on one of the many other fires she had to put out. 'Trust me, Nikky,' she said, 'Just trust me.'

What choice did I have?

CHAPTER 5

THE NEW NORMAL

The original commission for *Teletubbies* was about two hundred programmes, which meant that our target was around sixty-six episodes a year over three years. In that first year, however, we also had to film all the generic sequences: the titles, the Tubby Bye-Bye, receiving the tummy films, asking for the film to be shown again-again and so on. I can't tell you how often we were encouraged with the words, 'Yes, but just think – once you've done it, it'll be gone forever! You'll never have to do it again.' We had to do almost everything again. Again-again. There was something deeply unsatisfying about shooting the generics. Especially twice. They were bitty and out of context. We had very little sense of achievement or completion, and they were also incredibly technical.

The title sequence needed to look like fun incarnate, and to a degree, it was. Blasting the theme tune over the Warwickshire countryside, we danced in the sun as if at a bizarre and poorly attended festival. It looks simple, but in actuality was far from it.

The first task was to complete the other end of what we had shot in the blue screen studio. Popping out of the top of the dome meant you and your dresser clambering up the thankfully unslippery slide – though surely they'd have to do something about that at some point? – then huddling together at the top and manoeuvring around in the tiny space. It was like trying to get an elephant in a lift. Once we had popped out, like a quartet of brightly coloured champagne corks, we had to run down the outside of the dome and up the grassy bank towards camera. My fear of dying was in full force, my thoughts racing. Slippery paws down a super-steep Astroturf slope? Eek! Then 'Action!' and off I go. Okay, gently does it. Lots of baby steps. Don't slip. Don't fall. One last hop. I made it, hoorah! Run across the flat bit to the slope, and up then up it. Good God! Up the slope. Up. Come on. UP. Now why the hell can't I get up the slope in time?

Every single take, I gathered my energy and gave it my all. I did my very best to keep up with the others but my legs just wouldn't comply with my will. Every single take, I was miles behind everyone else. Even today I can't look at the title sequence without feeling ashamed of myself. I don't know why I found it so hard and I still curse myself for a shoddy job. Still, I didn't die.

The problem of the unslippery slide was solved by employing an army of slide-polishing elves to polish it for forty days and forty nights until it shone as if radioactive. In my role as guinea pig, I was the first one to try the new improved surface. It worked so well that I whizzed straight off the end and into the toast machine! Even when it had been re-stickified to a workable sheen, I found it a bit scary – though I didn't let on – and finally settled on tummy-down-feet-first as the most controllable and least harrowing technique. As a dancer, I could splay my legs wide enough to touch each side of the slide with my feet and employ them as brakes if needed. All that training . . .

Most of the shots of us coming down the slide were generic sequences, although occasionally a specific script would demand a particular style of slide-based entrance or exit and we'd have to shoot to order. Once I was over the initial trepidation, I rather enjoyed the opportunity to find new sliding methods. As a rule, though, our main access to and from the dome were the doors. Big, beautiful sliding doors, operated with a pulley by a man in a cupboard who occasionally needed a little prompt by someone screaming at the top of their lungs, 'DOORS!' If a Tubby had had a long run over hill and down dale to get to the doors, only to find they failed to open, that was going to be one unhappy Tubby. As far as I am aware, sliding door failure was the only thing we had in common with the cast of *Star Trek*.

Although, we did have a control panel of sorts. The central column of the dome housed levers and buttons and a practically obsolete phone receiver, along with the Tubby Sponges – primarily for cleaning dirty knees, so very rarely used. Its main function, however, was being the thing we ran around. Around and around and around, until insanity and exhaustion hit – often chasing or being chased by the Noo-Noo. The first few times the script called for this chase, we tried doing it at full speed and nearly killed ourselves. Thankfully, word came from Andy that we could go slowly, and then the footage could be speeded up in post-production – Benny Hill style (which is also funnier) – thereby giving us permission to shuffle round the dome at a sedate pace with the Noo-Noo trundling along steadily fore or aft. Naughty Noo-Noo. Who wouldn't want a magical hoover that tidies up any conceivable mess? The Noo-Noo was a stroke of genius – like a pet but way better. He was a comic foil to our antics, often marked in the script by the direction, 'Noo-Noo looks to camera, bemused.'

The Noo-Noo was operated by Mark Dean, a chipper lad from the Black Country who liked a singsong. Our signature greeting was, 'N'NooNooNoo, L'LaaLaaLaa, is all I want to say to you', and he gave a fair rendition of 'Total Eclipse of the Heart'. It should have been 'Total Elise of the Heart', because later he did indeed buy himself a Lotus car. It irked me no end that my domestic appliance drove a better motor than me. The Noo-Noo was a less glamorous ride, and tricky to manoeuvre. Mark sat inside, sideways on, with one arm puppeteering the nozzle, using a small monitor screen to see where he was going. The challenge was that the camera fed a reversed image to the screen, so he was constantly having to flip everything in his brain.

The use of monitors was a very common procedure for puppeteering at the time, and it was the system initially proposed for the Teletubbies themselves. Aside from the brain flip, which I personally found incredibly hard, there were issues with how to attach the monitors inside the puppet heads, and where they could be in order for us to see them. Also, when we jumped up and down or fell over, the monitor would invariably come loose from its housing, clonking us in the face and becoming instantly redundant. We all came to an agreement that we would do without the monitors and instead use our actual eyes.

Simple though it looks, one of the trickiest sequences to film was the 'Tubby Bye-Bye'. Andy wanted Teletubbyland to have lots of hills in order to give a sense of perspective. Not just because it's more interesting to the eye, but because it helps children to learn about spatial relationships. If one of us revealed ourselves gradually from very far away, with nothing else happening, there was time for the viewing child to see the effect of perspective, thereby averting that old far/near small/big confusion. These hills were also just the job for hiding behind. Above all other events, it was crucial that the 'Tubby Bye-Bye' was understood as a game. Young children can have a profound fear around object permanence. I'm sure we've all witnessed children being left at nursery or day-care, screaming their heads off because they can't be sure that mummy is ever coming back. Endings and disappearances can be terrifying to the very young. So, we gave plenty of notice that the end was coming. When it happened, the Teletubbies went away . . . then surprise . . . 'Boo!' they were back again. This was reassuring for the child: when they went away again, the chances were that they would come back again at some point. This answered a real developmental need, an answer which was layered underneath a simple guessing game, a game that children could play themselves at home. Who will it be that pops up again and says 'Boo!' today? Like much of the programme, there's deep reasoning behind the fun. This is a very hard thing to get right. Very clever people invented *Teletubbies*, and it was a privilege to work with them.

They got their money's worth though. That 'Tubby Bye-Bye' sequence was an absolute nightmare to film. That's the trouble when you try to hide giant puppets behind not very giant hillocks. Pui and Dave each had their own hill, but John and I were paired up and squished together behind the same grassy knoll, the ground below us sloping in two directions. We had to try very hard not to bash each other's ears when we popped up and, as we couldn't get our legs underneath us, it was all in the neck. This was absolute agony unless you could sneakily support your ears with your paws. I don't know if that even makes sense. Just know it was a really tough couple of days.

'It's a generic sequence,' they said.

'You'll never have to shoot it again,' they said.

They were not telling the truth.

Our comfort was that we knew the children watching would find it hilarious. It was simple and that's what worked best for us. The simpler it got, the funnier it was. We learned from watching playbacks that there was nothing funnier than looking straight down the lens and blinking. Nothing. We'd eke out that moment of eye contact for as long as possible. That's what I didn't understand about all the adults who criticised us later on – did they not think it was funny? I honestly don't know how anyone could watch it and not even raise a smile. Even if you couldn't see the educational value it's obvious that happy children learn, miserable children don't. The combination of humour and learning is a powerful brew, and our programme had it in spades. So far, this truism seems to be slow in reaching our education system.

The other generic sequence it took us a long time to get right was the game of 'which Tubby will be chosen to receive the tummy film?' It probably comes as no surprise to learn that the screen in a Teletubby's tummy is not a real TV – imagine the weight of that! It's just a rectangle of grey fun-fur onto which the film is superimposed in post-production, by the magic of video editing. Anne and Andy wanted the relationship with our audience to be two-way: if children were to access the Teletubbies via a television screen, then it made perfect sense for the Teletubbies to access children in the same way. There are limited areas on a body that are large enough to carry a television screen, and it would have been silly to have it behind us, so the tummy was the obvious choice. And if you have a television screen on your tummy, then you're going to need an aerial on your head. So really, how the Teletubbies look is perfectly logical when you think about it!

Each episode of *Teletubbies* included a short live-action film called the tummy film, which featured a child, a couple of children, or even a group, doing something interesting. For example, the film in the first episode featured toddler Ned getting ready to go on a bike ride with his dad. A separate department at Ragdoll were tasked with either locating the subject, or thinking up a suitable activity and then casting young children to take part. Then a specialist unit would film and edit the sequence. This was a highly skilled and sensitive area. No-one wanted to be coercing children to do something they didn't want to, we wanted them to look happy. No, we wanted them to *be* happy.

Every Teletubby tummy film started with children saying 'Hello!' over and over again, to enable the camera to zoom in from the Tubby's world to theirs. In order to fit the film onto one of our tummies, the screen had to be facing the camera in a most exact fashion. We were to look excited, but we also needed to ensure that the four corners of our screen stayed flat-on to camera and not twisted away. Our rectangular screens had to stay rectangular and not shift into any kind of rebellious parallelogram.

'Look excited.'

'Don't move.'

'Move more. But don't.'

It took bloody ages, but surely once done . . .

Shooting the four of us lying on the hilltop as our tummies glowed in turn was slightly more hilarious. Once lying down, we were incapable of subtly adjusting our positions, so the heroic dressers were employed to drag us about by our ankles into an exact configuration. We had to excitedly waggle our mostly numb limbs but not move the tummy screen – never moving the tummy screen!

When we first started working on the programme we were given a list of 'truths' about the characters, things like:

- Teletubbies love each other very much.
- Apart from one another, Teletubbies love children more than anything else.
- Teletubbies love to copy.
- Teletubbies do whatever they want.
- Teletubbies are funny.

Teletubbies' deep and profound love of children meant that when the films featuring them appeared on our tummies, it was the most exciting thing that could happen. Of course we wanted to see the films again-again.

Many parents did not want to see the films again-again. It drove a lot of people up the wall again-again. Anne always said that repeating the film was the bravest decision she made, but it was so smart. Very young children can struggle to take in aural and visual information at the same time, so having an instant replay gave them the opportunity to pick up on details they might have missed first time around. More than this, it allowed them to make predictions about what would happen next, and then to see those predictions come true. This was hugely important in building a child's confidence in his or her own ability to learn. For example, when watching the film for the first time, the viewer would see Ned put on his boots after sitting on the floor. Then in the second showing, the child would spot the same cue – Ned sitting on the floor – and think, 'Aha! He's going to put on his boots' and then that prediction would come true. Of course it would, it was exactly the same film. It might be obvious to us, but to a small child it's hugely empowering to have that thought process visually verified. When we are super-young we need to learn that we can trust our own brains.

The same attention was paid to the way young children process different kinds of sensory information, with regards to how a Teletubby makes an entrance. Before you see a character appear on screen, you will hear that character's signature song. This gives the child an opportunity to focus on the aural information and make a prediction about who is about to come into vision. They might hear, 'Lalaleela Laleelaleela', and then are given time to associate that sound with Laa-Laa and make the prediction that she is the one they are about to see. Then a distant blob of yellow appears in the landscape – that's the right colour, it's looking good for the prediction. As Laa-Laa comes nearer to say 'Eh-Oh!' the child recognises the signifying stance, the voice; the whole character is there and the prediction is vindicated. The child is given confidence in their ability to make sense of the world. This is crucial to all learning.

On occasion a Tubby might pop up unannounced, but that's just because it's funny.

The films on our tummies weren't the only things in Teletubbyland to be repeated, and they weren't the only source of complaint. Let's be honest, we used repetition a lot. If, at the morning's script read-through, I saw Laa-Laa discovering something fun – a special dance, say – I knew the chances were she'd be off to show each of the other Tubbies in turn. In Teletubbyland, things very rarely happened once. Why? Partly because setting up a pattern fulfils the prediction loop as described above, partly because the egalitarian nature of that pattern is very satisfying to a small child, and partly because it's just funny. A thing happening over and over again, especially if it's a funny thing to begin with, gets funnier and funnier to a child. Anne used to tell an anecdote about how, when she was a teacher, a little boy was spinning round and saying something along the lines of, 'You know how it is when you do a thing, miss, and then you can't stop doing the thing you're doing?' That. Kids love that. My pet theory is that adults sort of like that too. It's an interesting technique to play with in physical comedy. You do a thing once, it's funny. You do it twice or three times, it gets funnier. How many times can it be done before it ceases to be funny? If you keep going, can it get funny again? If so, when? I'm sure at some point you've played a game with a small child and grown tired of it way before they show any sign of becoming bored.

As the summer warmed up, *we* were in no danger of becoming bored. As well as the generics and the dances, we were now filming actual scripts. People still ask me, 'How long did it take to film one script?' and of course the answer is that it depended on the script. If the premise was, 'Everyone stands on one leg', we could knock it off in a morning. If it was, 'A cloud enters the dome and gets mixed up in the custard machine until the whole dome is filled with pink cloud, then Noo-Noo hoovers it all up except for a tiny bit which flies back into the sky', well, we could be there all week.

'Everyone stands on one leg' was one of the first scripts we filmed. Again it was a really simple premise and therefore very funny: we take it in turns to stand on one leg, then when Tinky Winky falls over, we all think that's a much better game so all fall over too. We do this over and over again until collapsing in fits of giggles. The end. Genius.

We filmed it on the grassy bank at the back of the dome, which was quite steep. This was when we found out how slippery the soles of our feet were on grass. There was rather more falling over than was originally in the script! To overcome this problem, Aunty Beth attached rubber circles to the soles of our feet for additional grip, so the distinctive appearance of the Teletubbies' feet was created to solve a practical problem.

Like many Tubby scripts, our game was ended by the interruption of The Windmill, rather than by coming to any kind of resolution – because that is what life is like for small children. Thc Windmill was our ovcrlord, to bc obcycd at all timcs. It hinged down to lie alongside the back of the set, invisible to any prying eyes, then was brought up into position when needed for a shot. It would have been a nightmare to have a permanent marker of Teletubbyland's location in later days when the press went bananas.

In Andy's mind, the four of us would stop whatever we were doing when we heard the whooshing of the windmill, look towards it, look to camera to let the viewing child know we were about to share something new, and then leave shot excitedly.

The challenge was how to make this happen in unison when there was no actual whooshing to hear and his performers couldn't see each other. If only there was someone on hand, skilled in directing physical movement, some kind of dancer or choreographer . . . Oh wait – Crazy Hair Girl!

So was born the routine that I swear the four of us could still carry off in perfect unison all these years later:

Stop, 2,3
Windmill 2,3
Camera 2,3
'Uh-Oh!'
and exit.

Typing it now vividly brings back the very specific heavy wobble that the puppet head made with the sharp change of focus.

The other classic ending of any given *Teletubbies* script was the 'Big Hug'. It looks so sweet, so warm and comforting. In reality, it was agony. That's all I'm saying.

It's part of the genius of the costumes that you would never for a minute imagine there was a contorted human inside, cussing and moaning and sweating and grumbling while the outer appearance is so cute. I had imagined that I would have to exaggerate my gestures in order to make them read on camera, especially given the space between my actual body and the padded puppet body. I was wrong. The more I watched back what we were filming, the more it became apparent that the suits were responsive enough to pick up even quite subtle movement. Very clever. This responsiveness broadened my repertoire of body language and gave me much more to play with than I'd expected. The ability to observe ourselves was crucial – we had no idea what our performances looked like from the outside at the moment of execution – but not that easy to achieve. Obviously, we couldn't just nip into the gallery to have a look at playback once we'd finished a scene. There'd be no nipping anywhere.

The schedule was too tight to accommodate waiting for us to emerge from our furry cocoons after each sequence, then traipse to the gallery, watch the take, traipse back and re-suit. We had to grab a peek now and again when the opportunity arose. We all had to learn and watching back the action together was the quickest way to get the hang of what we were doing. In those days, we were only semi-digital. We recorded onto actual physical tapes. These were very precious items, representing hundreds and thousands of pounds worth of expenditure. 'Give us that tape a sec, so we can have a quick look at it.' No – that was not going to happen. Once the tapes had gone off to Ragdoll head office and been transferred, if we asked very nicely, we could get them back to study. We also asked for a live feed into our cabin, so we could watch each other's scenes and see what worked and what didn't. This process was invaluable in allowing us to hone our performances.

Now that we were on set rather than in a church hall, distance was a new element to be incorporated, and though the costumes were reactive enough to relay our characters from a couple of fields away, I decided I needed something extra. It was the combination of my choreographic background – always thinking about the overall shape of a thing – and taking on board the question Anne had posed about how children would play us. That is to say, if a group of children were together and decided, 'Let's play *Teletubbies*!' what was it that they would do in order to be Po, or Laa-Laa or whoever?

One of the first sketches we shot involved each of us stepping in a puddle, 'Uh-Oh! Eurgggh!' and there was a shot tracking along four pairs of muddy feet. I thought, if you had a black and white TV – not unheard of at that time – how would you know whose feet were whose? I decided that whenever she was in place, Laa-Laa would stand pigeon-toed. I'd noticed young children doing it at the playgroup and it struck me as an instant indicator– the viewer would always know it was me even if they could only see the bottom half, and if they could only see the top half, well, there was the aerial. It worked at a distance and gave an instantly recognisable silhouette. It didn't do my knees much good, but in the name of art and all that.

Alongside exploring how to manipulate the costumes for the

camera, we were also starting to think about how to make them work better practically.

This leads me to the business of marks. When any film or television sequence is set up, there will be marks on the floor to let the actor/presenter know where they should stand in order to be in the right place for the camera. We had two problems with this:

- We could barely see anything
- We definitely couldn't see our feet

At first, we counted out our steps to make sure we hit our marks, and the voice in our ear would be able to give us instructions if we missed. After a while we became sufficiently adept at judging any distance between where we were and where the director needed us to be. Hitting my mark became a matter of absolute professional pride.

It was another crazy little skill for me to learn. Or, it was part of the crazy big skill we were all learning together. Some of the lessons learned were completely unexpected. I had no idea that filming *Teletubbies* would teach me something about the human body I can't imagine having the opportunity to learn in any other situation.

Pui and I in particular were developing a reputation for being bad-tempered. Whenever a Fab Four analogue came up, we were always the volatile Lennon and McCartney duo, with Dave as George and John as Ringo – the nice one. One day I overheard one of the director's PAs asking the line producer, 'Why are all the Teletubbies so horrid?' I had to ask myself too – why were we? I mean, we weren't. We weren't horrid people. We were perfectly lovely people in the general run of things. But there was something about being a Tubby that changed our personalities, that made us grumpy and difficult.

The answer was obvious really. After a certain amount of time in the suit, our skin became deprived of sufficient oxygen. I don't know about you, but I'd never thought about such a thing before – I'd never considered whether my skin was getting sufficient oxygen. Lungs yes, skin no. Sealed inside unrefreshed air, our skin would start to crawl, like only the worst of illnesses or hangovers can do to a person. Then a panic would set it. An almost hysterical need for air. Until finding out about the skin thing, it was difficult to understand. I could still breathe, but my whole being was telling me that I needed air, that I needed to get out of the suit *right now*. There was no room for manners. It was an urgent and unarguable request from my entire being. Get me out of this thing. Now!

That's why we were horrid. In later days, once we'd all learned what we were doing and didn't have to stay in the suits for quite as long, this ceased to be a problem. In that first year, the horror of it sometimes did result in our being horrid, and I'm sorry for that. At least I can explain it now. I remember saying during that first season, 'Any time you're not actually in the suit, it's the best job in the world, but when you are in the suit, it's a living hell.' Spirit of Yellow or not. These bumbling furry baby-giants had been designed on every level to make you forget about the human within as they cavorted around the countryside in the sun. Unfortunately, our directors sometimes had a tendency to forget that as well.

It should come as no surprise then that the sweetest sound to a Tubby innard's ear was the word, 'Cut!' It was also the word that triggered an almost Pavlovian response in our dedicated helpers. It warms my heart to think of our wonderful dressers, to whom we were never horrid, running up and down hills to reach us as soon as possible. This was partly out of a duty of care – they really did want to look after us – and partly because there was always the danger that we would sit down on the grass and get a muddy bum before reaching the allocated 'base camp' area, laid out with tarpaulins and blankets. There we would wait with flip-top heads, while the folk in the gallery watched back whatever we'd just filmed, to see if it was good and if it was a clean take. This would determine if we needed to go again or if we could move on. We'd spend a tense few minutes during which our beloved dressers would wipe our sweaty brows with towels, poke a fan in our faces or down our necks and feed us water, all the while juggling our massive heads. Heroes. Going again meant the head was flipped back on and we were led back to the start positions, ready to go again.

If the take was good, your dresser ripped open the back of the baby-gro – a swift job by now, thanks to the marvel of Velcro – and unfastened the back of the fat suit. As soon as there was sufficient freedom to move, you'd bring the mechanisms up the arms so that the pair of you could be free of the massive head ASAP. You'd then be free to wiggle out of the costume and get some oxygen onto your poor deprived flesh. You'd be soaking wet all over, despite the mythical wicking properties of our undergarments. With touching consideration, we were given colour-coded towelling dressing-gowns in order to cover our modesty when moving around the set. The boys made good use of these, but Pui and I were both way too interested in cooling down to immediately put on another layer, and we didn't give a toss about wandering around in what was essentially our pants.

May I dwell on the issue of the heads again? The fit of a Teletubby head was a really delicate thing. We each had two, in case of emergency, and there would inevitably be 'the one that fits best' and 'the one that is agony'. There were so many variables, and they all affected how the weight was transferred through all the easily injured bones and muscles in a human neck, into the rest of the skeleton. It would have been a disaster if we had sustained any serious damage to our actual heads, necks or skeletons, but the puppet heads had their own vulnerabilities. Emergencies that might befall the puppet heads included: a nasty fall or collision, which would squish the 'snout' of the face, making the character look like they'd been hit in the face with a frying pan; some kind of splishing or splashing with water or custard; or most commonly of all, the snapping of the elastic which fastened the eyes to the mechanism, causing them to roll backwards into the puppet head. This was in equal measure disturbing and hilarious. The laughter would soon die down if our head mechanic, Veronica, couldn't fix it with a new elastic band – we were very high tech – for then would come the dreaded words, 'You'll have to go into your second head.' This kind of surreal phrase had become workaday for us.

As the weeks rolled by, we settled into our routine and began to feel more comfortable with everything that goes into being a Teletubby. It seemed I was a proper grown-up after all and perfectly capable of getting up at 6.30am every morning. There were things about living in a hotel that were lovely, but there were also downsides. You had to transfer your belongings to and fro every week, Thursday evening was always spent packing, you couldn't cook for yourself, and if you wanted to stay in the countryside over the weekend or have loved ones visit, it was quite expensive. Nevertheless, we were all hugely relieved that we'd had the good sense to turn down the shared house. At least in the hotel we could enjoy a little privacy when we needed it.

The Three Ways were also supplying food to the set. The chef and one of the managers would drive over with the food and a rack or two of heat lamps. It wasn't good. I mean, it would have been okay if we'd all had cushy office jobs but it was tough physical work, and not just for the Teletubbies but also for a large percentage of the crew. The hours were long for everyone. The lunch tasted like what it was: food prepared as cheaply as possible, driven a few miles and heated up under lamps. It was heavy on greasy chips and low on the hardcore nutritional value we needed. In the evenings, I was desperate for a bowl of lightly steamed vegetables. However I was often more desperate for my bed, so supper wasn't eaten every night. A few months in, I contracted an infection and was laid up in London for a couple of days, under doctor's orders. My thinking was that I could have easily shaken off the infection if I hadn't been undernourished for the amount of work I was doing. Something had to be done.

Incidentally, from the beginning of rehearsals in London, we had had a young lad alongside us whose role was that of emergency understudy. I don't quite know how he got the job. He came across as rather an idle sort and spent most of the time dozing in a corner. During the time I was confined to my bed, he was finally called upon to take my place so that filming could continue. He was so appallingly inept that he was got rid of forthwith, and they worked round my absence instead. However, there are a couple of group shots from that first season where Laa-Laa is unusually tall and immobile. One for the Teletubby nerds to look out for.

Back on the farm, I felt the need to back up my stance on the food to make sure that it wasn't just me being precious. I did a little research, canvassing for opinion among the rest of the crew. The percentage split between people who agreed with me regarding the catering and those who thought it was fine was about 50/50. That was enough for me. At lunch one day, the series producer, Sue James, came over to ask if everything was okay and I mouthed off about the food being terrible. Later that afternoon, I was in the Portakabin on my own for some reason when Anne came blustering in, slamming the door behind her as a message to everyone else to leave well alone for a while. This was my toast machine moment. What did I mean by having a go at Sue about the food? Who the hell did I think I was? Well? All at some volume.

I had to decide who the hell I did think I was. Did I think I was someone who was going to back down and apologise profusely, keeping my employability intact? Or was I the sort to stick to my guns, knowing I was right but risking losing the only decent paying job I had ever had, or was ever likely to have? Plus, I loved this woman. I didn't want her to be shouting at me – I wanted her to love me back. But also to respect me. I took a deep breath and stated my case, at first at a lower volume. Anne didn't back down either – of course she didn't – so we carried on arguing for a while, both quite loudly. Then she screamed at me, 'So, madam, if there's a tray of raw fruit and vegetables in here tomorrow morning you'll be happy will you?'

'Yes.' Also screaming.

'Okay then.'

'Okay.'

Off she stormed, slamming the door behind her.

Then she was back for one last thing – like Columbo.

'And apologise to Sue.'

'Of course.'

'Good.'

We had forgotten we didn't have to shout that bit.

I went and found Sue straight away, apologised profusely and explained about being uncontrollably horrid, but also genuinely concerned about the food situation. She accepted my apology, because she is a lovely person. Lovelier than me.

Anne was as good as her word. The following morning there were two silver platters in our cabin, one full of fruit and one full of raw vegetables. I was happy. I buzzed around the site, offering the bountiful cornucopia to anyone who was in need, like a waiter at a posh do with a tray of canapés. When Anne arrived there was much obsequious and humble thanks on my side, and again, good grace on hers.

What also happened was that the chef from The Three Ways,

John George, came on board to cook for us on site and from then on our food was wonderfully good. Every chef we had thereafter was marvellous, and I should also say that on every other Ragdoll production on which I have worked, the catering has been nothing but top-notch. Thank you, Anne.

Most importantly, I still had a job and had staved off another way in which I might die doing it.

However, I wasn't completely out of the woods yet. My asthma had always been my greatest concern, and I thought my worst fears would be played out when I started suffering symptoms early in the working day. For those that don't have any experience of the disease: even in its milder manifestations, the tightening of the chest and inability to draw breath easily into your lungs is a scary sensation. Once I'd been out on set for a while, the symptoms would clear, but they'd be back the next morning, coming on as I did my warm-up on the floor of our cabin. I bumped up my medication, but that wasn't a long-term solution. I had to find out what was causing the asthma. I'd had genuinely life-threatening attacks in the past, and I was a long way from any hospital. Now things had got serious, I was not going to allow myself to actually die. I was convinced there was a specific trigger – probably an animal – but I needed evidence. My turn to Columbo.

One morning, while stretching out into the splits, I turned my head to the side and saw a thick layer of hair – dog hair, if I wasn't mistaken – along the base of one of our couches. It turned out that our security guard had been in our cabin, contrary to regulations, snuggling down for a snooze with his very hairy pooch during the night watch. Naughty security guard. Naughty ex-security guard.

We were lucky to have our spacious Portakabin to hang out in when we weren't on set, although on occasion we were thrown out to make room for any bigwigs who visited. Later on when we were a success and had proven our worth, an entertaining hut was added to our complex. It was no hardship to be evicted – it was a beautiful spot and there was always a corner of the countryside to sit and enjoy the resident yellowhammers singing, watching the sheep and other wildlife.

Not all of nature's creatures brought joy, though. The thunderbugs were especially attracted to the Citrus Posse, and I think John got the worst of it. When they were out in force, you were stuck between a rock and a hard place. If you didn't get a towel in place around your neck as soon as you went flip-top head, they would fly inside, between your body and the suit. You didn't really want a towel round your neck, because you needed the air, and insect repellent made you choke on chemicals. If you felt them crawling on you when standing around waiting for 'Action!', your only defence was to hit yourself as hard as you possibly could in the hope that you would be able to squish the insect against your body – or to try to make peace with the unscratchable itch.

Itching was not the only bodily function that wasn't best suited to being in costume. No matter how good you were at remembering to go for a wee before you got in, there was always going to be a mad dash to the loo the moment you got out. And you really didn't want to come on your period in the middle of a long and complex scene. Then there was sneezing, about which you really couldn't do anything. Your face was there, stranded, in a void. Your nose was both a long way and cut off from your hands. The thought of covering the inside of your head – not to mention the metal mouth mechanisms – with your own snot was too repulsive for words. I trained myself to direct the force of a sneeze totally out of my mouth, rather than down my nose. This was unpleasantly loud for anyone tuned into my microphone, but it seemed a better option than the snot. I only had a cold once during the whole six years of filming – it wasn't pretty. Neither was hay fever. We learned to keep a towel over the gaping neck of the heads between shots outside, otherwise they would fill with pollen – and/or thunderbugs – and render the associated Tubby innard incapable.

Aunty Beth was on every one of these little teething problems. She was also terrific fun and I was lucky that she was my first dresser. She offered an extra service every Friday night, which was letting me share a ride back to South London. So as not to completely rot the upholstery of her passenger seat, I would lay out a complex jigsaw of towels to absorb my sweat. We'd finish work at 6.00pm, get on the road by 7.00pm, and I'd still be sweating. I'd sweat for the whole journey. It was a curious thing that first year when my body got into the habit of producing fluid and didn't seem to know when to stop. It didn't happen in following years, partly because we had more breaks but mostly, I believe, because our body temperature adjusted. I swear that for the years I filmed *Teletubbies*, I could tolerate humid heat like an equatorial native, but was a freezing wimp all winter. I once wore a fleece and a woolly hat on Waikiki beach in Hawaii – in March – when it was around eighty degrees.

Aunty Beth used to drop me in Camberwell, where I could get a number 36 bus to New Cross. Once back, I'd go straight out to the Dewdrop Inn to meet pals for a drink and a pizza, then go up to the Goldsmiths Tavern's ska night, to skank in the weekend. By 11.00pm, I had just about stopped sweating from work and was ready to start sweating from fun.

In all the excitement of gaining my new career as a giant yellow puppet – move over Big Bird – I hadn't really taken into consideration the actuality of leading a double life. New Cross at the time was rough, but it was my home and I loved it deeply. It was in my heart, and in my voice too apparently. Anne described my non-Tubby speech as, 'Weird South London R.P.' I guess you can take the girl out of SE14, but you can't take SE14 out of the girl – even if she's dressed in a big yellow baby-gro.

Most of the other London dwellers on the show would make the journey up to the Midlands at the crack of dawn on Monday morning, but I liked the security of knowing I was already there and ready to start work. Plus, I was at the mercy of Dave's preference. Every Sunday afternoon I'd have to leave whatever fun I was having, to go and pack myself up and get myself over to Lambeth. It was always a wrench to leave home and loved ones. I didn't suffer from homesickness, but I missed having my support network around me when things went wrong or became too much of a challenge. I solved this problem to a certain degree by starting a 'special friendship' with our lovely sound man.

Talking of sound, the issue with recording still hadn't been fully resolved by this point. My trust in Anne was in danger of failing and reached a critical point when we heard it was likely that Ragdoll would employ four other actors to provide the voices for the Teletubbies, recording at Pinewood Studios and using our vocal track as a guide. I can't tell you what a blow this was. It felt like being given the best Christmas present ever and then having to watch Santa saw it in half. I know it sounds a bit 'luvvie' now, but Pui and I were absolutely distraught. We had spent months developing these characters and now we were to be reduced to being merely the innards, literally just puppets. It was heart-breaking. Anne wasn't on site at the time, so Pui and I took ourselves off to Andy's caravan to throw ourselves on his mercy. We begged. We pleaded.

'Please don't do this. It will completely take ownership away from us and that's bound to affect our performances. It's not what you promised. Please.'

We cried, people. They weren't pretend tears – we really cried. That's how much it meant to us. That's how invested we were.

John wasn't happy about the decision, but he wasn't as emotional about it as us girls. And Dave? I think Dave was aware that the main problem voice was his own and he still hadn't come up with anything Anne and Andy were really happy with. There were also issues with scheduling. When and where and how would we record a usable voice track when we were so behind with filming and therefore needed on set for as many daylight hours as possible? Andy listened, Andy sympathised, Andy understood, but Andy couldn't promise us anything. When I saw Anne later in the day, she only asked that I trust her once again. There were many on the shoot that didn't, but she'd given me fruit and crudités. If she told me to trust her, then I was going to take a deep breath and do just that.

It would all become clear at the end of our first season's shooting, which came at the end of October. We filmed more or less from clocks-forward to clocks-back for maximum daylight hours, but now the light was fading and the air was turning chilly. Filming was over for the year and there was a wrap party to be had. We were commandeering the Methodist chapel hall in Mickleton for the evening, which was conveniently situated opposite our hotel. The art department had decked it out and there was food and free drink and music and dancing and all the usual party stuff, plus something very unusual indeed. We were to be treated to the very first offline edit of a complete episode of *Teletubbies* – a rough-cut with the live soundtrack. We were beside ourselves with anticipation, eager to see what we'd all been doing it for.

I felt inexplicably nervous as the playback started, but I was well aware that Anne and Andy knew what they were doing. I tried to imagine how children would react to the opening sequence, and I pictured them bouncing along to its joyfully infectious tune. I cringed with embarrassment seeing myself fail to get up that hill. The tummy film featured the adorable Ned and his bicycle. The assembled throng responded with the appropriate, 'Aaaaah!' when Ned explained, 'I doin' sum werk!' and the whole programme was enchanting. Box-of-frogs-bonkers enchanting but enchanting nonetheless. I'll confess that I found the baby sun a little creepy at first, but hey, this programme wasn't aimed at thirty-four-year-olds and I'd been taught that children are always fascinated to see other children, especially on screen, even when they're still babies. I thought the symbolism of the baby sun was clear: she – actually a baby girl called Jessica Smith – is our God. Nothing happens until the sun has risen. She is with us throughout the episode and once she's set, that's it. Game over. Without doubt, this declared the importance of children to the lives of the Teletubbies. What a delightful baby she was. Those gurgling giggles and squeals of approval set the tone right from the start.

The reaction of the assembled throng probably wasn't that different to how the general public responded on first viewing the show. Amazed, amused, and surprised to a greater or lesser extent. I watched, spellbound, with the Tubbies and our dressers, unable to stop smiling. I stood by my original assessment: this was going to be huge. We Teletubbies were delighted. Well, three of us were delighted. One of us was distraught.

With timing that was at best insensitive, and at worst downright cruel, Dave had been given a letter at the end of the shooting day but before the party. A letter which informed him that his services would no longer be required for the filming of *Teletubbies*. I knew there were problems with his voice, I knew he was the weakest link when it came to the dances, I knew he had some trouble remembering instructions and hitting his marks, but I didn't see that coming. I really felt for him, especially being in an atmosphere of out-and-out celebration when he'd just been dealt such a blow. Needless to say, he left early.

I was surprised at Ragdoll. Not so much at the sacking, but at how they did it. They said they had their reasons and wanted to let him know as soon as the decision had been made so that he could get on with his life. It still seemed cruel to me, and perhaps a little short-sighted. In life, as in fairy-tales, if you upset someone with a tendency towards vengeance you run the risk of your actions coming back to bite you. Hadn't they read *Sleeping Beauty*? If you don't invite the wicked fairy to the party, she's apt to settle the score with some kind of evil spell.

But for now, there was too much to be proud of. Too much to celebrate. We partied until we were thrown out of the hall, stepping over the bodies who had overdone themselves, full of tipsy pride in ourselves for having transformed this ambitious idea into reality.

CHAPTER 6

and we're on!

I felt both pride and relief when we reached the end of the first season's filming. Not only had I not died, but for the first time in my life, I was able to book a proper holiday knowing that I had an actual paid job to come back to. For more than a decade living as an archetypal struggling artist, holidays had been thin on the ground – coming only when my dad had a more than decent win on the horses, or when there was a friend of a friend I could stay with. This was different. I could actually afford to go off gallivanting around the globe. I'd spent my summer hermetically sealed in fun-fur, and now I wanted to go somewhere I could exist wearing little more than a hankie. Southern Hemisphere, here I come!

I'd always been a little nervous of the tropics, knowing that my lungs thrived in a hot, dry climate, but now that I'd survived weeks on end inhaling my own sweat-soaked humid air, I figured I'd nothing to fear any more. I was not going to die. Possibly not ever. The wave of excitement, trepidation, gratitude and sheer amazement that I was actually going on this adventure made me clench my fists, grit my teeth and make an 'Eeeeeee' sound. We left for Thailand on Christmas day, had a singsong on the plane with Boney M. – I know! – and on arrival, I slept for an entire week. I slept while my friends explored Bangkok. I slept on the train south. I slept for days on a charming island, waking only to be spoon-fed small pieces of fruit. It's safe to say, I was knackered. After more sleep than should be humanly possible, a local Thai wizard with a comprehensive knowledge of traditional remedies, gave me magic tea of ginger, lemongrass and other more secret herbs, which I drank until I could once more exist in a vertical position.

After a long and recuperative trip, I was back in the UK and ready to get started on filming season two. Before that, however, we were told a solution to the sound issue had been found and we would be required to voice the material we'd shot in season one. Finally, confirmation that it was going to be us. Hoorah!

Schedules had been tweaked, budgets had been adjusted, and a system of recording had been put in place to enable us to do voice overs at Pinewood Studios. The relief came not just from the fact that I would retain full ownership of the Laa-Laa I'd invented, but also from my faith being justified. My judge of character had been correct and my trust in Anne well-placed. I could continue to love her.

While I'd been larking about in the holiday sun, Mark Heenehan had been employed to be the voice of Tinky Winky while Ragdoll continued to look for someone to be the physical presence. It wasn't an ideal situation, but the pressures of the schedule prohibited the luxury of waiting until the perfect person to be body and voice could be found. Mark was big, strapping even, but could access the higher end of his vocal range to give Tinky Winky a charming naivety and a gurgling chuckle in his voice. He was a professional actor and vocalist, more used to this kind of thing than I. Once again, I was in a whole new world, the world of ADR, which I would come to learn stands for Additional Dialogue Recording. Obviously.

I never got over the excitement of working at Pinewood. I was never blasé about it and entering through those famous gates genuinely thrilled me every time. The place had so much history and it still oozed a golden-age glamour that made you want to drive through it in a vintage open-top car in a cloche hat and a fur collar, possibly smoking but definitely drinking a cocktail – shaken, not stirred – when passing the legendary 007 stage. We worked in studio six, which lent itself to the fantasy. A small recording and viewing theatre at the back of the lot, you could smell the ghosts of a thousand cigars smoked while watching the rushes of classic English films. This was where sound recordist, Sandy Buchanan, was to capture our vocals, which would then be mixed and matched with the programme by Oscar-nominated lovely man Nick Le Messurier, ably assisted by Tim Vine – no, not that one. Because the studio was at the back of the lot – it's thrilling just using that language, isn't it? – we had to walk through all of Pinewood to get to work, checking out film sets that were being built in the proper sound stages along the way. At lunch, we'd eat in the canteen with all manner of aliens, spies and extras of every hue who formed the eccentric queue for food. On special occasions, we might be treated to a lunch in the restaurant proper, keeping our eyes peeled for actual famous people.

The ADR sessions became one of my favourite aspects of the job. The work took a great deal of focus but gave an enormous sense of satisfaction when successfully completed, and guess what? You could wear real clothes. Both John and I made the error of turning up to the first recording day wearing trousers that rustled – Utility Chic was big at the time – and we had to stand super-still so as not to ruin the take. Or be forced to do the session in our underpants.

The offline edit we worked to would still have the vocal track that we'd recorded on the day. This would be the first time we'd seen the finished sketch, so as well as paying attention to what we needed to say, we were also assessing our performances.

Having watched the sketch through to remind ourselves of

the script, we'd re-voice a clean version. That is, a version without the huffing and puffing and clanking of the mouth and eye mechanisms. A clean version had another meaning entirely when it came to John. Remember how we all thought he was the nice one because he didn't moan as much as the rest of us? It turned out that when he'd been running over the hills, he'd been vocalising his efforts: 'Fuckingfuckingfuckfuckfuckfuckfucking fuck fuck fuck.'

Of course, we hadn't been able to hear him, so we had absolutely no idea that he was the foulest mouthed of all. Ringo!

It was amazing how clearly we could remember what we'd done on the day. We were given scripts to work from when revoicing, but we barely used them, relying instead on memory. People can be cruelly amazed to find out that we had scripts, but of course we did – it was a very carefully crafted programme. The scripts were written in regular English, which we would then Tubbify. It wasn't gibberish, as many people suppose. It had proper grammatical structure, created in line with children's speech patterns. More than anything else, we were attacked for our use of language, and especially for the 'Eh-Oh!':

'Why can't they say "Hello" properly? It's dumbing down. They're teaching our children it's okay to use baby talk. If children watch this ridiculous programme, they'll never learn to speak correctly.'

What I think this reveals is a lack of faith in young children's ability to know what's what. It was our belief that from a very early age, most children realise what television is, on some level. We believed they would understand that the whole thing was a game. We used a play language based on emergent speech. We all know that babies babble, that they pick up on the cadence of language before they have the vocabulary or fine motor skills to articulate words. They learn the tune before the lyrics. This is what was at the heart of the *Teletubbies* language. Andy had chosen our linguistic repertoire carefully. If any words came up that lay outside that repertoire, we'd have a stab at an approximation just as any toddler would, but the tonal inflexion and rhythm would always be correct. There's an ongoing dispute in the world of language development as to whether adults should use baby talk with their children or speak to them in fully formed sentences as if addressing an adult. I'm not going to get into that argument here. We weren't adults speaking to children, we were fictitious playmates.

The 'Eh-Oh!' served a carefully researched purpose. We said 'hello' to the child at home and to each other at the top of every sequence, and this simple technique instantly made the viewer feel that they had a relationship with us. They could see that this friendly greeting was as reassuring to us as it was to them – we were all in the same gang and together from the off. Beyond that, it wasn't just a normal 'hello'. It was the sort of version that toddlers might use themselves, and instantly recognisable as Tubby. That sharing of a special codeword, a special language, is complicit: if you know it, you're part of the club and you can join in with the call and response protocol. We set this up, along with the other main protocols of Teletubbyland, right from the word go, from the top of the programme as an element of the title sequence. Even now, when people find out that I was a Teletubby, more often than not they will give me a cheery 'Eh-Oh!' and if they don't do it immediately, they will do it the next time they see me. The fact that the 'Eh-Oh!' was the stickiest of our trademarks wasn't an accident – Andy was deliberately tapping into the way that very young children learn and process language.

Andy was impressive. As an aspiring writer myself, I marvelled at how free he was able to be with his imagination, how he could open doors of invention that I hadn't even found yet. I wasn't the only fan. John would regularly express his admiration, declaring

Andy an unarguable genius. And Andy was funny. When there was laughing at the read-through, you knew it would be a good day's work. Ordinarily, when introduced to a sketch for the first time, part of my brain would start measuring the physical difficulties that lay ahead, but when the script was genuinely funny, that part of my brain just shut up. Instead I'd get excited about how I could maximise the funny. As I've said, most exciting of all was seeing the words 'Laa-Laa sings a song' or 'Laa-Laa does a dance'. I knew that Andy was handing me the opportunity to let rip, and it was a major boost to my confidence to know that he had complete faith in me to pull it off.

It was a huge responsibility to be the only writer on a substantial series like ours. More commonly, a team of writers would share the load. Although Anne encouraged Andy to share writing duties, in practice this was an uphill battle. During the first year, Anne established a writing group that met on Wednesday evenings, and as Dave and I had expressed interest, we were invited to join. It soon became obvious that Andy was not going to delegate. He was not going to share his baby. But while he turned down every script that anyone else submitted, I was the lucky one who somehow managed to get her creations past his metaphorical security gates.

Every episode had a long narrative sequence that comprised the main Teletubby action, such as 'Who Spilled the Tubby Custard?', and which sat at the thematic centre of each episode. This was the baby that Andy wasn't going to entrust to anyone else. There was also a short sequence, that we all came to refer to as a Quickie. This could be a simple visual idea such as popping up to say 'Eh-Oh!' from an unexpected position, a classic 'behind you' gag or something similar. I managed to get a few of my Quickie ideas accepted, so I can legitimately say I was the only contributing writer to get any material past Andy's exacting standards. I understood his stance. I know it was frustrating for Anne on occasion, waiting – expensively – for Andy to finish a script so that we'd have something to film, but there is a consistency and cohesion to *Teletubbies* which is a direct consequence of all the scripts coming from the brain of one man – well, almost all.

Anne and Andy had decided from the outset that the whole programme would be structured like a jigsaw puzzle with a selection of components to draw from: quickie sketches, main sketches, the dances, the tummy films (played twice) and the magical events. The magical event sections comprised either one of five animation sequences built around numbers, or a Lion and Bear chase, or later Bo Peep. A selection of these elements could be linked together with cut-away shots of the windmill or the baby sun giggling, or establisher shots of our beautiful landscape or the Noo-Noo tidying up, in order to create a programme. This format gave the producers plenty of flexibility in the edit. With children being children, it was impossible to predict exactly how long the tummy film of them would be, so the rest of the components could be assembled around this variable until the desired length of programme was achieved. But logistics weren't the only concern.

Ideally, all the material performed by the Teletubbies would be thematically linked to the children's activities, and this theme might also dictate if an animation sequence was to be included. The five animations were so beautifully idiosyncratic that you might not notice immediately that they were constructed around numbers, with each built around one of the first five digits. For example, a parade of animals could come marching through Tubbyland two-by-two, or the whole landscape would flood and three ships would come sailing by – that was my favourite. With these sections, as with the whole show, the educational content was buried within the overall aesthetic.

While the counting animations proved very popular, the Lion

and Bear were another thing entirely. The two giant cut-out characters, voiced by Penelope Keith and Eric Sykes, chased each other over Teletubbyland in what was intended as a playful game. However for some children, the tone tipped over into being genuinely scary. Eventually the postbag dictated that they were axed. This may have been a blessing in disguise as the much funnier Bo Peep sequence took their place. A traditional but over-sized Bo Peep figure searched for and found her wayward flock of sheep – the sheep declaring 'We are the sheep!' over and over like a ludicrously fluffy football crowd. Both of these sketches entailed hordes of crew lugging gigantic puppets over Tubbyland for days on end. It was deeply satisfying to see someone else have a go at that!

By early spring 1997, we were well into the swing of voicing season one episodes and now it was time to return to Teletubbyland to start filming season two. Everyone who was working away from home embarked on what was to become an annual ritual: fighting over the handful of decent, affordable rental properties within easy reach of Teletubbyland. After spending the first year housed in hotel accommodation, almost everyone decided that having somewhere to call their own, at least temporarily, would be infinitely preferable. Those competing for home-from-homes would spend every spare minute leafing through the classifieds and 'building a relationship' with estate agents in the hope of nabbing somewhere that would inspire envy in the rest of the exiles. As she was no longer my dresser, Aunty Beth and I had agreed to share a property, and I soon found a cottage in a neighbouring village. I liked the rhythm of its address: Woodlands, Blackwell, Warwickshire. The minimalism of this also rendered it virtually impossible to find for the first time on a dark March evening. But find it and rent it I did.

Beth and I lived happily together until personal matters took her off the show for a short while. We threw a truly rocking adieu party for her – the sort where you find unexpected bodies behind the couch the following morning and everyone is a little bit late to work. In Beth's absence I invited Ben, that year's 'special friend' and coincidentally also the sound man, to live with me. This arrangement worked beautifully for the duration. After all, Woodlands had a topiary rabbit in the front garden and who wouldn't envy that?

Everyone was ready to do it all again, but faster. Although we'd filmed as many episodes as was humanly possible in the first year, we were still very behind. After season one's teething problems, such as the toast machine and the voice issue, and the time it had taken to film all the generic shots, we found ourselves with a great deal of ground to make up before we even started the second season. The first year had also seen a few shifts in personnel, whether through choice or as part of the ongoing process of assembling the most efficient team possible. Foremost in the minds of us Teletubbies, of course, was the question of who would be the new Tinky Winky.

The big introduction was to take place at Pinewood, in one of my favourite rooms. The pool room was so-called not because it had a collection of green baize tables, but because in the olden days it had been an actual indoor pool. The remaining decor reflected that, with symmetrical steps and a balustraded balcony, and although the pool had been covered over and carpeted, I was always still aware of the empty tiled space below. I told myself jokes about being thrown in the deep end as I shook hands with Simon Shelton.

The first thing I noticed about Simon was his smile, springing readily to his lips and occupying the rest of his face in the twinkling of an eye. Anyone who could exude that much warmth and good humour with just a sprinkle of mischief had to be a great piece of casting. Having been in the Houston Ballet Company, he was also a proper professional dancer. This meant he would be strong, co-ordinated, dedicated and considerate. It turned out that he was also hilarious. I don't know anyone who didn't like Simon – he was one of those people it's just good to have around. A self-assured family man, he inspired confidence on a personal and professional level.

Once we were back in Tubbyland, Simon lived up to, and exceeded, expectations. He instantly grasped what was necessary to do the job, inspired Andy afresh and made everyone's life on set much easier than it had previously been. Poor Dave – I thought he brought a certain charm to the character of Tinky Winky, but it can't be denied that he struggled more than the rest of us. When Dave was doing the job, we could easily get up to eight takes or more, but when Simon took over it became rare for us to need more than two takes to get any scene right. This was an important development, both for the schedule and for our own physical comfort and wellbeing. We needed to be working faster and smarter, and as Simon settled into the role, we found ourselves making some headway through the backlog of material. Finally, the dream team was in place and work on season two could begin.

On March 31st 1997, the very first episode of *Teletubbies* was broadcast. You may be tempted to imagine that we all sat around the screen like one massive happy family to watch the big event, but it wasn't like that. Those of us who were free to, watched the first show go out, but most of us were far too busy filming to be able to take a break, naively carrying on with the task in hand. If anything, it was rather an anti-climax. We'd all seen the first episode, entitled *Ned's Bicycle*, at the wrap party and we'd had our excitement there. Simon had been treated to a private screening as part of his audition process, and the majority of the crew were seasoned old pros for whom this was all just part of the job.

There was no reason to get excited, not for the first few weeks of broadcast at any rate. Once it had bedded-in, we'd keep an eye out for anyone who was eccentric enough to review a little kids show but we didn't expect much. We had no idea what was about to hit our isolated little lives. I had always been convinced that the show would be a huge success, but I had no inkling of the media circus it would unleash. Anne and Andy hoped it would succeed with its target audience but had no reason to imagine anyone else would be interested. There were even people working on the show who wondered if anyone at all would pay attention.

Reviews started slowly. They weren't what you'd call enthusiastic, but for every column griping about what this new rubbish was, there would be an adorable drawing dropped off at the Ragdoll shop to be passed on to the Teletubbies. The initial signs were that the children – for whom it was made – loved the show. The adults – for whom it wasn't – not so much. In the beginning, we weren't that bothered about the opinion of the British press. We had no reason to be. We were focused on making the show and on keeping up the pace so we could catch up with our quota.

As a stand-up comedian, John liked to keep his finger on the pulse in order to make topical gags, and he read the papers every day. This meant he was the most aware of what was going on, and he'd act as our press agency, sharing juicy tit-bits with the rest of us. It was exciting to begin with. We were happy for the producers that the show was getting noticed – surely the attention would be good for the ratings? Once we were into 'silly season' and the press had nothing else to write about, we became front page news.

There were two main areas of attack. The first, voiced mainly in the broadsheets with a middle-class accent, was that the show was detrimental to children's development. We were accused of dumbing down language with our baby talk and preventing children from learning how to speak properly. As *Teletubbies* had been co-created and written by a childhood linguistics specialist, this was rather a hollow criticism. From their lofty perch, journalists with no specialism in child development looked down and pooh-poohed the slow tempo of the show, the endless repetition, the seemingly simplistic structure and the ridiculous characters. This wasn't a good use of licence-payers' money. Where was the educational value? How can this have been commissioned? This is children's television gone mad!

The educational value was everywhere of course, and our programme was for three-year-olds, who are surely allowed to have some fun and games in their lives. Underlying this often aggressive stance was a level of suspicion. What evil powers were we employing to have such a profound effect on such tiny minds? The grown-ups couldn't understand why children loved the show so much, why they ran to the television as soon as the first few notes of the theme tune began to play, how they sat transfixed throughout as if hypnotised – some malevolent force was surely at play. Far from the throwaway fluff our naysayers accused us of, the programme was put together with deep thought, educational theory, psychology, linguistics, years and years of experience, consideration and careful construction. The developmental heft was buried deep under many layers of love, laughter and the sheer joy of being three years old, so it was easy to miss if you were a lot older than three.

The second point of attack – from the tabloids – was much more straightforward: What on earth is this? What are they on? Who are those people? More importantly, can we get some dirt?

It took a little time for them to be absolutely certain that the characters were people inside suits. So smart was the bigging-up of everything else on screen that the initial presumption was that the Tubbies were too small to be actual grown humans.

Once that became clear, however, we were prime targets. This was when it all started to get deeply weird for the four of us.

Anne was determined that our identities should remain secret. Her main concern was that the illusion would be spoiled for the children if there were pictures of the thoroughly unmagical human innards plastered everywhere, breaking the spell she had so carefully crafted. The unpleasantness of this unwanted exposure was something of which I had personal experience. If I was 'outed' in some social situation – a parent declaring to their toddler, 'Look honey, this lady is Laa-Laa!' – the child would look me up and down and then turn to the parent with an expression of confusion and pity, as if to say, 'Are you drunk, Mother? This is obviously not Laa-Laa, this is merely a smiley woman.'

The statement 'This is Laa-Laa' when applied to myself without the yellow suit on, made no sense to the child. I understood that the adult was excited and wanted the child to feel that excitement too, but that's looking with adult eyes and not from the point of view of the child. I tried to avert this behaviour, but I wasn't always quick enough and a few baffled and disappointed children slipped through the net. When you scale that baffle and disappointment up to a national level, you have a problem on your hands.

We had signed non-disclosure agreements and very few people outside our inner circles knew who the Teletubbies were. Despite this, Ragdoll were taking no risks – they were going to protect their investment. This secrecy was like catnip to the gutter press. The more their investigations drew a blank, the more determined they were to discover our true identities.

It was interesting to learn how the tabloid press functions. Maybe I was slow on the uptake, but I had no idea how frequently the same sets of words would be passed around. This was especially apparent when the content was factually inaccurate. One journalist wrote that I had turned my South East London flat into a shrine to *Teletubbies*. I had one poster up on my kitchen wall. I was not obsessed. Nevertheless, this same untruth was reproduced, verbatim, in every other rag. Sometimes even spelling mistakes were transferred, in case there was any doubt the article had merely been cut and pasted. How lazy.

Once they found out where Teletubbyland was, we were in trouble. Security was increased. We had men out scouring local lanes that had any kind of view of our site and searching adjoining fields for the paparazzi wielding long lenses. Soon, we needed a full-time guard at the entrance, and not just to keep out the press but to turn away members of the public. A few of the papers printed a map of where Teletubbyland was, so people thought they'd pop along for a day out, not seeming to realise that this was a place of work. They didn't see it as an invasion of privacy, but rather that they had the right. What's worse was that if they'd seen anything, it would have ruined it for the children they had brought with them – a super-sized version of, 'Look honey, this lady is Laa-Laa.'

For obvious reasons, we were unable to prevent incursion from above. All at once and literally out of the blue, a helicopter would come flying over at low altitude with a couple of photographers hanging out of the side, dangerously dangling their expensive-looking cameras as they hung in the air. It was extraordinary. Helicopters cost a fortune to hire. We were just puppets! Where was the sense?

There were uncomfortable implications for the four of us. In order to avoid a surreptitious shot of us half-in and half-out of our costumes – the very worst thing a child could possibly see – we had to get entirely enclosed in the suit within the dome and then walk uphill to our start positions, do the scene, and then walk back to the dome before we could go 'flip-top head' and get some air. Obviously this extra effort sapped our energy for the important business on camera. What had started as a source of amusement was rapidly turning into a monumental pain.

Our families weren't spared either. One evening at around 8.00pm, a hack rang my parents' doorbell. My father – who'd been an ad man in the '60s and '70s, so knew something of the ways of the press – answered the door:

'Good evening, Sir. I'm from the *Daily Mirror*, is it true you're Laa-Laa's dad?'

'Go away. I'm busy watching television.'

Slam.

Good old Dad.

I had more reason to be grateful to my dad when, around about the time of our first broadcast, I finally managed to pass my driving test. After all those years of public transport, trailing around on foot and cadging lifts, I could finally get on the road under my own steam. Once our line producer had managed to get around the fact that being a Teletubby made a person uninsurable, I was all set to go. I rang my ex-racing-driver father to let him know he could stop being ashamed of his pedestrian daughter and he told me he had an old Vauxhall Carlton he was supposed to be selling for my Uncle Bob, but I was welcome to borrow it until he found a buyer. So Ben drove me over one evening to pick it up, and after a brief lesson in how to drive an automatic – essentially press go – I cruised back across three counties in a massive car that turned on a sixpence. I felt and looked as if I was in *The Sweeney*. I loved it. Sadly, the opportunities I had to drive it were becoming few and far between. Thanks to the attentions of the press, we were prevented from driving back to our digs in our own cars in case we were followed. We had to lie, out of view, in the back of a cab which would then drive around the country lanes until we lost anyone tailing us and could finally go home.

They soon found out that I lived in New Cross. I bet they drew straws to see which poor sod had to brave it down to SE14. Then again, maybe not – these are people who go through bins after all. Which they did. What were they expecting to find? Discarded pieces of Tubby toast? Rabbit corpses? Love letters to Po? They visited my local pub, the legendary Dew Drop Inn, spiritual home of all the old punks and freaks in the neighbourhood. The guy from the *Daily Mail* pretended to be an old friend of mine, asking for my phone number, checking which house was mine and generally smarming around. It was obvious to anyone who knew me that he was lying and my pal Gary, the barman, told the assembled punters that the incongruous stranger was the filth, which shut everyone up. This particular hack cornered my friend Anna with the old friend routine, 'Yeah, I haven't seen Nikky for years, I really wanna get in touch. Does she still live over the park? Is it the one with the plants?'

'Don't know. Don't know where she lives.'

'I heard she shaved all her hair off. Is that true?'

'Don't know.'

'How can you not know?'

'She always wears a hat.'

Class.

The folk in the Dew Drop were my drinking buddies, but they didn't owe me anything. No-one had any money and I couldn't really have blamed them if they'd tried to earn a few quid selling a story to the papers. But this was a high calibre collection of barflies. They knew the meaning of loyalty and being a mensch, for all that polite society would probably look down their noses at them. So successfully did this army of punks deprive reporters of any juicy gossip, the tabloids were reduced to printing the one detail they had been given: 'Wears a hat.'

Honestly, that made it into the papers.

Incidentally, I had shaved all my hair off. I had started *Teletubbies* with my hair in a thick bob – or tangled sweaty mess, as it soon became. There wasn't room in the skullcap to tie your hair back or up, so it stuck damply to your skull, providing an extra layer of insulation and heat. It absolutely had to go. I bought a set of clippers and every week I'd find a quiet corner to give myself a number-one shearing. This resulted in a pleasing Velcro-like effect within the skullcap, which helped to keep the puppet head in place. Being a skinhead for a few years was an interesting experience. People who didn't know me tended to look at me with pity, assuming I must have cancer. Sometimes there was fear and suspicion – at least one empty restaurant wouldn't give me a table, scared of all my skinhead mates arriving maybe. In Thailand people thought I was a monk, and I enjoyed utterly undeserved respect. In the Sinai Peninsula, everyone was concerned that it would be impossible for me to find a husband until my hair grew back. Perhaps it was just as well the press settled for 'wears a hat.'

Genuine fear set in at the point when the *Sun* printed a daily footer enquiring, 'Do you know a Teletubby? Call this number and we'll pay you for your story!' I asked Anne, 'What will you do if you open the paper tomorrow morning and the headline says, "I fucked Laa-Laa in drug-fuelled orgy!"?' She chuckled in an 'Oh Nikky, you are a one!' kind of a way.

I wasn't laughing. I wanted to know whether she intended to stand by her cast, or if those threatened easy-to-get replacements would be moved in. The story wouldn't have to be true – God knows drug-fuelled orgies were right off my agenda for the foreseeable future. I was too knackered for one thing. But even if disproved, the mud would stick. It was terrifying. The four of us lived our lives huddling out of sight, waiting for something to inevitably hit the fan.

In the end it wasn't a member of the general public who dished the fabricated dirt. No, it was one of our own. With the help of the celebrity publicist Max Clifford, jilted Dave Thompson saw his opportunity to take advantage of the press interest in the show. Hell hath no fury like a purple puppet scorned. My first inkling that something was afoot was when a model girlfriend of mine rang to tell me she'd been approached to 'feature' in a news story claiming sexual shenanigans in Teletubbyland. She'd turned it down. More proof that my friends had standards. Then another came forward with the same tale. And another. The press sure were having trouble finding anyone to join in with this charade.

When the story came out, it was a double page spread featuring a photo of Dave lolling about in the buff with a pretty model-type I didn't know, in her pants, draped all over him and, for some reason, the Noo-Noo. The whole story was about how the two of them 'did it' over and over again, all night long, in the Tubbytronic Superdome. Everyone involved in the show knew this wasn't true, but a story is a story I suppose. The knock-on effect of this exposé was that, just as everyone had got bored of talking about us, it all started up again. Perfect.

John told me that the tabloid press allegedly offered Dave even more money if he dished the dirt on his fellow cast members for public entertainment. He refused this offer on principle and I genuinely thank him for that.

With the bit between their teeth, the press would give us no respite now. They managed to cobble together a set of photographs of the mysterious Teletubby innards: Pui's was a press shot from when she was in Lenny Henry's sitcom *Chef!*, with a jaunty white cook's hat and everything; Simon's was a dashing commercial head-shot – of course; and John's was an action pose from his other life as a stand-up comedian. They all looked like fine upstanding members of low-level showbiz. God knows where they found the shot of me, I'd never seen it before. Clearly taken during a live performance, it was from a solo dance piece where I wore overly-exaggerated make-up and hammed it up for comic effect. Out of context I looked like a weird bag-lady. With context, I also looked like a weird bag-lady. Never mind, I was barely recognisable and that was definitely a good thing. The tagline read:

'Dancer Nikky Smedley: wears a hat.'

Even before the media circus, there had always been strict rules on and around Teletubbyland. Visitors were often blindfolded so they wouldn't know exactly where they were being driven to, and cameras and photography were banned on set for everyone except the actual crew. Under no circumstances could any member of cast or crew record an image of any of the Teletubbies only partly in their costumes. Shortly after the increase in media attention, we were informed that someone on set – although I don't think we ever found out who – took just such a photograph of the four of us, relaxing between takes in the dome. Our lower halves were Tubbies, our top halves humans, hanging out for air and water. Of course, this image was sold to the tabloids. It was so disappointing.

Ragdoll thought that if they met the press part-way, gave them a small amount of well-controlled access, then perhaps they'd go away and leave us alone. So they reluctantly agreed to allow the *Sunday Times* to visit the set, where they could take strictly monitored photographs, under supervision. They could interview the four of us, but on no account could they photograph us as our human selves. As the *Times'* photographer was escorted on to the set by one of our producers, he pretended to clean his camera lens and surreptitiously took a forbidden shot with Simon in the foreground with the legs of a puppet and the head of a man, like some weird nursery minotaur. I mean, if you can't trust the *Sunday Times*, who can you trust?

The attention was relentless. Everyone tried to forget it was there, tried to rise above it and get on with the show, but it was difficult. Anne said she felt under attack every day. She wasn't alone. The overwhelming feeling was that of being powerless. I had no control over how I was represented. My actual behaviour in the here and now counted for nothing and if the chips fell badly, I could be judged on things that weren't even true. I lived with a constant nagging fear and anxiety because of that powerlessness, which in itself was exhausting and tedious. It was something for which I was totally unprepared. We were a harmless children's TV show – we'd done nothing to court that kind of publicity and yet there we were, hounded.

People did – and sometimes still do – show me misplaced but well-meaning sympathy: 'What a shame that no-one ever saw your face . . . to be that famous but still no-one knows who you are. It's awful really, such a wasted opportunity. What a pity. Aren't you sad about that?' The question is always accompanied by a tilt of the head for emphasis.

Ha!

I had the merest taste of what it can be like to be famous, and it sucks. It's revolting. Why would anyone in their right minds want to live their lives like that? No, it's not a shame. No, I am not sad about it. The whole point was to be able to go and do a good job, to make some top-quality television that would make young children feel happy and loved and good about themselves and then go home and lead a normal life. Go to the pub, go to the shop, go swimming, put rubbish in my bin, go about my business freely and unhindered.

I realise that people associate fame with wealth, and almost everyone likes the idea of that. I understand that people crave love and attention. I am those people too, but it's just too high a price to pay. Maybe it's different when you get to the upper echelons of fame, maybe there are different kinds of attention, maybe there are ways of handling it so it doesn't become a total nightmare. But you can't trust the media and you can't control them, so it's a hell of a risk to take and we've all seen how badly wrong it can go. I was truly glad I wasn't properly famous – I just had one very famous outfit.

In my darker moments, I wondered if this was how it was going to be from now on, if this was the price I would have to pay for having a great job and being successful at it: the hiding, the stalking, the fear. I knew the press packs needed fresh blood, and we wouldn't be prime targets forever, but on the other hand, what if the threat was always there? Even from the perspective of my low-level celebrity, press intrusion was unbearable and there seemed to be no way of preventing it. There was no rational talking down to be done, it was going to take something earth-shattering to have any effect on the situation.

Something earth-shattering is exactly what happened in the August of 1997. Princess Diana was killed.

I found out one Saturday morning when I switched on my television to watch cartoons on Nickelodeon, but instead found a ticker-tape footer imploring me to turn over to BBC One for news of national importance. Which I did. After the initial shock and horror, a small selfish part of me started to realise what this meant for the Teletubbies. This news would be the main focus for the foreseeable future and we could go back to being anonymous puppets. In addition to which, the press were thought to have contributed to the death of our once future queen – surely that would lead to some examination of their methods.

I realise that the harassment I experienced pales into insignificance compared to what Diana had to endure, along with many others whose lives have been made unbearable by press intrusion, but even the modest level with which I had to contend was traumatic. I have absolutely no idea how we would have coped had *Teletubbies* first aired during the era of social media. Not only would we have had the press haranguing us, but the general populace would have had myriad platforms from which to berate us if they'd felt so inclined. Far from Diana's death marking the beginning of an era where personal privacy is more greatly respected, we now seem to live in a time where the very concept has become almost impossible to maintain, even for those outside the public eye. I am grateful for small mercies.

For everyone involved in *Teletubbies*, the last couple months of filming were much more peaceful and productive. We were still playing catch-up throughout the second season and we filmed beyond clock-back, running over into November. There were pros and cons to this. A new experience was being cold: the very special chill of having worked up a nice hot sweaty environment in the suit and then being exposed to the cruel November air. 'No, I'll stay in here, thanks!' were words none of us thought we would ever hear ourselves saying. Nevertheless, the extra effort meant that by the time we finished filming season two, we were more or less up to speed in terms of schedule and the entire unit was functioning more like a finely oiled machine. The plus side of filming so late in the year was that we could enjoy the positive sides of the show's success together in the run-up to Christmas.

With Santa needing to fill his sack for the festive season, our merchandising was in full swing, with all predictions being that Teletubby dolls would be the must-have items on that year's gift lists. As it turned out, I was the UK's best-selling toy of 1997, narrowly beating Po into second place. I know it's ridiculous and childish and petty, but I can't tell you how gratifying that was, and still is. The conversation with my father about how to be everyone's favourite reverberated in my ears and lifted the corners of my mouth.

If that wasn't satisfying enough, I started getting phone calls from all and sundry asking me if I could get a set of Teletubby dolls for them because the shelves were empty. All and sundry included former employers who had failed to renew my contract, late payers, companies who hadn't chosen me in the first place, those that had failed to comply with the agreed terms and those who never called back. I must admit, I enjoyed telling them that I was, sadly, unable to help. I could enjoy it with an easy conscience too as I really was unable to help. When the standard plush Teletubby dolls were first produced, we were each given a set of four, gift wrapped in colour-coded paper with a 'Love from Anne' card attached. My box is in the same pristine condition it was when I received it, still wrapped and everything. I may need to sell it one day for a tin of beans.

Anyhow, that was as close as we came to the merchandise side of things. Everything was licensed out. Golden Bear had the contract for the plush dolls – they made millions of pounds – and we had no contact with them, so we were powerless to help the toy seekers. The manufacturers were falling over themselves to keep up with demand and in that first year Teletubby merchandising outsold all other toy brands twice over.

Later on, when the toys were more readily available, I loved being incognito and watching children decide which character they were going to choose. 'Have Laa-Laa. She's the best. She's the one you love most.' I'd whisper when mummy wasn't paying attention.

All four of us marvelled at the extraordinary range of merchandising that was created, and we were probably unaware of the vast majority of goods being sold in our name: toast and custard and other food products and bath toys – my favourite – and clothing lines and Tracy Island style Teletubbylands and magazines and teething rings and rucksacks . . . and . . . and . . . and . . . The list was endless. Every country that the programme was sold to came up with a culturally appropriate range and of course plenty of goods were produced unofficially too. During the annual street fair in Stratford-upon-Avon – The Mop – ugly and cheaply produced Teletubby dolls were in evidence as prizes on many of the stalls. Not for long. They picked the wrong town to try and pass off unlicensed goods. All the Ragdoll legal department had to do was take three steps out of the office, and no stall-holder could run or hide that quickly.

When the talking dolls came out, my own mother picked one up in Toys R Us – or as I took to calling it, Toys R Me – and later asked me, 'Is that your voice?'

'Yes Mum, whose else would it be?'

I wasn't going to let on that there was a time it might indeed have been someone else's. My sister on the other hand took a fright any time anyone set off a talking Laa-Laa in a shop, startled to suddenly hear her sibling's voice out of nowhere. Pui and I had to do a special recording session when an American company developed a digital version of our two talking dolls. It was the most technical voice session I'd ever done, and I'd done a fair amount of over-dubbing by then. Each phrase had very specific parameters in terms of duration, pitch and tone. Again, I was given one of the toys to keep, which again, still sits pristine in its box in what I refer to as 'the pension cupboard'.

The merchandise probably earned more people more money than the programme did and there were those that believed the whole exercise had been a cynical campaign to sell toys – people who couldn't get a doll for Christmas, probably. Now our original audience are all grown up, it's not unusual to come across a person who will say to me, 'I've never met anyone I used to have a toy of before!'

Around this time, I started getting requests for public appearances.

'Please will you come to our school?'

'Will you come and open our library?'

'It'd be so good of you to attend our Nursery's open day.'

I had to turn down every one of these, 'No, I can't, I'm sorry. I'm too big.'

Then there'd be a pause while they considered the diva arrogance and who-does-she-think-she-is-ness.

'I don't mean too successful or important. I mean physically too big.'

A more forgiving but slightly confused pause would follow.

'I wouldn't get through the door.'

Then I'd explain that Laa-Laa stood eight feet tall from her aerial tip to her giant paw toes, and though I wasn't sure of the exact girth, it was a lot wider than most doorways. On top of this was the fact that the costumes were worth tens of thousands of pounds and there was no way I'd be allowed to remove mine from the site. Even now, people ask me, 'And do you still have the costume?' and I say no – partly because of its value, and partly because it would fill most of my house. It's pleasing that people didn't realise how big we were as it showed the trick of perspective and super-sizing everything had worked. The children needed to be protected from the truth – another reason why personal appearances were out of the question. Pui's three-year-old niece came on a visit from Hong Kong and was given special permission to come onto set, but she wasn't impressed at all – more terrified: 'I don't like Aunty's Po! I don't like Aunty's Po!' It was much better to keep us viewed via a television screen.

However, there was a way for us to appear to our public more broadly without having to show up in person. The BBC thought releasing a recording of the theme song, *Say Eh-Oh!* would be an excellent chance to capitalise on the success of the Teletubby merchandising boom in the run up to Christmas. Anne and Andy weren't very happy about the idea when the BBC first mooted it. As ever, their concern was that if the show was exposed on too many adult formats, it would lose its mystique and appeal for the very young children for whom it was made. Pressure was applied. After all, I guess it made sense to make as big an omelette as possible while the golden goose was laying. The songwriter, Andrew McCrorie-Shand, was very happy indeed.

Despite the fact that the accompanying video was cut together from existing footage, the four Tubbies were brought into the studio to rerecord the vocals for the single release. This meant that it fell outside of our original contract so we could claim royalties. Hoorah! I remember asking Anne if we could please have a point – one percentage point of sales – each and she said yes, but that didn't come to pass. I think we ended up with one percentage point between the four of us. Still, it was a lovely Christmas bonus.

I remember walking into my local pub in New Cross one evening, during the time that the single was everywhere, and being greeted with a merry group on the karaoke stage singing along to *Say Eh-Oh*! Once again I had been gifted the opportunity to anonymously enjoy people revelling in the show's popularity. It was one of the most surreal experiences of that time, matched only by sitting in front of the television and seeing our record repeatedly being declared top of the charts for yet another week on *Top of the Pops*.

We so nearly had the Christmas Number One. We kept Robbie Williams' *Angels* off the top spot, but having hung on until the actual Christmas week, we were knocked from our perch by the Spice Girls. Curse them. Nevertheless, we were in the top seventy-five of the charts for thirty-two weeks.

Right up until the point that I was cast in *Teletubbies,* I'd tried really hard to be a pop star and never come close to the charts. You could say that I'd had a failed career in pop music. I'd been signed to and dumped by CBS records, I'd played the pyramid stage at Glastonbury, and only the previous year, I'd still been gigging with my band Psychopussy. Nothing had worked. But there I was, having left all that behind me to behave like a three-year-old in a giant furry yellow suit, and I had a Number One hit single. I now have a double platinum disc on my lounge wall. Sometimes the universe has a very strange way of making dreams come true.

CHAPTER 7

Keep Blinking and Carry On

Before the third year of filming started, I wrote a note to myself in the back of my Filofax:

HOW TO GET THROO TUBS:

- Enjoy every minute.
- There's only one year left.
- It's my job to be FUNNY.

I'd had the first year of learning how to do this crazy job, of getting used to the physical work, of panic and hysteria and the constant concern that the whole thing would be the death of me. I'd had the second year of extreme pressure from press insanity and working my paws off as we tried to catch up on our schedule. Now for this third – and what I presumed would be the final – year, perhaps I could actually take a breath and make the most of it.

I wasn't the only one. Anne's face had changed colour with relief. She looked like she was breathing out for the first time in two years. Her gamble had paid off. She'd put in every penny from fifteen years' work, she'd been knocked about and genuinely hurt by the media bullying, but she'd survived it. Now, the general consensus among those who had been so quick to judge her negatively was that the show was a ground-breaking development in children's television broadcasting. Not everyone liked it, of course, but the media and the cognoscenti had to concede that it had value, and that the children certainly loved it. If anything, focus had shifted to discussion around *why* the children loved it so much and what techniques Anne and Andy had employed in order to engender such devotion. Positive responses from both parents and the children themselves reassured all of us – including the BBC – that we were on the right track and that the instincts of the show's creators had been proven correct. Now we had been accepted and our efforts validated, we could all go back to making *Teletubbies* in peace.

This isn't to say that the physical demands of the job had become any easier. Yes, the four of us had a better understanding of how much stamina was required and the whole unit were now working as a much more efficient team, but there were still challenges. We had a marvellous design department who created the most beautiful props, but who had a tendency to over-estimate a Teletubby's ability to hold things. Despite having spent thirty-odd years successfully holding objects, I now found myself surprisingly inept in this field. The main problem was that because the stomach of the costume was so big, it was really hard to get your paws to meet in front of you to carry anything.

Occupying top spot in my 'tricky to hold' charts were the Tubby custard bowls. Let me tell you about Tubby custard. In real life, it was the most disgusting concoction, made from a cheap catering pack of instant mash potato, watered down to the correct consistency and turned pink with food colouring. Failure to forensically clean out the custard machine after use led to an inhumanly gross stench the next time the back of it was opened. It was right up there with the Shit Wagon. Different, but equally gag-inducing.

There were all sorts of reasons why a script involving Tubby custard would lead to groans in the read-through. The custard machine was in a tricky position. There wasn't quite enough room for the four of us to manoeuvre ourselves around it comfortably. We all had to squish into shot, all bent out of joint, and for some reason we – I – could never remember how the thing actually worked. Quite often it didn't.

Green rocker for on.

Silver lever for the bowl coming out.

Pink knob for the tap coming down.

No, wait, yes . . .

Red button for making the custard come out.

It was important not to forget to put the tap back up and the silver lever in the first position – while juggling your heavy bowl of custard – or it'd be in the wrong place for the next Tubby. The custard machine was another piece of technology actually operated by Mark Dean, the Noo-Noo – squished into a small space. Thinking about it, almost all of the Teletubby appliances were operated by Mark Dean squished into a small space.

Our custard bowls were things of beauty and cleverly constructed to give the viewing child a sense of anticipation as they watched the custard get closer and closer to our mouths. In real life, the simulated sucking up of the custard was sufficiently suggestive to raise a giggle or two on set. It was actually achieved by an extended tube from the mouthpiece of the custard bowl being wedged through your puppet head, jamming against your face like some form of steampunk dentistry, before it reached the pump held in place behind you by . . . well you should be able to guess who.

Another downside to any Tubby custard sketch was that it meant having to wear a bib. I had an ongoing gag with Aunty Beth and Tessa M'Dresser that Laa-Laa hated her bib, exactly like a toddler might. I genuinely hated it too. It got in the way, was held in place by jabby pins, and was an extra impediment to reacquainting my body with fresh air as quickly as possible after a shot. Being totally in character and having a massive tantrum about it – 'Bloody bibbling bib! Blinking bibbing thing. I a big girl now. I don't even needed a bibbling bib!' – was an easy way to make the crew laugh.

This last was a lie. I did need a bibbling bib. The three worst things about handling Tubby custard were that it was surprisingly heavy, awkward to hold on to, and full of peril. After we had managed to serve ourselves a bowl of custard – what was the order of those controls again? – we had to stand politely waiting at the custard machine until everyone had served themselves a bowlful, and then we'd all go to the table together. Very civilised. Except for when you were holding a heavy bowl of spillable liquid straight out in front of you, with the weight of the costume pressing down on your shoulders and your pectoral muscles working like the clappers to squeeze the foam of your chest together sufficiently to allow your hands to make contact with the bowl – which was really quite slippery. When you added the bibbling bib to the mix . . . well. Bibbley Cheese! I found it very, very difficult. As soon as I heard the glorious word, 'Cut!' I'd yell, 'Bowl please!' hoping someone would be able to rush forward and take it from me before I dropped the lot. Sometimes I did drop the lot. Oh, the shame. The humiliation. It was like wetting yourself on set. Although I can assure you that I never did that. Even when managing to hold onto the mother-load, it was tricky to run excitedly to the table without sloshing a little custard over the side of the bowl, potentially making a time-consuming stain removal necessary. So yeah, the bib had to stay for practical as well as aesthetic reasons.

We were saved from repeated custard spillages by a genius in the art department who invented moulded pink polystyrene and latex inserts which perfectly resembled a bowlful of custard but weighed about a tenth as much as the genuine article. So once we'd filled our bowls – red button, green switch . . . no, wait – and got to our mark, the sloshy goo could be taken away and replaced with a light as air, unspillable facsimile. I didn't know who it was that invented the custard inserts, but my tendons and I were eternally grateful to them.

A Teletubby cannot live on Tubby custard alone. No, for a healthy diet there must also be Tubby toast. Tubby toast was good. It was comparatively easy to manipulate – you didn't need a bib and there was a nice simple machine with one knob. Also, a toast script would inevitably involve us sitting round the table. Sitting. Nice.

Rather than actual bread, a piece of Tubby toast was a large disc of expanded polystyrene, painted to look toasty with a smiley face on it.

Eating Tubby toast was a hoot. 'Nyum nyum, nyum nyum, nyum nyum.'

Until the instruction came: 'Freeze!'

We'd freeze, and someone – we knew not who, we couldn't see with our mouths full – would come and take the whole piece of toast out of our hands and replace it with a piece that had a section bitten out of it. Until we heard 'Action!' we had to remain motionless in order for the edit to work. Then we'd recommence 'nyuming' as if nothing had happened.

This process would be repeated several times over with the toast getting smaller and smaller until it was just a crumb you could actually shove into your puppet's mouth. Wipe chops. Smack lips. Ah! Tubby toast was great. We had plates that appeared out of nowhere and we rarely had to carry them. The toast came to us straight out of the machine, magically flying onto each Tubby's waiting plate. Yes, Tubby toast was superior to Tubby custard in every way.

For one sketch, the gag was that the toast machine delivered three slices instead of four. The script called for the Teletubby version of a very English tea-party: plenty of overly polite posturing in the mode of, 'No, no, do have mine . . .', 'No please, have mine . . .' and so on. What actually happened was Dipsy and Tinky Winky laying into each other in mock fisticuffs, finally rolling about on the floor together. It wasn't very often that a gag for the crew was worth any extra time in the suit, but I'm glad the boys decided that one was. It was featured on the end-of-term blooper reel every year.

Memorable toast sketch number two involved the toast machine breaking to the extent that it began relentlessly flinging its wares toward the table until we were knee-deep in smiley-faced discs. The four of us sat round the table while the entire crew lobbed toast at us for days. It started out with just the art department and camera assists doing the throwing, then the director decided he'd like more toast being flung. Word went out that anyone who was free and fancied hurling stuff at the Teletubbies should make their way to the dome. Uh-oh! I sensed possible pay-back for the 'being horrid' days. Time to find out who was bearing any kind of grudge. On the second day, while Aunty Beth was checking continuity to make sure that the piece of toast stuck in my aerial was replaced at precisely the right angle, I had one of those outside-yourself moments. It stayed with me through the next take, as I caught glimpses of the assembled throng delightedly throwing hundreds of smiley-faced discs at the four of us as we pretended to be having a wonderful time in the middle of this assault. I wondered how I had reached a point in life where this was my job. There are possibilities in the universe that are beyond our imaginings and this was definitely one of them.

Any action that happened around the table was challenging from the camera's point of view because there were limited options of where you could shoot from and get all four of us in frame. Obviously the director and the camera operators wanted to avoid monotony, so they were always trying to find new inventive options. Then, despite the action being indoors, the views through the window had to be lit and dressed with flowers, in order to look pretty and in keeping with the Teletubbyland vibe. This meant much waiting around which required us to be in situ. One of our favourite games to play while in that situ was imaginary moaning – by way of a change from the normal everyday moaning. All completely in character of course.

'Fucking council dome.'

'They still haven't fixed the bloody doors.'

'I've written to them over and over.'

'Dipsy was on the phone for over two hours – and nothing. Nada!'

'The paper's peeling down here, have you seen it?'

'That's from the rat piss.'

'Well why the fuck didn't Noo-Noo tidy it up?'

'He's been drinking again.'

'Oh God! Well we can't afford to send him back to the Priory.'

'Look, look, that puny human is trying to fix the doors.'

'Good luck with that.'

The majority of the puny humans would be getting on with the task in hand, so this game was chiefly for our own amusement. Except that as it was his job to listen, the sound guy got treated to our nonsense on a regular basis. Maybe that's where those special friendships with the sound guys had their roots.

We weren't the only ones on set to fall foul of a tricky prop, though. Logically, you'd have thought that when a balloon appears and Po chases it, catches it and then flies over Teletubbyland, the most difficult part would be how to make Po fly. But no, that was an easy half-day on a green screen studio floor. The big problem was the balloon arriving in Teletubbyland in the first place. An actual balloon would be too small, erratic in the wind and too prone to bursting so the art department fashioned a beautifully decorated, solid, Tubby-sized balloon.

Then the problem was that the balloon was too heavy to float unassisted or on a fishing line, so an expert in radio-controlled helicopter flight had to be employed to transport the balloon along its designated pathway. The art department were worried the balloon might even be a little too heavy for the helicopter – that it might not be able to achieve sufficient height. Mr Radio Control had no such concerns. He was very confident in his own abilities and that of his machines. Yes, he'd brought his two best helicopters with him – as he told us over and over again. You know when nerves bring out the worst in a person, so they compensate with excessive pride and forget that pride often precedes a fall? That was Mr Radio Control.

The art department expressed their concern and counselled him to proceed with caution. Mr Radio Control pooh-poohed them and said he'd be fine. When he set up a trial flight – just to get a feel for the air – he managed to fly his best helicopter straight into the Tubbytronic Superdome. We couldn't really fathom why he did this. I mean, there was a moderate breeze but nothing extreme. Perhaps it was those nerves again. Luckily he'd brought his two best helicopters with him. We watched as he got the second helicopter set up for its trial flight and again he managed to fly it straight into the dome. He did not have his three best helicopters with him. He was sent home and we filmed something simple like dancing around a tree. That was always the payoff. Andy could have a big production number if he balanced it with a couple of cheap and easy setups, and they would still be hilarious – often more so. In the end, the balloon went with Po to the green screen studio and it was all sorted out in post-production. That probably should have been the plan all along, but then we wouldn't have had such a brilliant laugh at that poor man's expense. Horrid Teletubbies!

The bigger the props got, the less the likelihood of us needing to hold them and the greater the probability of them needing to hold us. A massive prop was always a source of excitement. It was especially thrilling if the prop arrived before we'd seen the script, because we wouldn't know whose prop it was going to be. I'd watch a truly enormous see-saw being winched off the back of a truck and cross my fingers tightly: 'Please be me, please be me, please be me!' Mostly I'd be perfectly happy if a script didn't involve Laa-Laa as that would mean some time off to go for a swim, or sleep, or catch up on some real-life admin. When it was something that looked like fun, I always hoped it would be Laa-Laa who got to play with the big toy. No wonder I got the job – I essentially have the character of a toddler.

As it turned out, we all had a go on the see-saw, but I was on it for longest. As I rode up and down I was taken back to the child me who thrilled at a fairground ride, not wanting it to ever end, laughing my head off at the extraordinary and unique sensation that many man-hours of engineering prowess had made possible. It was mechanically operated – Mark Dean squished into a small space, of course – so we didn't have to do anything except sit there, act and enjoy the ride. Enjoy it? It was barely acting. Although, for John it was. I don't know how he was sitting or why he couldn't get himself comfy, but the whole experience was bollock-crushing agony for him, poor soul.

I thought the see-saw was the zenith of outsized playground props, but then the swing arrived. This was a two-hander for me and Pui. As ever, we started by blocking through the script without costumes, to establish positions for ourselves and the cameras. The outline of the script was: I find the swing, I teach myself how to use it, I am very pleased with myself, Po rocks up, she has a go, falls off, lots of times, we laugh, I show her how, she has another go, swings beautifully and the swing disappears.

There was a lot buried within this simple scenario: learning to share and how tricky that can be, the joy and confidence gained from attaining mastery of a skill, generous acknowledgement of seeing that skill in another, the playing out of the dynamic between older and younger siblings or friends, and in Pui's case the joyous hamming up of a fall or three. What a hoot to film.

More importantly, as a human it was possible to lie lengthways on the seat and swing gently from side to side. This was incredibly comfy and relaxing and I immediately wanted to take the swing home with me and install it in my back garden. Once Pui and I had finished being funny with the swing, I asked if I could have it. I could not. This happened to me quite a lot over the years – some props were so magnificent that I was desperate to take them home. I offered money and everything, but it was never allowed. Not even the giant orange lower-case 'e' that Laa-Laa's ball turned into in one episode, 'De letter 'e'? De letter 'e'? Das not-y shape a ball should be!'

No dice. I bet someone in the art department half-inched it.

I'd have paid very decent money for Laa-Laa's guitar – there can't be too many people in the world who own a toy guitar almost as big as themselves. Although, it didn't get off to a very promising start. I was initially given a beautifully made, super-sized replica acoustic instrument. But due to its thickness, I was completely unable to get my arms around it. I couldn't even hold it in place, let alone attempt to play it. When they gave it to me to hold, I dropped it. When they gave it to me again, I dropped it. I swear they thought I was doing it on purpose, but I really wasn't.

Give.

Drop.

Give.

Drop.

This happened way too many times before they skulked off in a cloud of barely contained frustration. Ultimately, the cloud cleared, the sun of persistence shone and they made a thinner version that I could just about hold in place. With the assistance of a secret fastening that clipped the instrument to my harness, I could indulge myself and rock out like a big kid. I know it's ridiculous, but I'd have been properly peeved if that prop had gone to someone else. I gave into my inner Hendrix and really let rip. Later on at Christmas time, I made it into *Guitar* magazine's list of 'Guitar Solos of the Year'. They even mocked up an imaginary Laa-Laa album, titled 'Bibbley Cheese!' God bless 'em.

The most-impossible-to-hold prop award goes to John. For the first Christmas shows we filmed, the script called for Dipsy to run over the hills with a cracker under his arm looking for Laa-Laa to pull it with. When the cracker arrived on the back of a truck, we marvelled at the craftsmanship. It was made of plywood, with exquisite micro-joinery forming the curved shape. It took five men to lift it off the back of the truck. John was not impressed. I had to feel for the design team, as they'd obviously got totally carried away with making a beautiful thing and forgotten that a lone human, already encumbered with several kilograms of fur and padding, had to run over hills with it under one arm. Aunty Beth knocked up a Plastazote version in a couple of hours. Plastazote is a chemically inert closed cell polyethylene foam blown with nitrogen, produced as a by-product of oil – but you probably knew that. My time on *Teletubbies* taught me to believe that almost anything is possible with some Plastazote and a Kimble gun.

Christmas episodes came with their own unique challenges and making programmes for the festive season in the middle of summer took the surreal-o-meter up a few notches. We filmed the first batch of Christmas sketches in our second year on site. There wasn't a cloud in the sky on the day Laa-Laa and Po were to film a sketch in which they played in the snow. This was good as it meant the animated snow cloud would show up really clearly. The two of us danced around on top of a hillock while Mark Dean – surprisingly unsquished – squirted us with foam from a junior water cannon contraption. How he managed to get it in my eye – yes, my actual human eye – I'll never know. It was very slippery and unsurprisingly I was the first to go over, taking Pui with me so that both of us were rolling around in foam, still being squirted by a small man and laughing our heads off, no longer acting. We were perhaps a little hysterical with the absurdity of it all.

The overall effect of this particular fake snow was a little underwhelming, so in the third year the production team really went to town. They hired a professional fake snow company with one of the best names ever: Snow Business. Whenever you see snow in a film, if it's not actual snow then the chances are Snow Business will have supplied it. They've really cornered the fake snow market. I don't know why I find that so funny. They covered the entirety of Teletubbyland with a white membrane, then trucks arrived and squirted fake snow over the whole landscape, from a proper grown-up water cannon contraption. And there it was: snow in summer, Christmas in August.

Everyone was required to wear masks to filter out any little fibres that might be floating around in the air, which felt like a great leveller to the four Tubbies. What we hadn't foreseen was that the snow upped the ambient temperature by quite a few degrees as the gleaming white surface bounced the sun's heat back up at everyone. It also bounced the sun's light around, so shades and squinting were the order of the day. The winter wonderland was to remain in situ while we filmed a week's worth of Yuletide episodes. Heaven only knows what the local wildlife thought of it all. Our wonderful chef Carlos cooked a full-on Christmas lunch on the last day with crackers on the tables and everything. I think we may even have sung carols!

We'd grown so used to the dazzling white landscape that it looked odd when Christmas was done with and we returned to our usual swathe of green. It was like trying to walk after you've spent too long in roller skates. The snow hadn't left us forever though, oh no. Hard though we tried, it had been impossible to prevent a certain amount of snowy ingress into the dome. Now, even after cleaning, piles of fake snow had collected in corners. Every time a panel was removed to lay cables or change bulbs, a heap of fake snow would be lying in wait. Fake snow would live with us until the end of filming. Even after that, when they dismantled the dome for good, I'm willing to bet that there were still some piles of fake snow lurking in nooks and crannies.

Fake snow was not the only precipitation to engulf Teletubbyland in 1998. Earlier in the year we had to deal with a more serious deluge. Easter was looming and everyone was looking forward to the long weekend. It was the Thursday before Good Friday and it was raining. Pui was shooting a scene in the dome and the rest of us were taking it easy in our cabin. Suddenly Pui wasn't shooting a scene in the dome. Instead she was bursting into the cabin, excitedly filling us in on the unfolding drama. The dome was flooding! Crumbs, had there really been that much rain? Evidently, yes. As the dome sat in the centre of a dip, water was running down the slopes of the surrounding amphitheatre from all directions. The body of it was only made out of plywood and Astroturf so it wasn't able to remain waterproof in the face of such a torrent, in addition to which water was seeping from beneath into the channels where all the cables were laid. Before long, the power to the dome was off and men were running around trying to rescue electrical things. It was quite possible that we would have to wrap early, which would mean we'd get to go home early! It was late morning and the puppet-masters in the bunker were going to make a decision at lunchtime. The production team were reluctant to lose another afternoon, what with two bank holidays coming up, but they were also keen not to electrocute or drown anyone – a frazzled Teletubby would not be a good look.

Costumes and props were run through the downpour to safety, hatches were battened down and bags were surreptitiously packed in hope. By lunchtime it was fairly obvious that rain had most definitely stopped play – or started it, depending on perspective. We stayed to fill our bellies with the lunch Carlos had lovingly prepared, before the first wave of people made their way off site in the minibus to the car park. Then the minibus returned with people still in it. The news was that access to the farm from the actual road was blocked. What was usually a common or garden cattle grid was now a raging torrent, several feet wide, carrying tree branches and other debris at not inconsiderable speed. A river, a brand new fast-flowing river, was preventing our early escape. Attempts to find ways through or round the water had all failed. Were we doomed to spend Easter trapped in Tubbyland with next to no alcohol or food?

Our teeth ungritted when word reached us that Rex the farmer was willing to ferry the four Teletubbies through the water on his tractor. We could then be met by a car to take us to the station where we hoped to get trains home for the weekend. Hoorah for being the Talent and having lovely people go out of their way to take care of us. We'd have to move sharpish because although trains were still running, that situation could change at any minute.

The crossing of the newly arrived river was alarming. Whole trees were being carried past on the floodwater where only six hours earlier we had gaily driven over dry land. The plan succeeded and the four of us drove in a Mercedes towards Stratford. It had stopped raining, but floodwater blocked the roads in many directions, and our route had become circuitous to say the least. Before long we found ourselves confronting the inevitable. We were in a narrow country road facing a large body of water. There were stationary cars on either side of the flood, who had obviously decided that it was too deep for them to ford. Our driver, however, was not to be thwarted.

'I reckon we can get through there. Whaddayathink?'

'No.'

'No. I don't think we can.'

'No.'

'I don't think so.'

'No.'

'No.'

The kingdom of the car was not a democracy.

'Let's give it a go!'

'NO!' All four of us yelled, making our opinion very clear.

Our opinion was ignored and our chauffeur drove slowly and carefully into the water until it started to pour in under the doors and the engine decided enough was enough. The driver, seemingly undeterred, lifted his handset to call for a replacement car and promptly dropped his phone into the water now filling the footwell. We had to laugh – it was beyond farce – and nobody's phone had a signal anyway. We also had to berate him for completely ignoring our request not to strand us in the middle of a massive puddle. Some lovely people in a little yellow jeep came to our rescue and, having clambered free of car and water, we were damply snuggled on sacks of coal in the back of the vehicle and driven to Stratford. We left the driver to think about the decisions he'd made.

Once within signal range, we used our new-fangled mobile phones to glean information on which hostelry was the designated meeting place for out-of-town refugees wanting to be placed with the locals who worked on the shoot. Also, everyone really needed a drink.

The mood in the 'M' bar was like the party at the end of the world: high spirits verging on hysteria. Well, we might as well make the most of it. Word started to come in that most of the surrounding villages were now cut off by floodwater so even the people who lived nearby could no longer get home. We started to consider the possibility of refusing to leave the pub until morning. Luckily, Simon's rented accommodation for that season was a spacious apartment in an old stately home – Clopton House, very sufficiently envy-inducing – on a hill to the north side of town. On a hill. These were very important words. He invited everyone back to his place for a party and sleepover, if indeed we could reach the house. This we managed to do, on foot, and Simon's generosity ensured an overnight safe haven for every waif and stray.

The morning was like a different world. Sun danced in and out from behind fluffy little clouds and apart from the gallant broom-wielders sweeping water out of the hallway, you wouldn't have known anything untoward had happened. This effect was magnified in the shared car – this time with a different driver – back to Teletubbyland. We clattered over the cattle grid back up the farm track to the car park. My mind watched the ghost of the previous day's deluge and it seemed beyond belief. Where did it all go? We were all reunited with our unharmed vehicles, which thankfully had rested overnight on high ground, and tootled back to our loved ones, who were living different lives, in a city. Lives without random displays of power from Mother Nature. It was very much like emerging from a dream. I mean even more than usual.

The dreamlike quality of Teletubbyland that we'd all become so used to was due in no small part to the constant parade of extraordinary props that Andy conceived of, which the art department designed and brought forth into reality. At the top of their game, they were able to make the objects themselves exude a kind of playful joy. The power of this skill was to make even the most seasoned and cynical television professionals working on the show become more childlike and playful in their attitude, akin to the mood we were trying to create for the viewing child. This in turn created a kind of unit solidarity, a sense of community and a shared bond throughout the whole unit that I believe contributed to the warmth of the programme that emanated through the screen. I have no idea how they managed that. When people think of the programme – whether they worked on it or just watched it – it's not just the characters they remember. It's also the dome and the colour and all the props that made it so iconic.

CHAPTER 8
again-again!

Towards the end of the third year's filming, there were strong rumours about our contracts being extended. Nothing was certain but my paws were crossed that we'd be returning in 1999. If I'd been forced to have a punt I might have betted against it, because although the BBC was understandably keen to keep that particular goose laying golden eggs, I didn't think Anne was especially eager to continue. But even if she was ready to move on and do something else, the temptation to squeeze every last drop of success out of the show may have been too great. It was hard to call and we left Teletubbyland that autumn not knowing whether we would be back the following spring.

I had trouble accepting that this could be the end. It couldn't be the end for me, surely? I knew I wasn't finished. I wasn't finished with children's television. I wasn't finished with *Teletubbies*. I certainly wasn't finished with Anne Wood. There was so much more I wanted to learn from her, and on good days I felt that I had something to offer her in return. Despite having had three years to do it, I feared I had failed to make myself indispensable to Ragdoll. Anne had hinted at the possibility of my being able to carve out a future role at the company – nothing firm, but it was enough to give me hope. One of her special techniques was to say something very important in a throwaway fashion, which had the effect of leaving a person a little dumbstruck. It was in this way, in the doorway of the canteen, that she told me she thought I had a real flair for children's television. I'd not received much praise in my professional life and this stopped me in my tracks, as if I was a five-year-old being told I'd done a good drawing. However, there was a proviso: she thought I'd do really well if only I could get rid of my anger.

My anger? I had anger? But I was fluffy! I was 'sweet in a surreal way' – the *Sunday Times* had said so. When I stopped and thought about it for a moment, I realised she was right. I had come to her as a dancer at the end of my career, having fought tooth and nail in every arena of my life. A kind of anger had fed that energy, had fuelled that drive and had protected me and kept me safe in the streets of New Cross. Of course a great deal of anger comes from fear, and I was terrified of virtually everything. I couldn't let anyone know that, so it came out as an edgy, defensive aggression sometimes. Maybe I thought I was hiding it – hey, I was an actor wasn't I? – but obviously I'd not managed to hide it from Anne. If I was going to carve out a future with her, I needed to soften those edges.

It wasn't only my love for and admiration of Anne and Andy that made me want to continue working with Ragdoll. I had become genuinely fascinated by what makes little human minds tick, what makes meaning for very young children and how that impacts on us as we grow. I'd learned something about what worked, and I wanted to expand that knowledge. I realised that the more I learned about children, the more I was learning about what it means to be human. Ragdoll were generous. They shared their knowledge and the techniques they used. They wanted us to understand and they didn't keep secrets.

For example, there were no focus groups in the traditional sense – Anne said she couldn't see the point of testing a thing once you'd already made it – but, throughout its development, Ragdoll would continually put their product in front of the target audience. The company had an ongoing relationship with several nurseries, schools and childminders, and periodically a member of staff – usually Annette Cunningham, who was in charge of this department – would pop round with tapes to show the children. Annette set up a small video camera on top of the television, facing the audience. As the children watched the film, the camera recorded a full and frank account of how they reacted to the material they were shown. Watching this film back – synced up with the video they'd been played – we could observe when they laughed, what grabbed their attention, if and when they joined in, and when they got bored and wandered off – all uninfluenced by any adult guidance or interjection. Most of them didn't even notice the camera was there. These days, now everyone is used to filming everything on their phones all the time, the process would be even easier.

In the early days in particular, these tapes were regularly shared with us. They served as motivation and gave us tremendous reassurance that what we were doing formed a connection with our young audience. With careful scrutiny, we could learn when the connection was strongest and feed that knowledge into our performances. We would have learned much less and much slower if Anne hadn't had the wisdom to educate us in the most direct way possible.

Now that the continuation of my education in this field was uncertain, I realised that I had to make provision for a potential future away from Teletubbyland.

I decided to curtail my usual off-season gallivanting around the Southern Hemisphere and put some effort into building my career. First job: get an agent. Pui and Simon had both had agents from the beginning, and they shared this handy resource when it came to negotiating deals that affected all four of us. John and I were used to working without a net, as agents weren't commonplace in comedy or dance at the time. I was on the books of a few low-grade model agencies and those that handled extras, background dancers and the like, but I'd never tried to find proper representation before. Now seemed like the time. I was on the telly, I was part of a globally successful show, I'd been on the cover of the *Radio Times*, surely someone would be interested. My role had been, um, niche, but at least I'd proved I could show up on time, learn my lines and hit my mark – even when blind! Surely all that counted for something.

All that counted for precisely nothing. I wrote a tonne of letters and got a tonne of rejections. Then one day, among the rejection letters, I received a postcard from my friend Fiona who had started a new life in New York. She loved it and thought I would too. She asked whether I would like to come and visit, since I finally had the dream combo of a little downtime and some disposable income? *Teletubbies* was even more successful in the States than it was in the UK. Maybe I could kill two birds with one stone and start trying to sell myself across the pond.

So it was that I embarked on my first visit to The Big Apple. I was incredibly nervous about the whole thing. I calmed my nerves with a little too much wine on the flight over so was already smiling when I got the full Manhattan skyline experience, tipsily sharing the cab from JFK with my airplane neighbour. Once in the bosom of the metropolis, I alighted at the east side of Grand Central Station and called my friend from the wrong-way-round phone box. Fiona only worked round the corner, but she was going to be in a meeting for the next half-hour and asked if I could amuse myself for a while. I sure could – I was in one of most amusing places on earth after all.

I love all stations, and what I'd seen of Grand Central in films and so forth had led me to believe it was one of the most romantic buildings on earth. I wheeled my case down the slope to the main concourse and sat on it, to look at the architecture, gaze at the wrong-way-round ceiling and watch the people coming and going. It immediately became my favourite building in the world.

My dad had visited New York in the seventies, in the bad days, and he'd been scared. He'd hated it. I thought about this as I sat there on my cheap luggage – I was still reluctant to fork out for expensive bags! I realised that I wasn't remotely scared of the city. I was nervous about what I had to achieve while I was there, but what I felt from New York itself was an overwhelming sensation of warmth, welcome and possibility. As soon as this feeling had made itself felt, it was borne out by a passing compliment, 'Hey! Your sneakers rule!'

You wouldn't get that in Waterloo station.

I spent a week in The Big Apple, and yes, I loved it. In seven days I managed to acquire somewhere to live, a yoga teacher, a lover, a lawyer to sort my legals and, most importantly, an agent who thought I could be the next Tracey Ullman. I don't think I stopped trembling with nerves for the entire week, not until my farewell drinks party anyhow. I flew home exhausted and overstimulated, but also pretty pleased with myself.

I didn't have to wait long before the news came through from Anne about the future of *Teletubbies*. She had agreed to film more episodes and offered me a contract for a further three years. She was happy to give me some time to think about it but not much. This news wasn't exactly a surprise, but it was a relief.

I think the surprise had been how well my New York trip had gone, and now I had a decision to make. Should I set the ball rolling with my permit to work in the USA, sign with the agent and gamble my future on the American Dream, or should I take a rock-solid offer for three years of well-paid work, after which I may be able to extend my career with Ragdoll and if not, one would hope, America would still be there? Surely a no-brainer, right?

Sometimes I wonder if my choice was a little cowardly. In truth I was opting for the security of the known rather than the major risk of the alternative. I sent thank you letters and little Laa-Laa dolls to everyone who had been kind to me in the States, letting them know my situation and that I'd contact them again in the future. I never did.

I hoped I'd made the right decision, but none of us really know how an alternative life choice might have worked out, do we? At any rate, all four of us came to the same conclusion, even before we knew the terms. We were signing up to film enough episodes of *Teletubbies* to bring our total to 365. The BBC had wanted more, but Anne figured that one for each day of the year should be enough for our demographic.

We would also make fifty-two *Teletubbies Everywhere* segments. These were ten-minute sequences, very graphic and more themed than narrative-based, to be shot in a studio at Pinewood during the final year. Dreamt up by Andy in collaboration with the BBC, these segments were graphic representations of more overtly educational notions. The characters would appear on plain coloured backgrounds and illustrate certain numbers, shapes, colours or concepts. Very simple, very clean, very clear. I wasn't party to the whys and wherefores of how *Teletubbies Everywhere* came to be, but it's my suspicion that the series was created in response to those who couldn't see the subtle educational values of the main show. This isn't to say that *Teletubbies Everywhere* didn't maintain the brand's playful atmosphere – with Andy in charge that was always going to be the case. For the cast, it was motivating to be given a different challenge after all those years.

Our second contract was sewn up tight, taking into account emerging new media and online platforms, as well as those as yet unimagined. Heaven forbid we should be paid royalties for a new hologram version, or a Teletubbies feed directly into the brain, or whatever else *they* might come up with next. On the plus side, our wages had gone up, we had all settled into our roles and the overall atmosphere was now that of a successful proven product rather than an out-there crazy-bonkers risk. We liked working with one another – not just the Tubbies but the whole team, many of whom had been onboard since the beginning. We had far more people eager to return year on year than those who left to find pastures new.

In preparation for this book, when I asked colleagues what they remembered about the time they spent working on *Teletubbies*, they all – yes, all – said that their over-arching memory was of a happy time. On several occasions I heard, 'It's over twenty years ago, and it's still the most fun I've ever had at work.'

Before we could return to our beloved pastures old, we had to endure the big studio photo shoot. Every season started this way and every season we hated it. It did, however, highlight what a tight-knit team we had become. By now the wardrobe department, the dressers, the art department and the first AD all knew how to wrangle the Tubbies. They knew what we could and couldn't do, what we could and couldn't hold and what we could and couldn't tolerate. Outsiders weren't in the know and tended to be rather a thorn in the communal side. You know how some photographers can be. You've been to a wedding.

We were never sure exactly who or what the photographs were for. Obviously some were for marketing, press and publicity, and others were for merchandising – to go on the packaging of various toys and so forth – but this was our fourth year. How many images of Dipsy in his hat did they need? Apparently, thousands and thousands and thousands . . .

The timing was bad from our point of view. The four of us would come back from our break with normal-sized necks, flabbier tummies and weaker shoulders. We'd not worked ourselves up to full Tubby strength yet – hell, we hadn't even got our eyes in. It always took me from three days to a week to get my Tubby eye in, to remind my brain how to process the minimal visual input to allow something approaching sight. There was always that nagging little worry that maybe this year my body would have forgotten how to do it, that over winter I'd somehow have totally lost my ability to Tub. I think this is why the bosses scheduled the big photo shoot for the beginning of the season – they assumed that because it didn't involve running over hills, they were easing us in gently. Unfortunately, this assumption was erroneous. There was nothing more taxing for the innard of a Teletubby than holding a stationary position for any length of time. When you were moving, you could shift the pressure and quite literally share the load around your body. In stillness, you had no options and once you were in that stance – that had the weight of the head balanced awkwardly through the side of your neck – you just had to grin and bear it until it was over. Also, standing still offered few opportunities to be funny. You couldn't really make people laugh holding a position for the label on a tin of spaghetti – although it was cool that Teletubby spaghetti shapes existed. Being funny was the thing that took the pain away – if you could make the crew laugh, it made you forget about the discomfort. The positive to focus on, was that we had two days of this painful tedium and then it was over for another year and we could get back to our natural environment: over the hills and far away.

By 1999, we'd had three years to get used to what being a Teletubby entailed, so even though it was rather a surreal form of employment, it had become a regular job for us and we'd developed a regular routine. Roughly speaking, we'd film for the duration of British Summer Time – as I've mentioned, clocks-forward to clocks-back – which was around eight months in total.

At the end of each filming block we'd have a BBQ on site, and at the end of the year a marvellous wrap party – safe in the knowledge that we had paid work to come back to. It is difficult to express how unusual and fortunate this state of affairs is when working in the entertainment industry, in my experience at any rate. I wasn't used to that level of security. It wasn't just the financial security that was important to me. It ran much deeper than that. I had a job that I completely understood, that I knew how to do and how to do well. My bosses were happy with my performance and the product we all made together was a major success. I'd never had this before. I'd always been the one driving, charging forth into the unknown with an obscure arty project experienced by a limited audience. On a personal level, there was also the absolute treat of knowing I was returning to a place of work peopled with colleagues I liked, some I'd call friends, who were also content in their work and therefore easy to collaborate with, year on year.

Naturally some new people were brought on board each season, but for those last three years the majority of personnel remained the same. Having tried out several potential directors, the producers had finally settled on Vic Finch and Paul Gawith – Vic and Mr G – who directed two-week blocks on rotation. Each spent a fortnight with us in the field before having to hide away in a dark editing suite while the other one had fun in Teletubbyland. Similarly, we had a team of trusted first ADs whose names I still see rolling past in prime-time credits. Some of our dressers had time to go to university and then come back to work with us through the summer. The camera, lighting, tech and sound crews were regulars, as were the art and production departments. In short, we were that enviable family that you hear referred to by film and TV folk, but I think we had an unusually large percentage of people returning year after year. Some members of the team would see each other outside of our filming seasons, but for the majority of us, we'd do the job, have the wrap party and that would be it until the next year. I'd go home and feel strangely bereft without my big, bouncy film family around me.

At home in our fields, we ran like a dog pack and drew a deep kind of emotional security from knowing we'd be with one another, day after day. There was always someone else's expertise to draw on if you had a problem, someone to cheer you up, someone you could help out in turn. Working that closely, that hard and for that long somehow meant you shared more with each other, became more intimate with each other than you maybe would in any other workplace. Bonds were formed that are still pretty strong over two decades later.

For us four Teletubbies, each year we returned was a year of getting to know one another even better. Over time, we watched each other grow up a little more, became aware of our development as performers, as people, as friends. Life took on a steady and predictable rhythm, which I personally found very soothing. The winters were spent out in the real world, coping with all that can throw at a person, and the summers back with the gang in a steady day-to-day job. This pattern was a welcome anchor in my life. I was anchored in the work, in the place and in the people. As the years rolled by, each spring felt like coming home. My heart warmed to see the friendly faces again and to be with the familiar personalities that already knew all the running gags.

The homely feeling of *Teletubbies* reached beyond the set too. Each year when we returned and started popping into local shops and pubs, we'd be greeted like the erstwhile regulars we were: 'Oh, you're all back filming again then are you? Nice to have you back.'

The relationship with the local community was important – at least to me. Although I felt some benefits to existing in a bubble, it was good to remind myself of the outside world occasionally. Working hard in a remote field for eleven hours a day can be isolating, and this was before the era when Wi-Fi was everywhere and everyone had a laptop to keep them connected to the rest of the world. Hell, there were still people in our unit existing without mobile phones. All manner of major world events could pass by with just the merest acknowledgement from someone who happened to be looking at a telly at the time.

But what a bubble we worked in! As evident from the wide shots in the programme, Teletubbyland was sited in a particularly gorgeous location. It couldn't fail to put joy in your heart when you were working outside in a beautiful swathe of the English countryside, in the fresh air, surrounded by nature. Of course, this also meant we were surrounded by actual weather. Luckily, we had to hand something of an expert in the vagaries of the English climate. Our Lighting Director, Chris Watts, also known as 'The Prophet', was often seen atop a hillock, protective lens to eye, gazing at the sky and predicting whether we had enough time to film a given sequence before a cloud covered or uncovered the sun. It was acceptable to film in either bright sun or cloud cover, but if the conditions changed halfway through a take, there would be a marked change in the lighting state, which would jar with the viewers' gaze. Just because they were young didn't mean they didn't deserve correct technical practice.

If it was a consistently dull and wet day, we'd opt to shoot an interior script, but we'd often fall foul of the capricious British climate. We'd start to film a sequence out of doors, then rain would hit, we'd decamp into the dome and the sun would come out again. The crew became very fleet of foot. It was perfectly usual to see large men running up and down hills with even larger lamps and heavy cables, trying to avoid that undesirable rain/electricity interface, while Tubbies and dressers would break out the golfing umbrellas and huddle together under them, waiting for the shower to pass. The memory of the Big Flood stayed with us, but the actuality was never to be repeated.

It wasn't always the weather that held us up. One year there seemed to be an inordinate number of bees buzzing around the Tubby Bye-Bye hillocks, and like all insects, they were especially attracted to the Citrus Posse. It was typical of the television mindset that the primary concern wasn't the welfare of the bees, although no-one wished them harm, or the cast and crew getting stung, although no-one wished them harm either. No, the primary concern was that little black blobs kept flying into shot and ruining the take. I loved that singularity of purpose. At the time, we had a kitchen assistant who was a keen apiarist, one of the country's top bee experts in fact, and an opera singer to boot – she was very talented. Taking time off from the vegetable preparation, she confirmed that the bees had indeed made a nest in one of the hillocks. A blast or two of 'The Queen of the Night' aria was insufficient to repel the swarm so she and her hastily assembled bee removal squad were called in to humanely dispose of them and find them a new, more suitable home – out of the range of even the longest, widest lenses.

Whether due to unwanted critters, inclement weather, or unforeseen snags, the time we spent waiting around for conditions to improve was filled with a panoply of ridiculous games. Pui Fan Lee was the absolute queen of the on-set diversion. She had worked in TV since she was a child, so she'd had plenty of time to build a repertoire of how to pass the time in the dead minutes that inevitably occur when filming. On top of which, she had a personality that lent itself perfectly to the role of games-master – persuasive enough to get everyone on board, and sufficiently charming and playful to make you want to join in. I was hugely admiring of Pui. She applied her positive energy and undeniable strength of purpose to all she did, whether in a professional capacity, or in the name of a bit of fun. With Simon as her foil – all winning smile and flirtatious goading – anyone who didn't play along just ended up looking churlish.

Sometimes the game was a simple showbizzy question asked of each person, 'Who's the biggest diva you've ever worked with?' or it might be something more personal: 'What was your favourite subject at school, and why?' My favourites were the prank calls. We'd huddle round one mobile phone and someone would ring random numbers with a local area code until we found a genuine one. Once we'd got a ringtone, everyone would fall silent and wait for the pick-up. As soon as we heard 'Hello' we'd all start to sing 'Happy Birthday' to a previously agreed common name and wait for the reaction. Inevitably the person on the other end would laugh and apologise for being the wrong number. We'd laugh and apologise back and hang up while they were still giggling. The ultimate aim was to overhear someone telling the story in a pub or café – ' . . . and I felt so bad telling them they'd got the wrong number . . .' – or to accidentally ring someone with the agreed name, whose birthday it actually was. Neither of these things ever happened, but the concept of well-meaning prank calls truly delighted me. Surely it couldn't fail to cheer somebody up, hearing twenty-odd people singing 'Happy Birthday' with total conviction to the wrong person. How very Teletubby.

My favourite game of Pui's was Bum Darts. Do you know it? If you don't, you should. A disposable plastic cup is placed on the ground approximately ten metres away from the contestant, who must transport a two-pence piece, clasped between his or her bum cheeks, over the distance and into the cup, with no use of hands – or any other additional part of the anatomy. The person with the most bullseyes wins. Simon was the undisputed champion. It must have been all that ballet. In addition to his highbrow history, Simon was the showbizziest of the four of us. Being married into the McCartney clan, a backing dancer for Sir Cliff of Richard for many years and one of Duran Duran's Wild Boys, whenever the on-set game involved tales from the trenches, he'd always win hands down: 'I had simulated sex with Joanna Lumley and it was wonderful!', for example.

It was a fortunate twist of fate that it was Simon who had to deal with the ridiculous media speculation around the actual sexuality of the purple Teletubby. Apparently, the fact that Tinky Winky carried a handbag and had a triangular aerial meant that he was gay. I mean, I ask you! This nonsense had been stirred in the US, primarily by Jerry Falwell (an American televangelist of the time). Whenever Simon had to deal with the homosexual puppet issue, in interviews and the like, he did so with aplomb, pointing out that anyone who genuinely thought there was any sexual agenda to these decidedly non-carnal creatures needed to have a bit of a word with themselves. We didn't even know who Jerry Falwell was, which might have been even more of an affront. That's how Simon became the life force of a gay icon. Despite the controversy, I think deep down he was rather chuffed about it!

An important factor in keeping up the pace of production year after year was making sure we could keep going physically. With just four Tubbies and no understudies, we needed to keep ourselves in tiptop condition. I chose to take regular saunas and swims. John was different. John was running his comedy empire while also filming the show, as well as doing stand-up gigs at the weekends. I don't know how he did it. Oh no, wait, I do. John had three modes: being Dipsy, being on the phone arranging gigs and being asleep. I'm not much of a napper, but John could nod off between takes one and two. He needed a stern dresser to keep him with us:

'JOHN!'

Once, he fell asleep in his Dipsy, in his bed, lying on a hand-held electrical fan. Thankfully, some keen-nosed attendant smelled the smouldering before a nightmare flaming Teletubby accident occurred. Conversely, John could do things in his suit that the rest of us couldn't even attempt. He'd be given a Dipsy solo and I'd marvel at what he *chose* to put himself through. Squats? When he wanted to, he could really dance up a storm – as if the suit weighed nothing at all. He also played volleyball at lunchtimes, which was more than I did.

We had a wide variety of extra-curricular activities: football, volleyball, quizzing, pool, tennis and so on. Aside from giving everyone a much-needed opportunity to let off some steam, these activities meant that the *whole* unit mixed together during downtime. Because members of the art department had a kick-about with the director and the Talent, the line producer and the cameraman, they all got to know one another outside their work roles and this meant the lines of communication within the realm of work became very free, open and relaxed. Which of course made the running of the show more efficient – and pleasant.

If I've made Teletubbyland sound like some kind of idyll, that's because it was. Every moment when you weren't actually doing the work was a total delight, but the work itself was tough. It was long and hard for everyone and we needed to release the tension. There was a serious side to our merrymaking too – we were supposed to be making a television show that was bursting with fun and love and friendship and out-and-out joie de vivre, which was easier to do if everyone involved was happy in their work. It's a credit to Anne, Andy and the entire production team that their attitude towards us all created such a positive atmosphere.

With Andy, we knew full well that we were working with someone special. Andy was quite demure as a character, but what came out of his brain could be raucously silly and delightfully daft. As time rolled on and we were exposed to more of his genius, what struck me most was how fearless he was. He had a tremendous amount of freedom in his imagination and there seemed to be no self-policing in terms of 'we can't do that, it'll be too expensive', 'that'll take too long' or 'there's no way that will translate from the page'. If Andy could think of it, then he was sure we'd all find a way to make it so. When I started my own writing for children, I found out that this expansive way of thinking is not as easy as Andy made it seem. It became something to aspire to, to try to emulate.

Nowadays people talk glibly about thinking outside the box, but Andy could think so far out that he almost went all the way round and back into it. And of course, Anne enabled him. He would never have had that freedom without her positive attitude and willingness to take risks, creatively and financially. Anne displayed some extraordinary super-human bravery. Can you imagine knowing that hundreds of people are working on a project that you have instigated, out of your imagination, all of them relying on you for their weekly wage, all of those livelihoods dependent on whether your wild idea for a kids' TV show is a success? The woman had balls of steel. Together Anne and Andy were a curious team. Visually they were rather Jack Spratt and his wife, but in the realm of the imagination, they were a match made in heaven. Once we were a bona fide success, Anne could relax and Andy could really let rip. We all could, really. We were doing something right because the children loved it, and as long as we kept doing it to schedule, all was good.

This isn't to say that working in Teletubbyland had suddenly become an easy-peasy breeze. It was still tough and the four of us had to make sure we preserved our strength, developed our stamina and just kept on keeping on. I did my best to conserve my energy, but I really felt the fatigue. I remember one time towards the end of the fifth season, I was in the dome, head off between takes of a Laa-Laa solo script which involved lots of dancing around the custard machine – yes, in the bibbling bib. I had reached the stage where energy conservation had reached ludicrous levels. Whenever I heard 'Cut!' I fell to the floor and lay where I'd fallen, my puppet head in my long-suffering dresser's lap as I gazed into the middle distance and breathed. Anne came into the dome from the viewing gallery where she'd been watching proceedings. She started to talk through what the script was about and the reaction they wanted from the child watching and how that should inform my performance and so on. She was trying to be helpful, I know she was, but I didn't even have the energy to listen to her. My facial expression didn't change, I rolled my eyes up to her face and with minimal mouth movement or effort, said, 'I know how to do it, Anne.' Anne bit her lip to stifle a giggle, and went scurrying back to the security of the director's lair. I apologised later and we laugh about it still.

All the way through, I kept that one viewing child in mind. On the days when I'd reach the turning to Teletubbyland and just want to keep driving, the days when doing as little as possible between setups was more important than playing a game, the days when fatigue ate my sense of humour and nothing was funny, on those days, I'd think of the small child in front of the television, eagerly waiting to see her favourite Teletubby friend. I'd know that child deserved nothing but the best I could muster. It may sound cheesy, but it's true.

Working in children's TV is not everyone's cup of squash. It's not the same as working in other branches of film and television. It's not taken as seriously by the industry in general, and usually the budgets are not as extensive. I can't deny that any kind of television has a glamour around it – even if you're a giant puppet in a field in the Midlands – but children's TV is a long way from the sex, drugs and rock 'n' roll ambience of some other parts of the industry. A keen observer may have been able to spot the occasional Friday morning hangover on someone who spent a little too long drinking beer and playing pool on a Thursday night, but overall we were a very well-behaved bunch. When the newspapers jumped to the conclusion that something so extraordinary and surreal must have been conceived and produced on an infernal concoction of recreational drugs, they couldn't have been further from the truth. It was almost more shocking that we were such a clean-living, innocent assemblage of characters.

I'm also proud that in all the years we worked together, the four Teletubbies never had a falling out. I mean, we got on each other's nerves or rubbed each other up the wrong way from time to time, but with a bit of space and a deep breath, we could carry on without event. It's impossible for me to imagine anyone else having played my fellow Teletubbies. When I think about them now, I automatically smile. The love I feel for them all is true.

In the first year of filming, nervous producers would threaten us with the fact that because no-one could see our faces, we would be extremely easy to replace. I'm not so sure that they would have found it so simple to find anyone else quite as perfect for the job as Pui, John and Simon.

CHAPTER 9

Teletubby Fever

By the turn of the century, unless you'd been asleep for the past three years or living in some remote corner of the globe, untarnished by modern media, you knew what a Teletubby was. As we conquered territory after territory, we were revoiced by local talent in myriad tongues. *Teletubbies* was shown in over one hundred and twenty countries and translated into forty-five languages. Demo tapes were sent to Anne for approval and she'd bring us choice examples to listen to, for sport. Some of the ex-Soviet countries' initial attempts were hilariously depressing. Stern, deep-voiced, gruff-sounding men whose facial hair you could almost hear. It was sad that they had conformed so much to stereotype and needed to be reminded that the whole show was about fun, so they should sound playful. It bears up what I said earlier about the importance of a joyful atmosphere among cast and crew seeping into the product. It's much harder to sound happy if you have little joy in your life. English speaking countries kept the same Teletubby voices but recorded home-grown narrators to reflect the local accent.

Sadly we only met our own narrator, Tim Whitnall, a handful of times as our ADR sessions took place on different days. For us to have narration to react to, Tim would go into the studio the day before us to record his lines. We heard so much of each other's voices, but I'm sorry to say I'd struggle to pick the real

Tim out of a line-up of Tim-a-likes. I daresay he'd say the same about me.

It wasn't just quantity we were enjoying – the quality of the programme was finally being acknowledged too. Ragdoll's award cabinet was filling up. I was beside myself with excitement when we were nominated for our first BAFTA, imagining myself picking out my red-carpet outfit and wondering whether I should wear a wig or go skinhead and proud. However, it soon became apparent that the Tubbies were not invited to the ball. I don't know whether this was to protect our identities or if more important people than us bagsied all the tickets! I expressed my disappointment to Anne, who assured me that all award ceremonies were incredibly tedious, that I wouldn't enjoy it and that she herself would give it a miss if she were able. I offered to go in her place, but no dice. The Children's BAFTAs are a separate beast from the BAFTAs proper – a smaller, more modest affair with a fraction of the showbiz glitz and glamour. Still, I would have enjoyed being there to receive the award. And the second BAFTA. And the two Royal Television Society awards. And the Japan Prize. And the rest. Ragdoll bought a new cabinet.

My favourite award was given in 2014, when *Teletubbies* won the Prix Jeunesse – an international foundation that promotes excellence in children's television – for 'The Most Edgy Programme of the Last 50 Years'. Isn't that marvellous? I bet Anne felt a special flavour of pride in being lauded for her level of risk-taking. The phenomenon of *Teletubbies* received all sorts of awards for marketing and merchandising and Anne even won Veuve Clicquot's Businesswoman of the Year award – her bafflement was priceless. As far as she was concerned she wasn't any sort of a businesswoman, she'd just wanted to make great TV for kids.

References to *Teletubbies* abounded. Comedians did skits and gently poked fun, people dressed up as us in sitcoms and in real life and we featured in *The Simpsons* – twice! That's when you know you're part of the cultural landscape. There were even press articles featuring those who'd had us tattooed onto their flesh. Tattoos, people! We were surprised at how many famous folk tried to associate themselves with the programme. Harry Enfield had a tongue-in-cheek attempt at taking credit for the whole idea, claiming that we had based *Teletubbies* on some alien characters he'd included in his sketch show. Celebrities all over the world were photographed with Teletubby dolls, and I can't deny the competitive edge as we rushed to see which of us was being held to the starry bosom of Britney Spears – Po – or Ivan Lendl – Tinky Winky. Simon was most definitely the Tubby du jour among the rich and famous, something that gave him an opportunity to wheel out his most gracious of grins. We each had our turn as a celebrity's favourite Teletubby, but I had to wait a while for the one that really made me thrill. On Instagram in 2015, Taylor Swift posted a throwback photo of her as a schoolgirl dressed as Laa-Laa for Hallowe'en. When the wider press picked it up, *Huffpost* added the tagline 'Laa-Laa would be proud' – and I was.

Not all the attention we received was entirely desirable. While it was always wonderful to read fan mail, I sometimes found myself on the receiving end of something more sinister. Such as the time I discovered I had a stalker. Well, more accurately, Laa-Laa had a stalker. It started after the *Daily Sport* printed a badly mocked-up image of Laa-Laa, dressed in black bra and pants – I know, weird – with the tagline 'FAKE: Saucy shots of Laa-Laa shock fans.' Under the headline 'Teletubby Laa-Laa's Leg Over! EXCLUSIVE Internet sex slur fury over BBC stars', the article revealed the depravity of internet images such as this one. My lingeried image cosied up to an advert for Sex Advice from Tony and Wendy – 'Britain's youngest brightest sexologists' – and girls offering '121 Pure Chat'. I wasn't expecting that. Then I started getting fan mail from a grown man telling me what a saucy little Teletubby I was and what he would like to do to me – with Tubby custard. Ick. I let the bosses know, in case I came to a grisly – and sticky – end, but after a few months, the letters tailed off and it became apparent that I was no longer starring in the stalker's creepy fantasies. Perhaps he graduated to a Tweenie.

I soon started lying about what I did for a living whenever I met someone new. I wasn't being grandiose, it was just that once people found out I was a Teletubby, they'd want to ask me all about it and I'd find myself spending all my free time talking about work. No-one wants that. So I decided to say I was a gardener instead. I liked talking about plants. The other Tubbies also tended to be evasive when similarly put on the spot. Simon was at a showbiz soiree trying to avoid a certain *Blue Peter* presenter who was badgering him about how much he earned, when he was approached by a man he didn't know. The stranger's opening line was:

'I hear you play Tinky Winky.'

'Oh here we go,' thought Simon, 'Now I'm going to have to have that conversation.'

He replied, politely, 'Yes, that's right, I do.' Simon was courtesy personified.

The man extended his hand. 'Pleased to meet you. I'm Madame Cholet.'

And there it was: a magical giant puppet bond instantly formed. You don't get a Teletubby/Womble interface very often.

Along with the weirdness, we also received heart-warming correspondence from children themselves. I think the mystery office people kept back most of the fan mail, but if they received something especially interesting or delightful then they'd send it over for us to see. One little girl sent us each a toy of hers, to say thank you for brightening her days. Mine was a small doll of Ariel from Disney's *The Little Mermaid*, one fictitious character usurped by another. It's normally impossible to persuade a child to part with any of their possessions, even when outgrown, so it was deeply touching that she had gifted us each a keepsake. I still have mine.

What took us all by surprise was how impactful the programme was for children with Autism Spectrum Condition. At first we received an occasional letter of thanks from a parent, describing how their child was soothed by the show and how many smiles it brought, how calming it was and how grateful they were. Then a pattern started to form. It hadn't been an intended outcome, but it became apparent that something about *Teletubbies* really worked for these children. The slow pace, the clarity, the colours, the gentleness, all these elements and more combined to make real meaning for autistic children. This development touched Anne and Sue deeply and as a result they went on to build an ongoing relationship between *Teletubbies* and major autistic charities. This unforeseen phenomenon had repercussions for me further down the line when I started working in education. I found myself teaching in schools catering for children with special educational needs, and on more than one occasion I saw children with Autism Spectrum Condition transfixed and smiling as they watched the Tubbies cavorting onscreen, then demanding to see the programme again-again, with me looking on, incognito and thrilled.

Once we were a sure-fire hit and the media lavished its attention upon us more positively, a visit to Teletubbyland became the hot ticket and we were blessed with the presence of the great and good from all over the globe. Mostly this was industry people, your Alan Yentobs and your Greg Dykes, alongside the heads of various television empires around the world. John took the visitors very much in his stride, maintaining his routine of having his eyes closed more often than open when between takes. Simon would be charming, as Simon always was, and Pui and I would grit our teeth and try to behave ourselves through the 'performing monkey' occasions. We didn't always succeed.

I quickly learned how to read the situation when being addressed by an important visiting human while in my Laa. Some people started off trying to be smart by talking to where they assumed your actual eyes were, but even they would be drawn in by the power of the puppet. Most people succumbed almost immediately. From inside the puppet mouth I could see their chin tilt upwards and then I knew I had them. I knew they had completely forgotten that there was a human inside. They had allowed themselves to buy into the fantasy without realising it. At this point, Laa-Laa had become real and they spoke only to her. As a result, I could say virtually anything and get away with it. I once asked Anna Hume, head of children's TV at the BBC, 'Did you buy that dress?' and she laughed, completely overlooking my rudeness. The power of the puppet had made her accept Laa-Laa as just being funny. Pui played this game too and to excellent effect, helped by her Po being just that little bit shorter, so she stood at a slightly more natural eye-line. She came running into the cabin one day after having been entertaining visitors in the dome. She threw herself face down onto the couch, pulling a cushion over her head.

'What is it? What's wrong?'

'You know when you're in the suit and you're a bit too cheeky to someone important, and it's fine, and then you get out and when you're just you again you're incredibly embarrassed about what you've said and you have to run away before they talk to you as you?'

'Yes.'

'That.'

Sometimes they deserved it.

Sod's Law meant it was always the trickiest, most tiring, most technical setup when visitors arrived on set. We'd suddenly become aware of a posse of extremely powerful and important television executives stationed on a hillside out of shot. The producers would have already talked them up, assuring them how special this experience would be and how few people had been thus privileged. So they were almost always happy and smiley and in a good mood. On arrival they might have witnessed a diverse selection of four people in their underwear walk into the Tubbytronic Superdome, and fifteen minutes later, see Tinky Winky, Dipsy, Laa-Laa and Po appear in front of them, larking about in real, gigantic life. Sometimes we were primed beforehand, and sometimes the request would come through our earpieces, seconds after 'Cut!' was called:

'Would you mind very much staying in costume after the take, in order for the visitors to meet The Tubbies? Please.'

'Yes, that's fine,' we'd always reply. What choice did we have?

Although, we did manage to create our own kind of entertainment during these 'Meet and Greet' events. Honestly, being encircled by four actual Teletubbies is quite an intimidating experience. People don't realise how massive we are, until they do. We'd occasionally surround and squish one of our own puny humans on set – a camera assistant or director or some such – just for a laugh. I always thought we'd make a terrific motorbike gang. You could punch us, stab us, shoot us, virtually nothing could get through, but then one head butt from Dipsy and you'd be floored. With Tinky Winky on top of you, you weren't getting up unaided. Cast Po as evil torture-meister and Laa as the wild one that has to be held back and it'd be curtains for you!

Sorry, I digress, but such things went through my mind in idle moments.

Back to our visitors. Having been flirted with and teased, gently maligned and generally charmed by four enormous furry space babies, some visitors would choose to leave it at that – to preserve the illusion – and clutter off to lunch. Others wanted the full shebang and would follow us into the dome to see what sorcery this was. As we perched next to our beds, our faithful dressers would remove our puppet heads and we'd recoil from the cloud of steam and stench released from within our personalised saunas. Our faces were flushed red, we were soaking wet with sweat and whatever hair we had was plastered to our heads. Despite all of this, and us panting and gasping for air, these denizens of international media, in charge of producing entertainment to mould the minds of future generations, would clamour around us, thrilled to be invited to share such intimacy, and ask *The Question*: 'Is it hot in those costumes?'

We'd nod politely, smile and confirm that yes, it was – just a bit. The internal voice was slightly different:

'Really? Really? Look at me! Look at all of us. The evidence is there, it's totally obvious isn't it? All that power you have, that enormous creative potential resting on your yay or nay, and the best you can come up with is, "Is it hot in those costumes?" You should be ashamed of yourself.'

Yes, I know it's ungracious, but as I've explained, the lack of oxygen to the skin did strange things to a person. A Teletubby shouldn't be snitty though, so we found a way to calm our peevishness. I loved my fellow Tubbies – and dressers – for their ability to take an irritant, shine a different light on it and change it into an entertainment. I have tried to learn that lesson, but it doesn't come easily to me. Our solution was to open a book. The wagers could be placed in one of two ways. If there was a group of visitors, we could bet on who would be the one to ask *The*

Question, or we could bet on how long it would take between the first Tubby head coming off and *The Question* being asked. There was no point betting on whether *The Question* would be asked – it always was.

The absolute zenith of the visitor experience to Teletubbyland came in the year 2000, which was our final full season filming on location. Let's call it the 'Big Event For The Americans' or the BEFTA. I'm not sure the four of us fully understood what it was all about, even at the time. What we did know was:

- A massive marquee was going up on the edge of Tubbyland – one of those with about a dozen pointy turrets, big enough to house a couple of circuses.
- Important looking people we had never seen before were strutting about with clipboards.
- The tension among our own bigwigs was increasing by the day.
- Loads – and I mean loads – of money was being spent.
- The local sheep were very concerned.

Surprisingly, we had been asked how much we would charge to appear in this extravaganza, which was to take place outside our usual schedule. This was unprecedented. The general run of things was that we got told what to do, we did it, and we got paid our decent weekly wage. End of story. We'd never had to negotiate a personal appearance fee before. Hoorah for the Americans!

To discuss our fee, we had a family meeting. Hitherto, it had mostly been my job to liaise with the bosses – John had appointed me 'Union Rep' following the food incident in the first year – but this was way above my pay grade. We needed proper representation. This was exactly the kind of situation when it was a jolly good job that Pui and Simon had actual agents and didn't mind John and I hanging on their coat-tails. Less happy campers might have looked after number one and sodded their fellow performers right off, but we were a tight-knit gang of four. This togetherness had increased over the years. We had each other's backs, always. And on this occasion, we knew, perhaps for the first time ever, that we held the aces. All four of them.

Simon's agent took the lead and negotiated our price for the event. Large, but not stupid. Fair. We weren't ingrates, but if we were going to be the stars then we thought we should each have a star-ish fee. This was our one opportunity to play those aces – we knew we were just giant puppets!

Preparations began to escalate in both speed and scale. A Ferris wheel was installed, extra catering wagons were brought on set, rumours were flying around about what lay in store for the BEFTA. Anne's neck turned red as it always did when she was stressed. Andy was having a ball. He was a man who enjoyed excess and grand gestures. Our contribution was to be the climax of the show. The crowd would be assembled on the high ground, looking down towards the dome. Various other entertainments would be presented and then for the grand finale, the four of us would be introduced. We'd come out, dance and wave for a while in a choreographed manner, then say our Tubby Bye-Byes and skip back into the dome. Twenty minutes tops. The rest of the evening we'd be free to enjoy ourselves, as long as we mingled with the crowd and made ourselves available for hand-shaking and general meet and greets. As we were all being paid an extra fee, I'd be happy to answer *The Question* as many times as they wanted.

The night of the BEFTA arrived and the four of us got some schmoozing under our belts while we were still just-out-of-the-shower presentable, and not just-out-of-the-Tubby sweaty messes. Riding on the Ferris wheel was marvellous – it was fascinating to see the lie of Teletubbyland and the surrounding countryside from this unfamiliar height. I had to have two or three goes. With candy floss, of course.

In the marquee, I was astonished to see ice sculptures of the four of us – literally the coolest thing to ever happen to me. There were light shows and lasers and then we had to go and get ready. Twinkly music played and an aerial acrobat floated over the dome, twirling around underneath a large helium balloon. Thank goodness it wasn't any windier. Then Bo Peep and her sheep made an entrance. In the programme, Bo Peep was a giant puppet character who occasionally herded animated puppet sheep through Teletubbyland, appearing much in the way of the Lion and Bear, only better. For the BEFTA, a silver-tongued producer borrowed some actual real sheep from a local farmer, along with an actual real shepherd. One man and his dog it was not. For a while there, it was sheep mayhem – are they supposed to be running over the top of the dome? Isn't that a bit dangerous? What if one of them falls?

After a few moments it was over, and thankfully no animals had been harmed in the making of this spectacle.

Then it was our turn. Hurry up, heads-on and off into the night. Like an idiot, I hadn't taken on board that this would be the first time we'd have to be Tubbies in darkness. How hilarious to have forgotten about this whole new visual challenge. Never mind – there was no time to worry about that. We made our entrance and the crowd went wild. All four of us played to them shamelessly – it was impossible to overact when being a Teletubby – and a good time was had by all.

It was the most extraordinary evening. As I never fully understood what the BEFTA was in aid of, I don't really know whether or not it was deemed a success. I must presume so because in the aftermath smiles were more abundant than frowns, and *Teletubbies* continued to be a rip-roaring success in the States for many years afterwards. All good.

It had taken such a lot of time and effort for all those people to organise this complex event, we'd become used to the massive marquee and the comings and goings, and then suddenly it was over. Like when the circus leaves town and all that remains is a patch of brown grass and a ghostly absence. The sheep were still there of course, but they would probably never be quite the same again.

CHAPTER 10

THE END OF DAYS

After four years of leading a double life, a curious thing had happened to this South East London girl. I started to miss the countryside whenever I was back in New Cross for any length of time. No wonder, you might think – it was New Cross, in the nineties. But I'd always loved it. Nearly twenty years of living with an SE postcode had made it my home. I loved its rough edges, I liked that outsiders were a bit wary, I enjoyed exchanging a chipper 'Good Morning' with local shopkeepers as well as with the drug dealers on the corner who were just variants of the retail trade. I felt the warmth of belonging and was secure in my surroundings. Then all at once it started to irritate me: the dirt, the stench and mostly, above all else, the noise.

I remember sitting by the old Seaman's Alms-houses in Greenwich, gazing at the Thames and verging on panic because I couldn't find anywhere quiet. I suppose it was partly my age – I was thirty-nine by this point – and partly because increasing numbers of my friends were leaving the area for pastures new. Hastings mostly. Times were changing and I was changing too. Deep down, I knew I'd grown accustomed to the pace and the peace of rural Warwickshire. I knew my blessed Teletubby adventure wouldn't last forever and though I desperately wanted to continue working with Anne after it ended, there were no guarantees.

In truth, there was a strong possibility that I would never be this financially secure again. If I was going to make a change and avoid growing old in this part of London, now would be the time to do it. I should say that New Cross is rather chichi these days, having been gentrified like most places in the capital.

So, I spent the first few months of the new millennium looking for a permanent abode in the vicinity of Teletubbyland. I am a Warwickshire girl by birth, though from a much less rural area. My parents were gracefully ageing nearby and my sister was starting a family of her own, also within striking distance. Being a lover of the coast and all things seaside, I never thought I would find myself returning to my landlocked beginnings, but once I'd made the decision it seemed to make sense. I began my search in earnest. I saw houses with damp, houses falling apart, houses falling down a slope, houses falling down and houses with too-new carpets – a sure sign of regular flooding. Then I saw a little round house, not much more than a glorified shed but totally charming and on the edge of a village a few miles from Tubbyland. It had been built in 1969 by a modernist architect for the headmistress of the village school on her retirement. I later learned from said architect that it was round because it had to be built snuggled into the hill – the rear windowsills are level with the ground. Working on the principle that the arch is the strongest structure, he'd built it that way to most effectively hold back the weight of soil under gravity. Also, he'd always wanted to build a round house.

On my first viewing of the property, as we sat drinking tea and watching pheasants meander across the garden, the owner – I liked to call him The Rev as he was indeed a man of the cloth – told me he'd been Bishop of Coventry and then Bishop of Birmingham, but that he'd had his first job as a vicar at St Margaret's Church in Olton, a suburb on the south side of England's second city.

'Oh!' I said, 'My grandparents lived in Olton.'

'Oh really, whereabouts?' The Rev asked.

'Meadow Grove.'

'What number?'

'Number three.'

Then he stopped to think before saying, 'Remind me now, I can't quite think of their names.'

'Tom and Jessie,' I replied, which was the truth and I liked saying it in that order so that they sounded like a cartoon. 'Tom and Jessie,' I repeated, partly to help his thought process and partly for fun. The pauses between each of us speaking were about to get longer.

The penny finally dropped, and he exclaimed, 'Morris?'

'Yes! That's right, Tom and Jessie Morris.'

'And Barbara?'

'Is my mother.'

He and my mother had grown up in the same street in a small Birmingham suburb and there I was, thinking about buying his house from him.

I'm a sucker for that kind of thing – big pointy fingers from the Fates saying, 'Do This. Dummy.' I tried to be rational and non-superstitious and all, but after a coincidence like that, I was always going to buy it. So I bought it. It still says 'The Very Reverend Canon Peter Berry' over my doorbell because, over twenty years later, I still haven't got around to removing it.

It had taken until the eleventh hour to find myself a proper home over the hills and far away, but better late than never, and it was worth waiting for a little round house that couldn't have been more suited to a Teletubby occupant.

I was all settled into my new home by 2001, which proved to be rather a hectic mishmash of a year. In addition to completing the last few full-length shows in Tubbyland, we also had to make those fifty-two *Teletubbies Everywhere* programmes at Pinewood.

The intention was to use techniques we're all familiar with these days, through the proliferation of green screen and CGI. However, we'd had trouble in the past using both blue and green screens as the former was troublesome for Mr Winky and the latter for Dipsy. Knowledgeable tech-heads were put together and a unique filming environment was created. A raised stage enabled us to be lit from below, as well as from soft light sources at the sides of the stage. Large diffuser lights – which looked like immense Chinese lanterns – did the job from above. All this resulted in an evenly lit white space that would do the job of a green/blue screen without presenting any keying problems for the troublesome Tubbies.

So we were to film Teletubbies indoors for the first time, on a proper sound stage to the rear of the studio complex. Our first day on set brought new routines and new challenges all round. The wardrobe department worked like dogs to get the costumes perfect, because there was nowhere to hide in this environment. The atmosphere among the crew was rather tense as this was not the normal way of doing things. Would it actually work? The four of us were quite excited, variety spicing up our puppet lives, and we had a finite area to work in for once. There would be no running to camera from three fields away, only to have 'Cut!' called because of rutting rabbits. And the surface was flat. No distance, no hills. This was going to be a breeze.

A breeze was what it most definitely wasn't. There was no air movement whatsoever to give us respite from the white heat of all those lights coming at us from every direction. The sweat came immediately and didn't stop coming, with no air to evaporate it even when we had a head break. What were those notes I'd written to myself only a couple of years ago – 'Enjoy every moment'? I was still determined that I would.

Working at Pinewood had always been a thrill, and now that delight would be daily. Romantic, faded glamour radiated from its creamy deco walls. In the new millennium however, it was undergoing changes. The way in moved from the old mock-tutor gatehouse to a new security-conscious entrance with a ginormous purpose-built car park. Increasingly, the dusty charm was being modernised to attract the next century's film-makers. My head understood this was the natural order of things, but my heart longed to hold onto all those reminders of past classics – I could almost smell them.

As is the way of the British weather, now that we were filming inside and no longer needed the elements on our side, the summer consisted of endless fine days. The crew would periodically open the massive roller doors of the studio to let in some light and fresh air, but it wasn't the same as being outside – especially if you were sealed in a giant furry suit. It's hard for me to put my finger on exactly what made the experience so different. Once inside the costume, you would have thought it wouldn't matter where we were, but there was an undeniable and intangible shift in the atmosphere of the whole unit. Perhaps we were just dome-sick, but the lightness of mood that permeated the shoot in Teletubbyland was harder to achieve in a sealed sound stage.

This is not to say we didn't manage to create our own special brand of fun between takes. One afternoon while waiting for a bulb to be replaced in one of the diffuser lamps, Pui instigated a game of Bum Darts outside the studio. While we were playing, a group of C-List celebrities rocked up, on a break from filming a commercial in the studio next door.

A dozen or so of us were sat in the gutter – some of us in our underwear, all of us looking at the stars – taking it in turns to competitively waddle over to a plastic cup. We must have looked a right old sight, but nevertheless they asked:

'What are you doing?'

I think they meant the question in a showbizzy way, as in,

'What are you filming? What's the project you're working on?' but we answered literally.

'Playing Bum Darts.'

Urchins!

Once we'd finished filming *Teletubbies Everywhere* we still had to return to Pinewood occasionally, to lay down the vocal tracks just as we did for the main programme. This was routine for us, but one sunny day in September 2001 was unlike any other we'd experienced.

The requirements for voicing *Teletubbies Everywhere* were quite different from the main show. If, for example, John was working on a sequence featuring the number four, starring Dipsy, a Dipsy would appear dancing in one corner of the screen and the narrator would say, 'One. One Dipsy.' Then a second would appear beside the first and the narrator would count again, 'Two. Two Dipsys.' and so on. Each dancing Dipsy was a separate shot and required its own vocal track. While the same sequence played four times over, John voiced each Dipsy in turn, with an 'Eh-Oh!', giggles, a repeat of his name, then more giggles, until all four soundtracks were playing simultaneously. Then each Dipsy disappeared one by one, counting down to the first, and a 'Bye-Bye!'. It was a long-winded process, but very funny.

After lunch, I was up first to voice ten Laa-Laas in exactly this way. Mark and Pui awaited their turn in the plush seats that lined the room. Our producer, Sue James, was overseeing the session. I was by the microphone waiting for the visual playback and for Sandy, the sound recordist, to give me my cue to begin. We had the traditional red-light system, so that people didn't interrupt a take. The light had obviously not been switched on yet because John suddenly came barrelling into the studio, more earnest and energised than I had ever seen him before, 'A radio! Sandy, have you got a radio?' His lack of composure stopped us all in our tracks.

'Yeah – there's one out the back there.'

John ran out and then ran back in with the radio, plugging it into a socket under the seats. He threw himself onto the floor, stomach down, facing the radio, as if it were the 1940s.

Sue and I looked at each other, baffled, until the words from the radio told us why our habitually cucumber-cool John was acting so out of character.

Two planes had been flown into The World Trade Centre. Reports were coming in of a third crash at The Pentagon. Suddenly, everyone was still and silent, trying to comprehend what was happening. We all had friends and loved ones in New York, John more than most. Sandy pulled the news up on the monitor and we watched aghast. Some time passed. It seemed we knew as much as we were going to find out for now, and these programmes weren't going to voice themselves. The others went outside with phones, to try and fail to reach those they were worried about, leaving Sue, Sandy and me to get on with the job in hand.

I voiced the first Laa-Laa, giggling playfully. As I worked through all ten it seemed at best bizarre and at worst heartless, to stand there laughing my head off while all those people perished. At the end of the day, I drove through the swanky new gates of Pinewood and found myself suddenly unable to continue the journey. I pulled over in front of a parade of shops, overwhelmed by the horror of the events of the day. The emotion I had stifled earlier in order to complete my professional responsibilities refused to be contained any longer and rose to the surface. I sat there sobbing.

I was glad to be able to return to my little round house in the countryside and hide away from man's inhumanity to man.

In addition to completing *Teletubbies Everywhere*, we needed to return to Tubbyland to finish some outstanding work on the main show. Shuttling between the little round house where I now lived and the big round house where I worked was such a treat. It warmed my heart to be back out in the open, but those last few weeks on location were bittersweet. While we had more work to do at Pinewood, these would be our last days in Teletubbyland, the last days for the whole unit in the particular beauty of our home away from home in the middle of the English countryside. We'd brought a surreal kind of magic to this corner of Warwickshire, but it had an inherent enchantment all its own. The blanket of dew-covered spider webs that lay over the hillocks twinkling in the early morning sun, the shooting star of a barn owl swooping across the perimeter at dusk, the secret opera sung by yellowhammers and sheep, the neuron-firing freshness of the air – there would be plenty to miss.

The BBC had pleaded with Anne and Andy to make even more episodes, but they were adamant in their refusal. It was time for us all to move on and put our energies into new projects. I recognised the truth of this and part of me felt the same way. I mean, there's only so many times a grown woman can get excited about custard. Nevertheless, I can't deny it was a wrench. While it was exciting to wonder what the next adventure would be, I couldn't ignore the sadness I felt to see the end moving inexorably towards us. No more dog-gang of idiots careening around the locale, no more production team to help out with any life admin that got in the way of me working, no more jolly chef giving me redcurrants for breakfast and allowing me to not have to think about feeding myself for the whole summer. No more John and Simon and Pui and all the other good friends I'd made over the years. No more being the Talent. No more being special. No more being Laa-Laa. Boohoo.

The end of *Teletubbies* wasn't as much like the last day of school as I thought it was going to be. More of a whimper than a bang.

We just carried on working until one day, we stopped. I don't know what I was expecting – fireworks, a parade, some kind of definite ending I suppose. The truth of the matter was that the obligations of the various departments finished at different times. Once the last footage had been filmed, camera, lights and sound were done, but the directors still had episodes to edit and we Tubbies still had vocal tracks to lay down – something we were still doing well into 2002. The wardrobe department had to clean, clear and store the costumes, and once the sweat of our toil had been removed as much as possible, they were taken to a theatrical store in Yorkshire. The location was chosen because it was close to Aunty Beth's home. Could she not bear to be too far away from the costumes, or did she know something we didn't?

From an emotional point of view, perhaps part of the reason for the lack of a clear-cut ending was that we had become so accustomed to the rhythm of our year being dictated by the *Teletubbies* filming season that any other pattern of life seemed incomprehensible. I took it for granted that I would see my fellow Tubbies again, there would be social occasions where various groups of friends from the show would get together and the likelihood of us being called on for extra photographs or something in the future was strong. I didn't feel a definite sense of an end, because I didn't imagine a definite ending had taken place. Plus, I lived round the corner now and I drove past the set every day. Its presence still loomed large, even during its destruction.

As I've said, the initial planning permission for Teletubbyland specified that the set had to be restored to Mother Nature after filming. It took weeks for the entirety of our fields to be cleared of all evidence of our occupation in order to make way for diggers to move in and finish destroying the fantasy. Teletubbyland is now a picturesque lake, I'm told. People ask me why it didn't stay as a visitor attraction but imagine the work it would have taken to make that happen. Health and safety would have no doubt been tricky too – that dome was an insurance lawyer's dream! No, it was better this way.

I've never been to see it. Andy and I were going to go together, but in the end we couldn't bring ourselves to do it. I think he eventually paid a visit, but for me the time had passed and I preferred to remember Teletubbyland in its pomp.

During those end days, it occurred to me that I may not have been sufficiently explicit about my desire to continue working for Anne. I was determined to find a place for myself at Ragdoll, so I made sure that I left no doubt about this. I arranged to have tea with her at the Shakespeare Hotel in the middle of Stratford. She was telling me about the garden she was creating at her new house and I said, 'Well, if nothing else comes up, maybe I can come and do your weeding?'

Her reply was, 'You'll always have a job with me, Nikky.'

She went on to reiterate her feeling that I had a natural flair and real talent for making work for children, and that we should stay in touch. She'd certainly be willing to employ me in some capacity should the opportunity arise. She noted that I seemed to have lost the aggressive edge I'd had when I first came to her. She asked why I thought that was. In a flash I was reminded of our argument over the catering all those years ago. From that moment on, I'd found it impossible not to be straight with Anne. On top of which, I'm not very good with praise. I find it disarming to be told I'm good at something – especially by someone I admire. So I told her the truth. Without overthinking it, I just let the honest words come out of my mouth: I thought it was because I didn't have to fight so hard any more. I wanted to cry. Speaking the truth about myself always makes me want to cry, especially when it comes as a bit of a surprise. I managed not to blub, but I know I welled up, and when I looked into Anne's eyes, I saw that I wasn't the only one.

That memory is very dear to me. In that moment, unspoken

but understood, was all my gratitude to Anne for making me feel worthwhile. She was the only person of authority in my life who had made me feel that what I had to offer was of value, that I was of value. I knew that she saw me, for good and bad, and I loved her for it. I wasn't going to give that up in a hurry. That's a hell of a way to create a devoted employee.

Anne was as good as her word, and before long I received a phone call from Sue James asking me to come to a meeting at Pinewood. Sue asked me if I'd like to have a go at directing some of the tummy films for *Teletubbies Everywhere*. This was it. This was the opportunity I had hoped for, a chance to carve a path into a future working for Ragdoll in as yet unknown ways. It didn't matter to me really *what* I was asked to do – it only mattered that I could continue learning from this extraordinary company. So yes, I accepted. I did want to have a go at that, please. I had no idea whether or not I'd be capable of doing it, but I couldn't think of a good reason not to try.

Although I'd worked as a director in the theatre, I'd never directed for screen before, and I certainly hadn't directed children, so the prospect was rather daunting. Nevertheless, I understood something of the ethos of the company and I'd seen enough tummy films to know the style and what worked for the show. I knew that the important thing was that the child or children being filmed felt comfortable and relaxed rather than forced to behave or act in a certain way. Again, it was about keeping in mind the needs of the child who would ultimately be watching. What the viewer wanted to see was happy, enthusiastic children engaged in some intriguing activity and in order to make that so, the process of filming had to be enjoyable for the children taking part. I saw this as my main function. If my camera operators had a clear understanding of what we needed to get in the can, I could concentrate on giving them joyous children to film while they focused on capturing the action. Thankfully, I would be working with an experienced and supportive camera crew who I knew well, because they had shot many episodes of *Teletubbies*. I also had support from Annette Cunningham, Anne's expert in the practicalities and logistics of working with children. Annette had television in her bones and I learned lessons from her that she didn't even know she was teaching.

Moving behind the camera was a major transition for me. For the last six years I'd been following someone else's instructions and my role had been to help someone else's vision become a reality in a very clearly defined way. Now I was the creator, the ultimate responsibility for every aspect of this project lay with me. I was used to this in the theatrical realm, but I had no experience of how that translated across to the world of television. At least I understood the need to be creative to a deadline. Even in the artsiest of art forms, more often than not, you can't afford to sit about waiting for the muse to arrive – there are still deadlines to meet and expectations to live up to. I was used to that discipline. Although I must confess I was struck by the immediacy of everything, procrastination was anathema. I watched how Annette worked and there was no mucking around – if she needed to source something, she just got on with it. I realised that I would be expected to work at the same pace, which was a very different experience from frolicking around to order in our Teletubbyland hillocks. While the physical demands of my new job might not be as great as in my old one, the mental pressure had definitely been turned up a notch.

I knew I needed to come up with clean, clear visual ideas that fitted with the overall look and intent of *Teletubbies Everywhere*. I'd been so focused on being Laa-Laa for the previous six years, I'd almost forgotten that I had a latent skill to draw upon. As a choreographer, I had been used to arranging bodies in space in a way that allowed the meaning to become clear to the audience, and it was this physical and spatial clarity I could aim for in the films. Then all I had to do was inspire the children to genuinely enjoy themselves, and make sure we captured that on camera. How hard could it be?

My first outing as a director was filming brave little children jumping up and down a flight of concrete church steps in Hastings. It wasn't the easiest shoot in the world. The weather was bitterly cold, and I was worried that the children wouldn't want to play outside in the biting wind. Somehow we managed to persuade them, and even managed to make it fun, but we had to be quick before the poor little tots ran for the comparative warmth of the church. In the edit I had limited footage to work with, but nevertheless I managed to assemble an acceptable sequence. I had passed my trial as a children's director.

In order to achieve the visual clarity I was after, I needed clean and uncluttered locations, but I also wanted those locations to inspire joy and excitement in the children. Consequently, I earmarked Brean Sands in Somerset for a couple of days shooting. Some of the children we were filming had never been to the seaside before and when one little girl saw the sea for the first time she shrieked, 'What's THAT?!' while hanging onto my legs for safety. Before long she was running around on the beach, squealing with delight. Sadly we didn't manage to capture that excellent moment on film. I quickly learned to switch the camera on as soon as possible and to not turn it off until I could no longer see a child anywhere. Sod's Law says that as soon as you stop filming, children will do something brilliant!

Directing small children was a curious balancing act and I needed a quick-witted and sensitive team to pull it off. As the grown-up in charge, I had to make sure the children knew they could trust me completely and that they were in safe hands. It would be impossible to capture natural responses if they didn't feel totally secure. On the other hand, in order to inspire activity that would intrigue or excite the viewer, I had to be a viable playmate. In fact, the whole crew had to exude an air of playfulness, while also concentrating on getting the required action in the can. Whether overtly or by stealth, I had to get those children to do exactly what I wanted them to.

As always, I had to keep in mind the young child who would be watching the finished result at home on television, to make sure what we shot was going to make sense and also transport them to the delightful experiences the children on the screen were having. Even the smallest children need the comforting soothe of escapism, beyond the cares of the day. It was my job to provide the means of that escape.

I delivered my collection of films, unsure whether they would make the grade, and waited anxiously to see if I had managed to make the leap into a new line of work. They were accepted – hoorah! I'd done it. With a supportive team who'd helped me obtain a positive outcome, I'd got my metaphorical foot in the door. There was no way I was letting that door close now.

CHAPTER 11

TELETUBBIES ON TOUR

It was undisputedly a good thing that I had proven myself capable of directing the *Teletubbies Everywhere* films, but not that useful in terms of continuing my career with Ragdoll. My films were the very last ones required to complete the commission, so there was no need for any more and I had made myself redundant once again. This stop/start – or rather start/stop – state of affairs was to become something of a pattern. I foolishly allowed myself to get excited when Anne offered me the role of a cartoon mad-scientist baddy in a new show called *Dogman*, but the show fell into difficulties in the development stages, and it turned out to be another false start.

Such things were not unusual in my line of work, but they were also indicative of Anne's personality and methods as a producer. Once she'd found a person or a project she believed in, she wasn't afraid to invest time and money in them to see where it led, but she was also brave enough to pull the plug on anything not coming up to scratch. She approached every pocket of potential with a positive 'let's try' attitude, knowing that success was never a given. The writer of *Dogman* benefitted from her support until he failed to deliver the scripts and was given short shrift. She then pinned her hopes on the wonderfully named Cao Hamburger, but eventually had to admit that she was throwing good money after bad, and nothing ever came of that project either. I was determined not to be these people – I was hanging in there until my niche found me and when it did, I was not going to let her down.

Around this time, she asked me what I considered to be my métier, my forte. Thinking back to my days running a dance company, I told her I thought I was good at gathering a group of performers together and moulding them into an ensemble. She said she'd consider that.

Summoned to the Ragdoll offices one afternoon, I arrived to find Robin Stevens busying himself with an arrangement of various white spheres in the car park.

I had met Robin at the very beginning of *Teletubbies* when he gave us all lessons in puppeteering. In my meeting with Anne, it transpired that Robin was working on a new show she was going to support – that would explain the spheres, I suppose. She thought she could do something with it, and she was keen to treat her boys equally: Andy had been allowed to create his baby, so now it was Robin's turn. Anne had an inkling that Robin and I would work well together, and she was keen to get me involved with the show. She asked me to have a meeting with Robin to see what I thought.

As the idea for the show developed, the big cheeses decided that movement and dance should be at its heart. The Boohbahs were to be non-verbal, dancing little atoms of energy, metaphorically made of movement, who travelled the world in a magical sphere. During the show we would see children from around the globe, narrative puzzles played out by archetypal story-world people and the Boohbahs dancing, dancing, always dancing. That sounded like my niche. Dancing? I could do that.

I knew that *Boohbah* would suffer from tricky-second-album syndrome, but that just made me more committed to it. Robin's responsibility was the overall structure of the show, along with the story-world segment, and I was to be in charge of the Boohbahs themselves. Yes – in charge! Good Lord. I wasn't used to anyone having this amount of faith in me – I was going to give this my all. Now *I* would be on the bigwigs' table at the audition, *I* would be running around with a clipboard looking important, *I* would be looking at tapes of children watching clips of content that *I* had created. Well, not just me, but I'd be there. I'd be right there. I had become Ragdoll's resident movement expert. I had found my niche all right.

At the beginning of 2002, I started working with Robin, and Anne's son Chris, to cast the show. Being the boot on the other foot taught me more about the process of applying for and getting a performer's job than all the auditions I had attended as a hopeful. Sifting through hundreds of CVs was time consuming, but the choices were mostly easy to make. Applications came through from individuals and agents alike, some with no attempt to answer the specific brief. Anyone who sent a standard pack, exactly the same as they would send for any job, went in the bin, but there were plenty of good people to choose from. Having decided we'd see our potential Boohbahs one at a time – rather than all at once as for *Teletubbies* – we whittled down the enormous heap to two days' worth of auditions. I had no idea how tiring it would be.

You'd imagine it would be quite pleasant – spending the day sitting in a chair, watching hopeful performers give of their best – but every auditionee deserves your absolute full focus. Those that come at the end of the day are entitled to as much of your attention as those at the start, so your concentration can't flag for a moment. It's a mark of respect.

When I'd attended auditions, I'd always thought it rude and cruel to be told 'Next!' the minute I walked in the door, but suddenly I understood. We didn't actually do this to anyone, but there were some people that we knew weren't right for us – as much as we weren't right for them – as soon as they arrived. This instinct was *always* proved correct once they launched into the piece they had prepared for us, and it became obvious we were wasting each other's time. I could see how, casting a film, or a big West End Show, you'd just cut to the chase. Next. Not anything personal, or a judgement of anyone's talent, just whether that particular person fitted that particular job. I'd remember that the next time I was auditioning for a part.

As it was, we found a cast of five amazing performers and I set to work moulding the promised ensemble. Aah Boohbah! The process of creating the show was an unbelievable treat: going out and holding movement workshops with four-year-olds; going to a studio and making up sixty dances based on their movements; teaching those dances to my cast of talented, daft, strong, hilarious, capable performers; and then observing children getting up off the couch and dancing along to what we had made. I was even allowed – no, encouraged – to get my Boohbahs flying. I doubt I will ever again be given such freedom and support to make a creative vision into an actuality. What a lucky girl. Better even than getting to play the mad-scientist baddy.

It was 2002 and I was right there. I was in all the meetings. I was in on everything. I was learning so much. I was having high-powered discussions about exactly which farty noise the Boohbahs should make. I was even inventing toys. I was a medium-sized cheese/wig. Finding myself in this position surprised no-one more than me, but I did come up against some deep-seated prejudices along the way. Once all the Boohbah dances had been filmed, I was reassigned to produce the story-world sequences on location in the Canary Islands, in order to free up Chris who'd been doing the job to date. When the first crisis happened, one of the actors flipped out because I was now producer. He was aghast, 'YOU?! You're just a girl! You're producing?!' Yes me, the scraggy dancer from New Cross, so behave.

As producer, it was my responsibility to make sure the videotapes made it home safely. Crumbs. I remember how our line producer on *Teletubbies* got nervous when she had to take our tapes across Stratford – imagine the anxiety levels when carrying a month's worth of footage across Europe. I was like a meerkat – a drug smuggling meerkat. Despite the airline double-booking my flight, the ensuing delays and the lack of a cab at the other end, the tapes were safely delivered to the editor. Despite my being female.

The creative team behind *Boohbah* was nominated for a BAFTA, and this time I got to go to the ceremony. I got to wear a nice frock, swan about, eat steak and watch celebrities drunkenly collect awards. I didn't get to win, but I do have the nomination certificate on my wall. *Boohbah* was indeed something of a second album in the UK, but was hugely successful globally, including in countries not known for embracing our cultural exports, like China and India.

When American broadcaster PBS bought *Boohbah*, the length of their programme slot was longer than the length of the shows we'd made for Europe, so we had to make a new segment to extend the running time. I invented 'Look What I Can Do!', which involved a child – or two – proudly showing off a movement they had mastered. The viewer would see the demonstration from the front, from behind, and from each side before it gradually got faster and faster. The idea was for the movement to be clear enough for the child at home to copy, fun enough to make them want to, and performed with such infectious joy that the viewers wouldn't be able to stop themselves getting up and joining in. After trialling it in the trusted Ragdoll manner, we knew it worked. We had footage of children all over the world leaping off their sofas and copying the images on the screen. The executives at PBS were sceptical.

'So the performing child starts by saying, "Look what I can do!"?'

'Yes.'

'And there's no other words, no instructions?'

'No.'

'So how will the child at home know they are supposed to join in?'

'They will see the child on screen having such a marvellous time that they'll *want* to join in. Allowing the viewing child to take that decision is much more powerful.'

'Hmmm. Can we not add an adult voice-over after the child speaks, which says something like, "And you can too!"'

Anne and I failed to respond because we were busy rolling our eyes – it was not a video call – so he reiterated.

'So the kid goes, "Look what I can do!" and then a grown-up says, "And you can too . . ."'

Anne had held her counsel until now but could contain herself no longer.

'No! In my experience as soon as you tell them they're supposed to do a thing, any self-respecting child will point-blank refuse to do it.'

The words of an ex-teacher.

So, we won the battle. Good – we were right.

I'm super proud of that programme for getting children up and dancing around in front of the telly, without an adult telling them that's what they're supposed to do.

'Look What I Can Do!' proved to be such a success in America that I was once more flown over the pond. This time I travelled alone to lead live events in Maryland, New York and Las Vegas where huge rooms of children danced along with me of their own volition. There is almost no greater joy than inspiring children to dance and seeing how much they enjoy it. PBS even ran a competition for children to win the opportunity to star in a segment that would be included in a televised show. The winners would be directed by me in their hometown, and they turned out to be a brother and sister in Peoria. 'Look What I Can Do!' brought me closer than I'd ever been to the audience. I could see them and talk to them and interact in ways that taught me even more about what floats a young child's boat. I also met up with the educational consultant who was advising on the teacher's pack that accompanied *Boohbah*. The whole experience opened my eyes to the possibilities televisual creative output could have beyond the screen.

In 2004, *Boohbah* came to an end. The process of its creation had made me truly feel part of the company – I even had a desk. Ragdoll had moved premises to a building with a studio space to enable them to make *Boohbah* and as one of the first into the building and with no-one to tell me I couldn't, I'd snaffled myself a little desk. It felt good. I felt I belonged. Now that *Boohbah* was over though, I was going to have to find a reason to continue working at my little desk. I was going to have to stake my claim.

I started flexing my creative muscles again, devising new programme ideas and bringing scratch pilots to the bosses, but nothing seemed to take. Having proved myself capable of the cat-herding task of directing children, I was brought in to direct on other people's projects, including an experiment to see if it was possible to make a Ragdoll show featuring only toddlers as performers. Spoiler alert: it wasn't.

Around this time, I became aware of a gnawing somewhere in the depths of my soul. There was something inside me that had now had its fill of coercing children to perform for the camera. It's not that I didn't like working with kids – I really did – but something nagged away at me that it wasn't quite right. Not for me, anyway. Ragdoll always treated the children and their families extremely well, and I always made sure they had a great time and that shooting was lots of fun. Still, the bottom line was that I needed them to do my bidding, and that had started to sit wrong with me. If anything, I'd become more interested in the children – in observing them, playing with them, learning from them – and less interested in making television with them. Which was, after all, my job.

I was hugely grateful for the years of employment and for the level of security I'd been given by Ragdoll. I'd never imagined I could feel so financially, creatively and personally secure, and in return I'd given the company years of loyal labour.

When Ragdoll gave me the news that they'd like my little desk back and would have to let me go as a permanent member of staff, I knew – we all knew – that something had run its course. I wasn't thrown out on the rubbish heap. I was still part of the creative team as a freelancer, still a member of the family – just more of an estranged aunt than a favoured child – and I was still brought in to fulfil certain specific roles.

After *Boohbah*, Ragdoll's next major project was *In the Night Garden*. Andy's creative energies had been replenished and he and Anne were throwing themselves into the next big thing with gusto. Anne had mentioned that a new show was in the offing and she thought I might suit the role of one of the lead characters, but then nothing happened. I was not offered the part. I can't deny that it stung at the time, but in retrospect, I think they were probably right not to cast me. As it was more skin work, perhaps they were worried that I wouldn't be able to differentiate my performance sufficiently from the one I had given as Laa-Laa.

So no, I was not to be Upsy Daisy. However, I was brought on board *In the Night Garden* to help train up the cast. This time I'd not been involved in the audition process, so I was intrigued to find out who they'd chosen and in particular who it was that had nicked my part. Rebecca Hyland that's who, with Nick Kellington playing the male lead. I could see exactly why they'd been chosen. Rebecca's generous smile and ready laugh betrayed her gleeful nature – she even had playful hair, falling in enviable bouncing curls. Nick's mischief was wrapped in a warmth and softness that belied considerable physical strength; he looked like he'd be really hard to push over. These two and the rest of the ensemble brought a purposeful, focused energy to rehearsals. They were as interested in the philosophy behind the show as they were in the practicalities: in the *whys* as much as the *hows*. This thorough attitude would stand Nick and Rebecca in excellent stead later on in life when they were up to play Dipsy and Laa-Laa in the reboot of *Teletubbies*.

I worked as movement director on *In the Night Garden* and supplied the choreography for the spectacular carousel set piece. More than anything else, this was a feat of mathematics for Dirk, the director, Andy and myself, because we needed to make complex calculations to ensure the enormous motion control camera rig would enable the characters to appear on screen simultaneously, being different sizes but dancing in unison. People wonder how the show justified its multi-million-pound budget, but that sequence alone must have cost a fortune. It was worth every penny – it looks wonderful. As ever, nothing but the best for the child who watches a Ragdoll show.

After *In the Night Garden*, I was busying myself with real-life children – educating and storytelling – when a surprise phone call put a special kind of smile on my face that hadn't been there for a while. A performer's kind of a smile. 2007 would mark the tenth anniversary of *Teletubbies'* first broadcast and the BBC wanted to put together a world tour of publicity events to commemorate this milestone. Spread throughout the year, the four Tubbies were to make personal appearances in three continents – live and on TV. It was the first time the characters would be seen outside of Teletubbyland and interacting with actual human beings. I was asked whether I'd be willing to take part. Well, what do you think?

On a weekday evening in London's Holland Park, the old gang were assembled for the official launch of the tour. Aunty Beth had driven a trunkful of Laa-Laa down from the stores in Yorkshire and I was thrilled to see them both. Over five years had passed since I'd last been in my Laa, and roughly seven since Beth had been the one to put me in her. Nevertheless, we slipped back into the routine as if it had been only last week.

The same words and noises were spoken when raising my arms to shift the costume up:

'Hup!'

'Say please.'

'Hup!'

Running gags made a welcome return: 'Tongue me baby!' The same ripe language that made Aunty Beth laugh. All in character, as ever. It was spookily easy for us to work together, even after all that time. Our physical memories took over and put us in the right positions for one another straight away. Our intricate surreal ballet, embedded in muscle and bone. The human body is a truly amazing thing.

For the four Tubbies, the intervening years since our last meeting became similarly meaningless. Of course we had plenty of news to catch up on and there was the excited speculation about our forthcoming travels, but in all the important ways the absence didn't matter one bit. As ourselves and in character, we felt that lovely sense of comfort you get from seeing an old friend after a long time and being able to just pick up where you left off.

After being suited up, we were once more in the dark – metaphorically and literally – and now in a contained space with lots of camera flashes. We were shoved into position, and all four of us posed like the professionals we were, with our specially made Teletubby passports – I wish I'd managed to pilfer mine. It was amusing to hear the press photographers call to us in the way that the paparazzi do to proper celebrities:

'Po! Po! This way, Po!'

'Over here Laa-Laa!'

Then we were moved through to another area where various celebrities, sundry VIPs, and their children – who really should have been in bed! – came to have their photographs taken with us. A long time passed without breathing external air, but with the old familiar sweat in eyes, sore shoulders, aching backs, confused blur, gasping – then we were herded out of sight and released from our damp prisons. Phew! What had just happened? I wasn't entirely sure, but it was going to happen again and in lots of different places. We were on our way.

The first stop on our grand tour would be New York, for a week of events centred around the date of our broadcast anniversary in the States, March 28th. The mayor would declare this official Teletubby day, before giving us the keys to the city. Wow! I mean, a ticker-tape parade would have been nice, but the keys to the city wasn't bad. It was one of the most brilliant and exhausting weeks of my life.

We stayed at the Park Lane Hotel on the south side of Central Park, and most mornings we were picked up before dawn for an early morning TV appearance. Each day I stood on the pavement – usually the first one up and ready – waiting for our minibus to arrive, singing 'The Apple Stretching' to myself and sharing 'Good mornings' with street sweepers, delivery guys and the fellows with the tourist carriages giving their horses a morning nosebag. It felt like a privilege to be included in that secret part of the day, before Gotham really got going.

For *Good Morning America*, our segment was filmed in the street, in a cordoned-off area, but we had to change into our suits inside the building. When push, quite literally, came to shove, we couldn't fit through the doors so they had to remove the entire revolving door apparatus in order to get us outside, while we sat in the lobby waiting, fully suited up, gently expiring. It was worth it. The reaction of the crowd was beyond enthusiastic, and it's true that a responsive audience lifts you as a performer and enables you to find hitherto untapped reservoirs of energy.

As well as the TV appearances, we stopped the traffic to have our photo taken crossing Times Square, we 'sang' our single at record shops and we launched a whole new range of merchandising. Unlike previously, these products were meant to appeal to older children and adults as well as the little ones. There were cool t-shirts and bags and specially commissioned trainers by the hippest street designers, all of which sported a funky new graphic representation of the Teletubbies – swinging sixties London with a hint of Tokyo style. Most popular of all were the headbands with our aerials sticking up from them. These became a symbol of the tour and the profits from their sale were donated to autism charities. As part of our fundraising for these charities, we also created four Teletubby Build-A-Bear Workshop bears which were then auctioned off. We did this live in the store, with the public in attendance. When a young autistic boy broke free of his parents to hug Tinky Winky, we all knew that behind the smiling puppet face Simon was moved to tears.

Early one crisply bright morning, we sailed to the Statue of Liberty on our very own boat for a photo shoot. There was no-one on it but us and we ran around the whole vessel like the gleeful toddlers we were supposed to represent. Even though there was no actual audience, playing Teletubbies on holiday – New York edition – was so much fun that we actually stayed in our suits even when the official shots had been taken. The steady breeze over the water certainly helped our stamina, as did the waving and cheering from any New Yorkers who spotted us from shore, some from their office blocks.

My greatest thrill was making an appearance at Grand Central

Station, which you may remember is my favourite building in the whole world, and John was similarly delighted by a photo shoot at the Apollo. We were a very happy Citrus Posse. For some of these appearances we could get changed in some forgotten corner of a building, but for others we had a low-loader truck which acted as our dressing room. All four of us could – at a squeeze – get suited up in the back of the truck, but only two of us could leave at a time. It was hilarious to watch one another being unloaded like an early morning meat delivery. Aunty Beth and another of our dressers – also named Beth – had come with us from the UK and we had a couple of American dressers who were also puppeteers themselves. As soon as they let us know they'd puppeteered Bert and Ernie in *Sesame Street*, we were putty in their hands!

A *Teletubbies* pop-up shop popped up on the Lower East Side and this – alongside the truck – became our base for the trip. It was where we held our first media interview as actual human beings. Hitherto we'd been in strict media purdah, but obviously Ragdoll thought the time was now right for us to show our faces. For those interested in such things, the four of us being revealed was a pretty big deal. For us, it felt most peculiar having a camera pointing at us whose lens we could clearly see. The whole experience made me feel rather vulnerable and exposed – naked even!

On the official Teletubby day however, we were back safely inside our furry armour. Crowds had gathered outside the front of the pop-up shop to witness Mayor Bloomberg give us the key to the city. I was a little disappointed that the key to the city wasn't an actual key but a framed certificate instead, but I was absolutely thrilled that the mayor chose to hand it to Laa-Laa – that old Tubby competitive streak hadn't completely vanished. It wasn't just an honour for the Teletubbies, but also for the charities we were supporting.

That evening there was an invitation-only Gala at the shop, where we made a personal appearance and proper celebrities lined up to have their photograph taken with us. The reaction was extraordinary. Some people had brought their children with them, but mostly it was grown-ups who really wanted a shot of themselves with the Teletubbies. Cool people too. I mean, Run DMC! There was no sense of irony in people's response to us, only genuine warmth, natural enthusiasm and delight. We did our duty until the wee small hours and after that, our final engagement, hit the sack for a deep, deep sleep.

In the airport on the way back, our little group – by now somewhat delirious with exhaustion – were spending the last of our dollars on a few beers and having a fairly raucous debrief, when suddenly Aunty Beth yelled out, 'Shut Up!' We did, for she is little but fierce. She was frozen in position with her eyes searching the air in front of her as if following a fly, 'I thought I heard our names . . .'

And then the announcement came again. It *was* our names. We bundled ourselves off to the information desk as requested.

'Oh there you are, I was about to give up. I've called several times.'

Thanks to Aunty Beth's superior hearing we were upgraded to business class. As someone who'd only ever flown economy class, I can tell you it's a whole other experience when you can lie down on a plane. It's most definitely the way to travel and after that week, we'd earned it. My feet didn't even swell up.

The next stop was Holland, where we were accommodated on the top floor of the Grand Hotel Krasnapolsky in central Amsterdam, the oldest and widely acknowledged as the classiest place in town. For our first photo shoot, we waved down to the square from the top floor balconies, with me channelling my inner Evita. Then we were sightseeing Tubbies again, on the prettiest bridges over the cleanest canals. We travelled to

Keukenhof for a photo shoot with cute children who were all snugly wrapped up and giving us beaming smiles despite the drab and drizzly weather. Together we planted the brand new 'Teletubby Tulip' in flowerbeds laid out in the shape of our four heads – with the correct aerial shapes and everything.

It had been decided that we would make a double appearance on the Netherlands' most popular chat show for our grand European unveiling. On the first evening we would be the fab four – the first time Teletubbies had appeared on a talk show – and on the second, we'd appear as our normal puny human selves. This was a bit of a coup. And a thrill. I'd never been on a chat show sofa before, and now I was going to do it twice.

We'd been warned that the host liked to shock and was likely to push the boundaries. It was a live show, so once we were on, we were on our own. In reality, he couldn't have been sweeter. I think he must have been a family man. There was something in his attitude that suggested he could have taken the mickey out of us, but he understood that as daft as our job might be, we brought joy to an awful lot of children. His desire to join in with our playfulness certainly seemed to outweigh any temptation to taunt.

This was how I interpreted the audience response too. On both nights they greeted us with tremendous whooping and whistling and a standing ovation. If only I could get that kind of response every time I got up on stage. What really stuck with me though was the waving. No-one tells you that when you make your entrance onto a chat show, and when you get you get up to leave, you should wave at the audience, yet you do. None of us had received any how-to-be-on-a-talk-show training, but the waving instinctively happened. I had a little out-of-body experience looking at myself.

'We're waving. I don't remember us deciding to do that?'

'I don't think we did, it just sort of happened, like someone else was operating that arm.'

I had always thought the Teletubbies would have made great chat show hosts, but that appearance was the closest we got.

Coinciding with our global celebration, the BBC launched its cable package in Asia, so we were booked to go to Singapore as representatives of the CBeebies channel.

This would be interesting. I wondered how we would be received, in contrast with the effusive Americans and the warmly playful Dutch. I didn't have to wait long to find out.

For a start we were incredibly well looked after and didn't stray far from the lap of luxury for the entire duration of the trip. My vast hotel room in Raffles Plaza overlooked what would have previously been the edge of Singapore island but was now a river running through the bustling city.

As it was the entire BBC Asia cable package that was to be launched, other proper celebrities were also in Singapore. Our first engagement was a spectacularly good dinner, up in the hills where most of the black and white colonial houses are. I embarrassed myself by accidentally referring to the Hairy Bikers as the Fat Bikers after getting them muddled up with that other pair of TV chefs from *Two Fat Ladies*. They took it on the chin and were good company throughout. When our paths crossed again in the future, it was rather fun to answer, 'How do you know each other?' with 'We worked together in Singapore'.

Ray Mears was also on the trip, but didn't attend that dinner. In fact, I only met him once during the whole week. I imagined him shunning our bourgeois practices and camping out in the nearest bit of green, keeping it real. James Martin was there with his drop-dead gorgeous girlfriend who turned heads every time she crossed the room. He himself was much more handsome in real life than I'd ever thought him on the telly, but a bit grumpy about getting his round in. When I got home and was lolling on the sofa watching TV the following weekend, the Hairy Bikers were guests on *Saturday Kitchen* – James's show – and the three of them were comparing notes about being upstaged by the Teletubbies at an event in Singapore. Ha! How funny. They were upstaged too. We couldn't help it really, it just happened – it's what you got when you let us out of Teletubbyland.

The launch night itself was really quite the occasion, peopled with the great and the good from all branches of the BBC and the Asian television industry. Our live appearance as Tubbies went down well, and then once we'd changed into our party frocks no-one knew who we were and we could enjoy happy anonymity. Except for Pui, who was working as a continuity announcer for CBeebies by then, so she appeared on stage once with us and again in her human guise, giving double value for money. I was glad the bigwigs were happy with the event, but it wasn't real – it was media people. I was looking forward to an audience of regular folk and of course, children.

Our photo shoot at Raffles Hotel gave us an opportunity to notice how the residents and staff reacted to us. While there was some pointing and laughing and taking of snapshots, there was a greater degree of calm than we had experienced hitherto. Staff politely helped keep people out of our way – for fear of us bashing into bodies we couldn't see more than anything – and a certain class of clientele was clearly too cool to show any discernible reaction. We were not cool. I think I was hotter and sweatier than I had ever been before.

Our final appearance was performing our song at a large – and thankfully air-conditioned – conference hall. The audience clapped and sang and danced along with us and were clearly having a wonderful time, but there wasn't the level of a-whoopin' and a-hollerin' that we'd previously experienced. Everything felt more reserved, which was rather lovely.

Our globetrotting extravaganza also included bookings closer to home. When told our schedule would take us to Suffolk, Cornwall and London, I was quite excited. The two out-of-town engagements were performing our single at agricultural shows, which seemed like an odd choice to me, but I've always been fond of a pig and it would be nice to have a home crowd. I don't know if it was the inclement weather, if the PR company had mis-judged our appeal to that particular audience, or if the Great British Public were just over us, but in comparison to our reception in other countries, we were given rather an insipid response.

In London we had a couple of days of photo opportunities around the city, the highlight of which was making an appearance on the London Eye, if only for the looks on the faces of passing tourists when they saw us playing up to the crowd from our little pod in the air. Tourists were interested, but the Londoners themselves were way too cool to pay attention to the giant fur-babies. I'd have been the same to be honest. No, the disappointment wasn't as much with the public as it was with the company in charge of this section of our tour. There had been so much potential. A home-grown success story that still generated massive interest around the world was surely worth more than a couple of promo shots? I suspect that the PR company thought we were rather below them – not trendy, not fashionable, not hip. I think this goes back to what I was saying earlier about how, in the UK at least, children's television doesn't have the same status as the grown-up version. Perhaps this is a reflection of how we think of children, in contrast to some other cultures.

Our final stop on the tour was Paris, with a trip every bit as chic and classy as you would hope. There were the usual photo shoots around iconic city landmarks, interviews and TV appearances, and then an appointment at a fashionable jewellers at the top of the Champs-Élysées where we were presented with silver Tubby-sized pendants of each of our characters and more chichi human-sized charm bracelets featuring all four of us. Here, more than anywhere, the people were not only kindness personified, but there was a knowingness about their attitude. Like they got the gag. Like they saw how the whole affair was both sublime *and* ridiculous. Like they knew the value, but also had a sense of perspective.

Then, almost as quickly as it had started, it was over. We had one last group shot with everyone involved in this part of the tour, most of whom had been on board for the whole shebang, and then it was back to the hotel to pack up and head home.

It had been so interesting to interact with our audience in person. How the adults treated us varied, but the response of the children was pretty consistent everywhere we went. They recognised us as their friends off the telly, and they behaved accordingly. Some expected us to have intimate knowledge of their family lives, having completely bought into the two-way connection through our tummy screens, 'You know how my baby brother doesn't like beans . . .'

It was truly heart-warming to feel how loved the Teletubbies were around the world. We knew the show was popular of course, but the personal connection that our tour allowed gave us a chance to experience it first-hand. It was a credit to the genius of Anne and Andy that even after so many years, interest in and love for the show was intense.

On an individual level it was a delightful little coda: one last chance to get inside the suit, one last chance to have all the fun of playing Laa-Laa. A beautiful, wonderful, hilarious treat of a P.S. The mood was different to filming the shows. Everyone involved was secure in what they were doing, in the strength of the characters, in the bond between us all. The pressure was off and the atmosphere was relaxed. Any problems or unforeseen issues were dealt with without panic – by this stage in proceedings we could cope with any challenge thrown up by the life of a Teletubby on tour.

At the time, I wasn't sure I truly believed that those days in

Paris would be the last time the four of us would be together – as humans or as Teletubbies. Rather than taking time to process that this was the end of the line, I think I was more concerned about whether my body would be capable of the work when they got us back together for the twentieth anniversary. I really expected that to happen. I never imagined we would lose ownership of those characters. I suppose in truth, they were never ours to lose.

CHAPTER 12

THE AFTERMATH

Being Laa-Laa was a peculiar job to move on from – a peculiar job even to describe. I mean, what *was* it exactly? It was sort of skin work, but not like Disney or Doctor Who. It was kind of acting, but not like in drama. It was puppeteering, but not really. It was comedy, but not in any recognisable way. It was physical, it was mental, it was trivial and it was profound. People had a reaction and formed a bond with something that was me but then I was unrecognisable to them. It was – and still is –bizarre. Once you're part of a project that enters people's lives like *Teletubbies* did – something that enters the culture so completely – it never goes away.

But move on I had to, so I followed my heart. I decided to stick with the children and began quietly building an alternative life for myself, studying and retraining to work as a creative educationalist. While still at Ragdoll, I'd been spending more and more time in schools and nurseries researching projects, and had wanted to get a qualification under my belt in order to do this in a more legitimate capacity. So I did exactly that.

Once out in the field, I started with EYFS – Early Years Foundation Stage – as this was the area where I was most comfortable. However during my decade on the educational frontline, I also worked in most other settings: primary, secondary, special needs and higher education.

With this career change, I was embarking on something completely new and that required of me a completely different set of skills to those I had been deploying over the last two decades. If it hadn't been for the time I'd spent at Ragdoll, it would never even have occurred to me that I would be capable of teaching. I had learned all that I could about communicating with children by being exposed to the expertise within the company. You may not think there are many useful transferable tools from being a Teletubby to being in the classroom, but the basics are much the same. You need the child to engage, to be interested in what is put before them; you must leave space for that engagement; you must help them feel confident in their own thought processes; you have to remember it's more about them than it is about you. Most importantly, you must be happy. Be happy so they can relax, feel secure and be happy themselves, because an unhappy child is not a learning child. I have Anne and Andy to thank for laying the foundations of my pedagogical beliefs and practices, and for inspiring me to write and perform my own stories for children. Everything I had learned about rhythm and repetition, about pace and tone, about creating for that one child, I fed into my teaching, my writing and my storytelling. I learned it all at Ragdoll.

Although my job wasn't wearing a big yellow suit any more, I'd still get a showbizzy *Teletubbies* booking from time to time. Pui always turned down requests for Po-related appearances and Simon seemed to be harder for researchers to find, but John and I were – and still are – enthusiastic contributors. It's always such a treat to be able to dip my toes back in the waters of being the Talent, but it doesn't feel straightforward. I feel I am occupying a strange hinterland: more than a member of the public, more than part of the audience or fanbase, but not quite a proper celebrity. I can't deny the frisson of excitement when television appearances allow me to rub shoulders with *actual* talent even though externally I endeavour to maintain my cool.

My cool was tested to the max when I was asked to take part in a quiz show hosted by Donny Osmond. Now, I was crazy about Donny Osmond when I was a kid in the seventies. I loved all the Osmonds. I liked how their hips looked in those white jumpsuits. But Donny was easily my favourite. Every night I kissed the classic purple-bonneted image of him above my bed, willing him to love me, believing that if I felt it deeply enough he would pick up on it and one day return my love. So obviously I said yes to the gig.

The name of the show eludes my memory, but the setup was this: a bank of about twenty people who all had something notable about them, and a screen to the side listing what those things were. The contestant's job was to match the 'thing' to the person. I was a person and I had a 'thing', hence my inclusion in the line-up. On the evening of filming we, the people with a 'thing', were assembled and made-up and walked to our places – I wished I'd worn shoes with lower heels. There was a Marilyn Monroe impersonator, which struck me as a bit patronising, guess-wise.

'One of these people is a Marilyn Monroe lookalike, can you guess which one?'

'Could it possibly be the one who's done up like Marilyn Monroe?'

The Milky Bar Kid was there – he was always there – as well as someone who could tear a phone book in half with his bare hands. I had to stand there for what seemed like, and probably was, hours – those shoes were a real mistake. Donny's brother Jay was in town and he showed up as a surprise guest who was almost as easy to guess as Ms Monroe.

After the shoot, I'd done everything I was obliged to do and was strolling down a corridor towards the exit, when I heard footsteps running behind me. A voice called out, 'Wait, wait, don't go, wait, stop, I love you! I love you!'

Yes, child me, it was Donny. Donny – bowled over to be in the same vicinity as adult me. Well. It was only a matter of time. This is what I actually thought to myself.

I waited. Donny and Jay caught up with me and hugged me and kissed me and told me how much they loved *Teletubbies*, and how Laa-Laa was their favourite. I never tire of hearing that. Jay even has a daughter who is named Lalla, after me. I was modest but they were gushing – their faces were not quite as I remembered and neither were their hips, but they were still Osmonds and I was on cloud nine. The whole time we were talking and hugging and grabbing at hands and kissing on cheeks, I was thinking of nine-year-old me and how the world had delivered unto her, her dream.

I played it cool, cooler than them, which was ridiculous, and when they were called back to the studio to film the next segment, I was gracious as they reluctantly let go of me. Later, when I was snuggling down under the covers, I touched the place on my cheek where he kissed me, and whispered into the night air, 'Yes, Donny Osmond, you love me now, you love me now.'

As I said before, the world has an odd way of making dreams come true.

Laa-Laa is always out there, always with me. Sometimes, she'll leap out at me unannounced, as she did when I was in the audience of a Flaming Lips gig.

It was a packed house at Birmingham Academy and everyone in the crowd seemed to be having a wonderful time. The whole spectacle was a masterclass in creating a convivial atmosphere at a performance. At one point the lead singer, Wayne, asked if there was anyone in the crowd whose birthday it was and a voice called out from above. It was a chap on the balcony whose name was Oliver, and Wayne conducted the crowd as we all sang 'Happy Birthday' to him. I didn't see anyone not joining in. There was a massive video screen behind the band, which had been showing eclectic and entertaining clips throughout the gig. When the band started to play a song called 'Do You Realise', Wayne turned to face the screen, arms aloft, as gigantic images of *Teletubbies* frolicked in front of the crowd. The crowd in which I was standing, looking at a man on a stage who was looking at a me on a screen, a screen that I was also looking at, looking at a giant yellow version of me, who was looking back at actual me. Wayne turned to look out at the crowd, at me looking at him while big me behind him was also looking out at him and at me. I was frozen in time, caught in a bizarre quantum cyclical thing. I pondered Heisenberg's uncertainty principle, the effect of the observer on the observed, what the individual protons were up to and how funny and strange the whole thing was. I was chuffed and smug and big and small and insubstantial and atoms. I don't think this kind of thing happens to many people.

In the wake of our global tour, the stringent rules about never seeing Teletubbies anywhere except in Tubbyland were no longer enforced so vigorously. I'm sure plenty of requests were turned down, but we did get to see each other from time to time for a TV appearance or interview or suchlike. Whenever we were reunited, we slipped into the easy camaraderie we had always shared, as if no time had passed at all. We understood things about one another that no-one else knew, we shared some pretty surreal memories and I was always thrilled when a new booking came through.

In 2009, the four of us were invited to join Peter Kay's Animated All Star Band for 'The Official BBC Children in Need Medley'. The track gathered together popular children's television characters of the day to perform a medley of marvellous tunes. Now, Simon had had a running gag for years revolving around The Jackson's song 'Can You Feel It'. Whenever he spotted our energy flagging and felt the need to give us a boost, he'd sing the hook, 'Bum Bum Bumbum, B'Bum Bum Bumbum', while dancing like a dad at a club and chanting, 'Keeping it up! Keeping it up!' Imagine what hilarity ensued when it turned out that this was the very tune we were to perform on the record. Even more of a treat was the fact that Simon's voice was recorded with us. All those years of being only half of Tinky Winky – in exactly the way Pui and I tried so hard to avoid – and finally, he was there, standing round the microphone with us, singing his heart out. This time, he'd be able to say that he too had scored a Number One single. I didn't know that it would be the last time I'd see him alive.

Regardless of shifts and changes, *Teletubbies* still pops up everywhere. There are questions on quiz shows, mentions in the press, jokey allusions and casual comments. Barely a week goes by without me hearing a reference to the show and it thrills me every time. Other people are thrilled too when they find out my 'thing', either from their own or their children's relationship with the show. It makes people look kindly upon me and makes me want to live up to their expectations. People are sometimes apologetic about their continued interest in the show, concerned that I might be weary of answering their questions. I'm not, apart from *The Question*, and I'm even pretty chilled about that these days. I have swathes of friends who call me Laa-Laa, and not necessarily because they worked on the show – hey, even my niece and nephews call me Aunty Laa!

How could I possibly mind? I'm proud of my involvement with the show and grateful for what it has afforded me. Aside from its impact on me personally, aside from the positive effect it's had on all those little ones, *Teletubbies* shifted and progressed the conversation about children and television. The media landscape is completely different from those early days when we were the evil product of devil-incarnate Anne Wood, hell bent on turning future generations' brains to mush. The methods in our madness have been vindicated. *Teletubbies* no longer gets any kind of bad press – no, if we are mentioned at all it is with warmth and the rosy glow of childhood nostalgia. This was a relief when bad news came in 2018.

I still keep a physical element in my work-life by teaching Pilates and I was at the studio early one morning, preparing for an eight-hour marathon shift, when I got a phone call from John. This wasn't so unusual. We were still in contact with each other and had been trying to arrange a date to meet for some time. He asked me to sit down, which I did, and good job too. The last thing I was expecting was the news that Simon had died. Beautiful Simon. Fit, funny, fabulous, younger-than-me Simon. Gone. All John knew at that point was that he had fallen and hit his head, and that this would be newsworthy so we should brace ourselves. I thought it unlikely that anyone had let Anne know, and I wanted her to find out from one of our own. I explained the situation to my first client of the day and sent the saddest email I'd ever sent to Ragdoll.

Other words started to emerge around Simon's death: Liverpool, docks, night, hypothermia, alcohol. No-one will ever know what really happened, but on the coldest night of the winter, in February, in the street, the life force of Simon Shelton faded away.

The shock was the news itself, but the surprise was how kind the press were. I spoke to everyone who asked me for comment, out of a sense of duty to make sure the media wrote about the most positive aspects of Simon's life and personality. I was expecting them to probe, wanting some dirt to dish, but that wasn't the case. The overall tone was one of sadness, pity and warmth. Even the *Sun* was respectful. It totally reflected the shift in perception over the years that these four previously vilified characters, and the people who brought them to life, were now dear to people's hearts.

At Simon's funeral, Pui and I clung to each other weeping. Those of us from his Tubby life in attendance smiled those strangled smiles of people who are pleased to see one another, but in whom grief is the dominant emotion.

I really struggled to come to terms with Simon's death. It's a cliché I know to say I just couldn't believe it, but I couldn't – it seemed impossible that such a thing could be true. But it was. It is. I felt guilty when people told me they were sorry for my loss. I didn't feel that I deserved their sympathy. I knew how awful the loss was for Simon's family and that my grief paled into insignificance by comparison. But loss doesn't work that way and I came to realise that people needed to express their sympathy because of the love they felt for the four of us. They were sorry not just for my loss but for their own and for the greater loss of a magnificent soul. For those of us who attended the funeral, it was a reminder of days gone by, of the passing of time and of the joyous bit of life we shared. It was the last time so many of us would be gathered together.

It's possible that losing Simon made it easier to come to terms with the characters being re-cast for the reboot of *Teletubbies*. Even if they had thought it was a good idea to get the original cast back, one of us was now missing so it would never have been the same. I am however extremely grateful that I had the opportunity to work on the new version of the show.

It was satisfying to feel I had some input to the next generation, as it were, and touching that the cast of 2014 were so eager and willing to take my advice. I think those four performers have done a pretty good job. They have taken the foundations that we laid and used their own personalities to build on them and create *Teletubbies* for a whole new cohort of little viewers.

I was a regular presence on the shoot for the first block of filming, unsure of whether to feel sorry for them for not being outside in the beautiful English countryside, or envious that they never had to travel the extreme distances we endured. Then pretty soon, as teething problems were overcome and everyone settled into the way of Tub, I was no longer needed. Like the four of us solving the problem of being stranded on our backs in that church hall so long ago, the new Tubbies were now up and running. I think it's a measure of how strong the concept of the show was, that it can stand up to being modernised without losing any of the allure of the original.

Just after I started work on the reboot, I bumped into Anne in Stratford-upon-Avon. I felt her customary warmth as we chatted, mostly checking in with one another that we were happy and healthy. Then she asked me if I knew about the new version of *Teletubbies*. I didn't know what to tell her. I didn't want to lie but I didn't want her to feel I had betrayed her. Anne interrupted my internal panic.

'I'm not going to watch it!' she said, 'I don't need to see what they've done to it.'

She waved away the subject, we exchanged a few more pleasantries and she was gone. I knew the whole hand-over was a peculiarly intense experience for me, but I hadn't really considered how it felt for Anne. Andy had moved on and *In The Night Garden* had become his Magnum Opus. But it was different for Anne. In our short exchange, I had the definite feeling that she couldn't even bring herself to think about someone messing about with her baby. I have no idea if she did ever watch it. If she did I don't know what she thought, but I could have a pretty good guess.

Time marches on and change happens no matter how any of us feel about it, and the twentieth anniversary of our first broadcast came and went without anyone needing to contact me about it. If anyone was celebrating, they were doing it with four other Tubby innards – we were yesterday's Tubs. What a peculiar thing. To have breathed life into a character, to see it become part of people's lives, and then to pass it on and no longer have any involvement whatsoever. Of course this is part and parcel of a performer's life, but on the occasions when the role you play has real resonance, it hits home more intensely.

It makes me think about soap opera stars, especially those who stay with a show for decades, perhaps even growing up in character. I can understand why it's tempting to stay put – why an actor can be reluctant to abandon a personality they've worked so hard to create. I particularly enjoy the ones who have a substantial run in a soap, then leave – I imagine they feel the need to stretch themselves in other roles and settings – but after a few years there they are, back again. Whatever it was they were doing in between times seemingly failed to live up to expectations. I like that they have the courage to realise they were better off where they were.

Would I have gone back to *Teletubbies* if they'd asked me? No, I don't think so. My ageing dodgy knees might have had something to say about it and a person knows when the time is right to move on. I mean, it's lovely when random journalists and the like, from all over the world, get in touch to ask me for an interview. I always say yes. I'm more than happy to talk about *Teletubbies*. But I think it's safe to say that I'm never going to be back inside the suit.

In a peculiar way, I rather miss it. I'm not romanticising. I haven't for a minute forgotten that inside the suit is a living hell of uncomfortable, but beyond that, it was a truly profound experience. It's already paradoxical to be employed to show off while sealed away, in isolation from those around you. Being left totally alone to do your job, when your job revolves around effectively communicating, is a strange dichotomy. There was also comfort to be had in the ability to remove yourself so entirely. I don't think it would be an exaggeration to say that hiding inside a puppet, I found myself. The confidence I gained from finally having a job that everyone agreed I could do consummately was immeasurable. I didn't even know it was something I lacked until I gained it. Sure, it's brilliant being the Talent, but if deep down you don't feel that you deserve that hallowed position, it's a hollow victory. Perhaps that's what's going on with those celebrities who earn a reputation for being difficult. It kind of makes sense.

At the onset, I was too concerned with whether or not I could actually do the job without dying to notice whether or not I deserved it. By the time I thought about deserving the job, I'd learned how to do it. Fortunately, it was me-shaped to start off with. Well, not entirely. The wonderful thing about playing Laa was that what came through the costume, who Laa-Laa was, on camera, was the best of me. Who gets to do that for a living? To put your failings aside and exude the nicest parts of your personality – for children, for laughter, for love. *That* was the biggest gift of all.

Even now, if at any point I'm feeling rather worthless, it's a hell of a way to cheer myself up to be able to think that it's more likely than not, somewhere in the world, a small child is looking at Laa-Laa, at my Laa, and is laughing.

CHAPTER 13

TIME FOR TUBBY BYE-BYE

2022 marks the 25th anniversary of *Teletubbies*' initial broadcast. Not bad for a show that many were writing off as an insane experiment within its first few weeks. I can't even guess the number of children who have enjoyed the programme, but the figure is in the billions and they're all over the world. That's a hell of a legacy on its own, but *Teletubbies* did more than just garner an enormous audience – it changed the conversation about children's television and the look of future shows for very young children.

When the success of *Teletubbies* was at its stratospheric peak, a slew of copycat programmes were hurried onto our screens. Very little thought went into their creation, and I suspect the motivation was more about replicating our merchandising income than about producing quality television for toddlers. These programmes came and went with a speed that drove home the fact that it took more than a selection of performers in brightly coloured fun-fur living together to fire up toddlers' imaginations. After this initial knee-jerk reaction, more serious attempts were made to take the lessons of *Teletubbies* to the next level. First came *Tweenies*, then *Fimbles* and *ZingZillas*, and of course Ragdoll itself learned lessons from its home-grown global behemoth that it could feed into the programmes it made thereafter.

Of course there had been carefully created, beautifully made, smart and adored children's television before *Teletubbies*. But there was something about the combination of focusing on the very young, high production values, educational understanding and out and out love – all the things, in fact, that Anne outlined during those early auditions – that has never been replicated before or since. The timing was perfect for a show with exactly the right attitude. What luck to have been along for the ride.

What about the long-suffering innards – was there life after *Teletubbies*? Of course there was. Before his fatal accident, Simon had managed to turn his passion for photography into a second career and had also gone to that place in which so many of us ex-dancers find ourselves: Pilates Land. John continued, and continues, to work in comedy and touring theatre as well as organising and promoting events – I'm still in regular contact with him. Pui's television career continues apace but I can't say we've really kept in touch. We've no reason not to, it's just the way life sometimes is. Andy is still creating genius-level televisual treats for very young children, and Anne? Well, she's finally having a well-earned lie-down.

And what about Crazy Hair Girl? I'm more Greying Hair Girl these days to be honest. My life is good: I get to create, I get to perform, I get to write and I get to teach. I think I do all of these things better than I would have done if I hadn't been Laa-Laa. I certainly do them more comfortably. Fancy that decision not to be poor any more working so effectively! I'd been looking for something to save me and *Teletubbies* did. There it is – *Teletubbies* saved me. At the beginning I worried that I might die doing the job, but in the end it gave me a life. I dread to think how things would have turned out if I hadn't had that lucky break, if that me-shaped job hadn't existed, or if I hadn't looked in the *Stage* newspaper the week they ran the advert, or if they hadn't chosen me, or if children hadn't loved the show, or if . . . or if . . . or if . . .

But all those things did happen, and I'm extremely grateful that they did. My time as a Teletubby still feeds into every aspect of my career. Whether I'm storytelling for children, teacher training in nurseries, making theatre pieces or even giving a TED talk, I'm drawing on the knowledge I accumulated while working for Anne. And although I may not be in the suit any more, Laa-Laa will always be my creation.

Laa is the gift that keeps on giving. Professionally, she has opened myriad doors and even in my day-to-day life, people tend to look upon me more kindly when they find out my big yellow puppety past. When I go and work in schools, I never say that I'm an ex-Teletubby, but – probably thanks to Google – they always find out. In every school, I walk into the staff room one day and see that shift in facial expression that tells me they know. Whenever someone finds out, nine times out of ten they will give me an 'Eh-Oh!' Ten times out of ten, they will be smiling.

Teletubbies is a point of connection for so many people, whether they watched it themselves or had children or grandchildren who watched it. It's not uncommon for people to apologise to me for asking questions about my time as Laa, imagining that I must be sick to the back teeth with the whole Teletubby thing. They could not be more wrong. I am proud to have been part of such a special creation and it's always a delight to see the joy on people's faces when they're given the opportunity to revisit their relationship with a TV show full of silly fun and love.

I'm happy that I will always be associated with a big yellow puppet and I will answer *The Question* with a smile on my face, for as long as people are still interested enough to ask it.

Thanks, Laa-Laa. Thank you for all you gave me and all you allowed me to be. I hope that in whatever guise, all the Teletubbies will be putting plenty more smiles on plenty more children's faces for many years to come.

And now, there's only one thing left to say.

Time for Tubby Bye-Bye.

Bye-bye.

ACKNOWLEDGEMENTS

Well, we're at the very back of the book and I'm extremely grateful to the following, without whom I'd never have got here:

Inga Gaile for giving me the prod I needed to write this in the first place. Lockdown for giving me the time and headspace to do it. Laurie Robertson for her support, belief and determined but smiley agenting. All at Sandstone Press for being so certain and happy-looking when they said yes, and for making it come true – especially Nicola Torch for a marvellously thorough and thoroughly enjoyable editing process. John Simmit for helping my memory and not hating the first draft – Citrus Posse forever! The many *Teletubbies* alumni that I contacted at the outset and who gave their blessings and offered up snippets of memories I'd forgotten. Everyone else who worked on the show and made it such a blast. And to Anne and Andy, of course.